3 1994 01282 7397

1107

SANTA ANA PUBLIC LIBRARY

MINERAL SPIRITS

ALSO BY HEATHER SHARFEDDIN

Blackbelly

FICTION SHARFEDDIN, H.
Sharfeddin, Heather.
Mineral spirits
31994012827397

MINERAL SPIRITS

A NOVEL

HEATHER SHARFEDDIN

BRIDGE WORKS PUBLISHING
Bridgehampton, New York

Copyright © 2006 by Heather Sharfeddin

All rights reserved under International and Pan-American Copyright
Conventions. No part of this book may be reproduced in any form
or by any electronic or mechanical means, including information
storage and retrieval systems, without written permission from the
publisher, except by a reviewer who may quote brief passages in
a review.

Published by Bridge Works Publishing Company,
Bridgehampton, New York

Distributed in the United States by National Book Network, Lanham,
Maryland. For descriptions of this and other
Bridge Works books, visit the National Book Network
Web site at www.nbnbooks.com.

FIRST EDITION

The characters and events in this book are fictitious. Any similarity
to actual persons, living or dead, is coincidental and not intended
by the author.

Library of Congress Cataloging-in-Publication Data

Sharfeddin, Heather.
    Mineral spirits : a novel / by Heather Sharfeddin. — 1st ed.
    p. cm.
    ISBN-10: 1-882593-98-7 (alk. paper)
    ISBN-13: 978-1-882593-98-9
  1. Montana — Fiction. I. Title.

PS3619.H35635M56 2006
813'.6 — dc22   2006000762

10 9 8 7 6 5 4 3 2 1

The paper used in this publication meets the minimum requirements of
American National Standard for Information Sciences— Permanence
of Paper for Printed Library Materials, ANSI/NISO Z39.48 – 1992.

Manufactured in the United States of America

For Salem,
whose support and devotion make all things possible.

MINERAL SPIRITS

1

AN ACRID BREEZE SWEPT UP FROM THE RIVER — a hint of rotting flesh. Enough that the sheriff braced himself. The boy had told him that an animal died down there during the summer, but no one went to see. There were a lot of animals out there: deer, coyotes, even a bear wasn't out of the question. It wasn't such an unusual odor.

Cottonwood leaves blanketed the corpse in a steady rain of yellow. The boy paused and stood with his hand over his nose, pointing down at the elbow joint protruding from the leaves. Bone meeting bone in a triangular arc that might've been any combination of parts on any sort of creature. The boy was unwilling to go any farther. Just stopped and pointed.

Sheriff Kip Edelson trudged down the soft slope toward the corpse, pausing a few yards distant to take inventory of the surrounding area. A large stick lay near the body. He guessed it belonged to the boy, was the instrument he'd used to unearth his grisly discovery. The sheriff glanced back at the child. He looked about ten.

"Thanks. You can go if you want," he said. But the boy stayed where he was.

Edelson guessed the damage was done. The nightmares would come, maybe worse so if the child was denied the outcome. The sheriff walked a wide margin around the skeleton, still partially clothed in rotting flesh. The skull twisted off to the side facing the river, the jaw gaping. Other pieces were strewn haphazardly about, the handiwork of coyotes, probably.

"What's your name?" he called up to the boy.

"Gray Dausman."

"Where are your folks?"

"My dad's at work. My mom lives in California." The kid paused. "I didn't tell anyone about it."

"Good. You did the right thing." Edelson assessed him a little more closely. His pants were muddy and too short, the knees ripped out. "You looked after by someone?"

The child shot him a defiant look. "I'm old enough. I don't need a babysitter."

He nodded. "Why don't you go call your dad?"

The boy disappeared over the upflung bank, toward the housing tract.

The sheriff turned back and scanned the wide, fast-moving Clark Fork River, an opaque gray-green. High clouds raked the pale sky, air crisp and crystal-like, a telling sign of autumn. His eyes followed the thickly forested mountain on the far bank to a high meadow, a pause in the timber where a handful of handsome, upscale homes overlooked the river. Too far up to see a rotting corpse. He stepped carefully around the bones and headed for his cruiser. Better get a forensic team out of Missoula before it got too late in the day.

He waited on the bank where spectators were congregating. The boy had apparently changed his mind about telling the news, which had run through the development like lightning down a wire fencerow. Edelson cautioned them to stand back and carved a line out of the dry earth with his boot sole to mark their boundary. The boy eventually reappeared, but the sheriff saw no affiliation with any specific adult, though the crowd plied him with questions. He simply pointed and shrugged. Said he was playing by the river, that's all.

"You the new sheriff?"

Edelson turned to find a slight man with a thick red mustache and a head of wheaty hair standing in all directions. "That would be me."

"Thought you'd have it easy here, eh?"

"Never thought anything of the sort."

"Edelson, isn't it?" The sheriff nodded, and the man thrust his hand forward. "Randy McHugh."

They shook, but Edelson stood his distance and maintained his sober expression.

"We haven't had a murder here since this place was just a stage stop," McHugh offered.

"No one said it was a murder." Edelson tried to imagine the place when it was a stage stop. It hadn't grown much since, the housing tract hammered up in the early 1980s notwithstanding. An optimistic undertaking for a dying town forty miles from gainful employment. Magda, Montana, was pinched between Interstate 90 and the Clark Fork River in a narrow strip of meadow, once the last outpost before the expanse of mountain wilderness stretching a hundred miles west to Spokane.

The housing tract was the poor section of Magda, a place so small residents of the development had only to look across the road to see their more fortunate neighbors. Rusted-out car bodies in fender-high weeds littered the yards, and not a speck of landscaping ornamented the cookie-cutter dwellings. It was home to impoverished citizens who'd migrated from everywhere but Montana itself, none the descendants of those who'd built the town, whose mark could still be discerned in the precision alignment of nineteenth-century buildings lining Main Street. These chipboard houses in electric colors with their window screens tossed onto roofs or gone missing altogether screamed of impermanence.

McHugh shifted back and forth on his feet as if they hurt sufficiently to give each a rest in turn. He wasn't from the housing tract. He owned the saloon. Same quarter-sawn oak bar, passed down from his granddaddy, that trappers and miners had bellied up to when the town still had promise. He was apolitical — or at least claimed to be. Spit in the street when the sheriff came through to make his bid for office.

McHugh stood next to Edelson, shoulder to elbow, as the sheriff was a man of considerable height. Six foot three. "Who we waitin' for?" McHugh inquired.

"*I'm* waiting for the coroner and a forensic team from Missoula," the sheriff said.

McHugh smiled, seemed satisfied. "Well, I guess I'll head back to the Silver Dog. Bound to see some business tonight. Nothin' like a gruesome discovery to get the whiskey flowing."

"Take 'em with you now," Edelson called to him, waving toward the crowd.

McHugh was already headed for town, a clip in his pace. He waved a hand back, but didn't turn around. "They'll come when they've gotten an eyeful."

As Edelson contemplated the nature of one man's good fortune, the coroner and crew arrived. "Okay, folks, you've seen enough," Edelson said to the steadily building crowd. "Go on back to your homes now. Let these men in here to do their work."

The crowd stepped back a pace or two, but largely ignored the sheriff's directive.

An attractive red-head brushed past him lugging the front end of a gurney. "And women," she corrected.

McHugh served drinks to a larger-than-usual crowd that evening, keeping the bar open late, listening to graphic descriptions told and retold of the corpse. Armchair pathologists asserted their theories. No one questioned that the victim had been murdered.

He filled a beer glass and set it on the counter, listening to

4

a regular named Walt speculate about the corpse's identity.

"Bet it was one of those Youth Corps workers came through last year," Walt said. "Bunch of fucked-up city kids, those are. Probably all killed each other before the summer was out. Bet if he keeps lookin', Sheriff'll find more than one body down there." He looked at McHugh. "You know this new sheriff?"

McHugh shrugged. He thought Edelson was a bit arrogant for a newcomer, but he didn't want to let on to his patrons that the sheriff hadn't been by the Silver Dog yet. McHugh had expected Edelson to drop in on his first or second day in town. The tavern was the center of everything going on in Magda, after all. If Edelson wanted to know who was doing what, he'd only find it here.

"Seems like a decent guy," Walt said absently.

"I guess we'll find out, won't we?" McHugh said. That body couldn't belong to a Youth Corps worker, but he didn't share his opinion with Walt. The YCC was a government organization. They would've kept careful accounting of their charges. A missing teen wouldn't have time to rot to bones under their supervision. McHugh didn't believe Edelson would figure out who the corpse was, though. How could he, with just a bunch of bones for evidence?

As he thought about it, another man stepped up to the bar and slid two crisp twenties toward McHugh. "Take the usual, Randy."

McHugh glanced at Walt, who shrugged and turned his eyes on his beer glass. McHugh pulled a baggie from beneath the cash register, folding it into a small square and cupping it covertly in his hand. He looked off toward the front door and commented about how early dusk arrived now that it was getting late in the year. He slipped his hand over the man's in a silent transaction, swiftly whisking up the cash and sliding it into his jeans pocket. "I can't believe summer is over. You?"

5

"Nope." The man shoved his hand into his coat pocket, nodded at McHugh, then at Walt and headed for the door.

Edelson sipped coffee on his back porch the following morning and gazed out at the Clark Fork River as it rolled past this new place he and Robin called home. A secluded few acres on a grassy knob overlooking the river. The house sat too far from the road to hear the semis heading for the coast. But with a westerly wind he could sometimes hear the Jake brakes blow before the truckers made it down the pass coming the other way. The sound reminded him of a distant train whistle, far off and haunting, but comforting with the thought that he was a little less alone in the world. Which could be a serious affliction in a place like this.

He thought about the body found just a few miles upstream from where he sat. It pulled at him to get going, pick up the trail. The morning was cold in a bright, snappy way. Yellow ground beneath a pale sky — parched and expectant. Steam blew off his cup as he raised it to his lips.

He went over in his mind the short list of clues he'd jotted in his notepad the night before, wondering if the body had been a man or a woman, adult or adolescent, criminal or loved one. It was too long left in the muck of the river bank to have those answers today. So this would be his first test as sheriff of Mineral County — a vastly vertical county with a one-to-100,000 ratio of people to pine trees.

"I'm driving in to Missoula this morning," Robin said through the screen door.

"What for?"

"To see the university."

Edelson turned and tried to locate her, but couldn't see into the dark kitchen. "That's fifty miles away. You can't drive that every day."

She appeared suddenly, taking up the full screen. A tall

6

woman, big boned. Not fat, but a far stretch from petite. She stared at him as if he'd slapped her across the face. "But you said . . ."

He turned back to the river. "I didn't make any promises."

"Kip, you did."

Her cat jumped into his lap, and he tossed it back to the floor as quickly. Couldn't figure out why it never got the hint. Why did it keep trying? "Can't hurt to check it out, I guess."

Robin disappeared again, and Edelson could hear her gathering her things. Then the front door slammed and he closed his eyes, wishing he'd just let her go without comment. She would've seen for herself it was too far to commute. Now she'd be bent on doing it just to show him.

Edelson scoured the site where they'd unearthed the skeleton. The light had slipped away before they had finished the night before — or at least before he was finished. The forensic team seemed satisfied long before he was ready to call it a night.

He bent low now, walking slowly. Creeping, really. His eyes jetted back and forth like a line printer, leaving not an inch unobserved. He turned at the perimeter of the site and started back in the opposite direction, a foot closer to the river. At last he squatted and used a stick to turn the mud up around an object of curiosity, poking out like a gray shard. As he uncovered it, he realized it was an arrowhead. A small one, about an inch long. He wiped it clean with his handkerchief and examined the stone, then tipped his head back and scanned the river bank. Edelson stood again and took new inventory of the landscape along both sides of the river. He looked for tipi rings, circular areas flattened by hand to accommodate a lodge. But he knew they wouldn't be necessary here, not with the level meadow above the river, the meadow that the town of Magda now occupied.

Edelson studied the arrowhead. Had it been there for a

7

century or more, or was it part of the crime scene? He recognized its construction: Nez Percé. An Idaho native, Edelson had spent his childhood traipsing behind his forest-ranger father, splashing through wild streams and rivers, climbing lookout towers. He knew the Nez Percé were a mobile tribe, adept riders, and their territory stretched from the Wallowas in Oregon to the Montana Bitterroots south of where he stood. But wasn't the Clark Fork too far north? Wasn't this Pend Oreille territory? He took another look at the arrowhead. It was a Nez Percé birdshot, or his name wasn't Clifford James Edelson.

He slipped it into a plastic bag and put it in his breast pocket, then resumed his search. As his eyes worked over the landscape, his mind worked over his knowledge of the Nez Percé. He couldn't make a link between those people and this place, but wasn't positive about the boundaries, either.

On his way back to the cruiser, Edelson wandered through the housing tract. It was nearly eleven o'clock, and children were riding bicycles in the streets. He looked for the boy, but didn't see him.

As he turned to go, a little girl called to him. "Gray lives in that house."

Edelson looked back at her, then in the direction she pointed. A bright, robin's-egg-blue house at the end of the street with an oxidized orange Land Cruiser up on blocks in the yard. "Gray?"

"Isn't that who you're lookin' for, mister?"

He nodded, wondering if it was, and started down the street. No one answered when he knocked, and he stood awkwardly on the porch, children openly gawking at him. Watching his every move. Edelson cupped his hands around his eyes and peered through the dirty window into a squalid dwelling, something a rat might need to tidy up before occupying. He circled around back, where he found the boy crouched over a small flame in the dry grass, matches still in his hand. The boy jumped to his feet, forgetting his fire.

Edelson crushed the flame with his boot, scuffing the ground in exaggerated fashion, making certain it was out long after the smoke had died away. He turned to the boy with a squint that deepened the creases in his brow. "Good thing I showed up when I did, or you'd have the whole place burnt down."

The boy looked up at the sheriff, but just as quickly looked away. "You gonna tell my dad?"

"I think that'd be a good place to start." Edelson looked the boy up and down. Waited for him to make eye contact again. "Do you have any idea how dry it is out here?"

The boy shook his head and stared at his feet.

"Not only could you have burned down your own place, but all your neighbors', and then you'd probably start a full-on forest fire. You'd burn everything from here to Canada."

The boy looked out at the treed slopes across the Interstate, eyes wide.

"Do you know what happens to people who start fires?" The sheriff leaned in toward the boy's face and gave him a hard stare. Could see him working to keep tears back. "Do you?"

"I wasn't gonna start a fire."

"So I guess that's not what I stomped out with my boot just now?" Edelson pointed at the charred earth.

"I mean I wasn't gonna burn anything down," the boy stammered.

"Doesn't matter what you were meaning to do."

"Please don't tell my dad."

"I *am* going to tell your dad. He'll probably tan your hide. And I'd say you've got that coming." Edelson straightened up and yanked his handcuffs from his belt. "Unless you'd rather I arrest you and haul you in."

The boy eyed the shiny bracelets. Tears brimmed at his

9

lids, but he kept them from spilling. "Okay," he said, and put his wrists out before him.

Edelson scowled. It wasn't supposed to go that way. "You want me to march you down the street handcuffed, in front of all your friends and everybody? You want me to take you to jail?"

The boy thrust his wrists forward. "If you don't tell my dad."

2

SHERIFF EDELSON EYED THE BOY through his rearview mirror.
Gray Dausman sat quietly in the back seat, staring out the window as they pulled onto I-90. His dark hair looked as though someone, perhaps even himself, had cut it with a bowie knife.
He had two circular cowlicks an inch apart at the forefront of his scalp, forcing a rogue lock straight down over his eyes. An otherwise unremarkable face, plain-featured, smooth-skinned.
Deep brown, almost black eyes.

Edelson wondered what he would do with the kid now.
He wanted to make an impression on the boy, make him understand how seriously flawed his choice of recreation was. This one had surprised him. Maybe he should've forced the boy into a reckoning with his father. But there was something about the way the boy chose — something that pulled at the pit of his stomach.

"Where does your father work?"

The boy looked at the back of Edelson's head. "You said you wouldn't tell him."

"I didn't say that."

The boy's mouth gaped.

Edelson shook his head, his lips pressed into a tense line.
"Fine. I'll just take you to jail. But I still need to know where he works."

"At the mill."

11

"What time does he get home?"

The boy shrugged. "Suppertime."

"Do you have any other relatives around? Is there a friend of the family that looks in on you? Anyone?"

"No." The child turned his attention to the window again.

They wound through the tiny town of Peerless, where the county jail, a cinderblock building in the shade of army green, was located. The sheriff hated the squat structure with its flat roof. He missed his old office in Sweetwater, Idaho, an elaborate nineteenth-century bank building of oak and marble that had high ceilings with crown molding. Not like this . . . this thing Mineral County officials called a jailhouse. Another problem with the jailhouse was that it kept burning down — three times in the last hundred years. And after the last time, the town fathers approved a fire-resistant eyesore, an *economy of resources*, they liked to call it.

Edelson led the boy inside, through the empty front office, down a short corridor to a barred cell. The boy paused in the doorway and Edelson removed the handcuffs.

"We usually cuff people behind their backs. You're lucky I'm in a good mood today."

The boy went to the bunk and sat down. "Do I have to piss in front of you?" he said, pointing at the toilet.

"Yup."

"That sucks. I'm not using that toilet."

"You're under arrest, not on a field trip." Edelson glowered at him. "Want to change your mind and have me call your dad?"

"No."

"Suit yourself." He closed the door with a loud clang.

"Do I get lunch?"

Edelson turned back to the boy and thought a moment.

He wished he had an assistant, someone to fetch a meal for his prisoner. Aside from the dispatcher, who worked out of her house, he was a one-man show. The county commissioner had told him they hadn't kept anyone in the Peerless jail in 20 years, anyway. They usually released them on their own recognizance or took them to Missoula.

"Bread and water, you know," the sheriff said.

The boy shrugged. He had the look of a starved-out cat.

"How old are you?"

"Ten."

Edelson frowned at the boy. He pocketed the keys and walked across the street to the supermarket, where he wandered the aisles for a loaf of white bread, a small jar of mustard, and a package of sliced bologna. As he stood in the express line behind a chatty, elderly woman with twice the permitted number of items, he stared at the comic books along the bottom of the magazine rack. He reached down and picked up a modern rendition of Superman, remembering how much he loved comics as a kid. He put it back, telling himself that this boy was in jail for committing a very serious crime. The woman in front of him pulled out her wallet, but instead of paying, she showed the clerk a school picture of a pale teenage girl with pimples. Edelson looked again at the comic, then at the sandwich fixings. They weren't exactly the most nutritious items he could find, but he was hungry too and a bologna sandwich sounded good right now. He picked up the comic book again and slid it under the bread. He shook his head, disgusted with himself for being too soft, then added a Twinkie to the pile.

The boy wolfed down the sandwich in minutes. The sheriff watched. He had wanted this to be an unpleasant experience for the boy, a punishment that would make him swear off fire-setting forever. So why hadn't he let Gray Dausman go on being hungry? The boy licked the crumbs off his fingers and started picking them from his stained shirt. Edelson made him another sandwich and handed it through the bars with the Twinkie and the comic book.

"I have business to attend to. You sit here and think about your crime."

"Okay," the boy said, without bothering to contain his smirk.

Edelson spent the afternoon at the Mineral County Historical Museum, digging for facts about local Indians, and was surprised to find no record of Indian habitation in the area. There weren't even any known trails. The president of the historical society and museum curator, a woman who appeared old enough to know firsthand, claimed the original travelers through the narrow county were John Mullen and crew, chartered to build a road from Fort Benton, Montana, to Walla Walla, Washington. The sheriff found this hard to believe and jotted a reminder in his notepad to check another source.

Shortly before three-thirty he unlocked the jail cell and escorted the boy out. "C'mon, you're going home."

The boy followed amiably at his heels. In the car he asked, "Did you find out about that skeleton?"

Edelson looked up at his mirror and caught the boy's glance. "No. Not yet." He sat quiet a moment, then he said, "You okay with all that stuff yesterday? I mean . . . it was pretty gross."

"Yeah."

Edelson thought he ought to say something more, but didn't know what. He didn't know anything about kids. Never had the urge to find out, either.

In the boy's driveway, the sheriff turned and gave him a mean stare. He wanted the kid to feel properly chastised. "You understand why I arrested you today?"

The boy nodded.

"If I catch you again, I'm gonna be a lot harder on you."

The boy fidgeted with his hands and gave the sheriff a weak nod.

"You can go now," he said.

The boy hesitated before climbing out of the cruiser. Edelson waited. "Are you gonna come back tomorrow?" the boy asked.

"You think I need to?"

The kid gathered his comic book and shrugged. When he got to the door he stopped. Edelson glimpsed him in the rearview mirror, just standing there, watching the cruiser pull away.

Gray caught the evening news with Brian Williams. He hated those two hours between five and seven when the only thing on all three channels was news. He wondered if the policeman who arrested him knew Judge Judy. He liked to watch Judge Judy because she yelled at grown-ups, sometimes even called them stupid. She seemed like she'd be nice to kids, although he'd never seen a kid on her show.

The phone rang and he ran to pick it up. "Hello?"

"Gray?" It was Mrs. Anton. She lived in the yellow house on the corner.

"Yeah."

"Why was the sheriff at your house today?"

"I don't know."

"Did he have more questions about that body?" There was a long pause, then she said, "I have a book for you."

Gray jumped up and down on the balls of his feet. "What's it about?"

"Two orphan boys in Venice."

"Where?"

"Italy. They solve a mystery. If you want it, come down and get it."

Gray slammed the phone down and dashed for the door,

then darted back and picked it up again. "Sorr —" He heard only the dial tone. "Oh." He dropped it again and ran outside just as his father's dented four-by-four pulled into the driveway.

"Hey, where you goin'?" Jim Dausman hollered out the window.

"Mrs. Anton got me a book," Gray said without looking back.

The old woman was waiting with the door open, wearing her flowered housecoat and slippers. She leaned outside and looked up the street at Gray's house. "Where did the sheriff take you today?"

"I gotta go," Gray said, glancing back at his father's truck. "My dad is home."

She handed him a scuffed hardback book. Hefty. He held it in both hands and grinned. "Thanks."

"You're welcome. You enjoy it, Gray."

At home Gray settled into the big chair in the corner, the one with the stuffing that was pulling out of its arms, and cracked open the book. His father sat with a beer, watching the news. When Gray got up to use the bathroom, the football game was on and his father was in the same place. Still drinking beer. It was dark outside.

"You eat, Gray?"

"Yeah. I had a sandwich."

His father nodded, staring at the TV.

Robin Edelson lounged in one of the cedar Adirondack chairs Kip had made and set behind their new house overlooking the river. The chairs were hand finished with Danish tongue oil — black walnut stain. His favorite for its forgiving hue. Edelson stood on the porch a while, watching his wife browse class schedules and brochures from the University of Montana. Her dyed-blonde hair sparkled gold in the evening sun, and Edelson hoped she was no longer angry.

16

"How was Missoula?" he said as he joined her, settling into his own chair. He looked out at a dense thicket of lodgepole pines across the river. He was suddenly fascinated by trees. They appeared new and full of oblique symbolism, an oddly tardy perspective for the son of a forester. A red-tailed hawk kited overhead, slinging its shadow across them. Edelson tipped his head back, squinting into the late afternoon sky, trying to glimpse the bird.

Robin thumbed through glossy pages. Finally, "It was okay."

"What'd you find out?"

She turned to him. "It's not that far."

He winced. She might as well have said *told you so*.

"I think I'll enroll for fall. It's not too late to get some of the classes I want."

"How much is that going to cost?"

"Is that all you ever think about? Money?"

He sighed. "It's not like we're rich, Robin." Edelson found a stick near his foot and heaved it overhand toward the river. It fell short a few yards, silently swallowed up by weeds. The answer to her question was increasingly *yes*. "Last I checked we don't have a money tree growing out here."

She folded her arms tightly across her chest. "What do you want me to do, Kip? Sit here all day while you're out roaming the county, chasing down drunks and digging up dead people? And don't forget we picked Montana over Nevada because it was close to the university so I could go back to school. You've been promising this since we got married. If I'd known how hard it was to get you to keep your word, I would've made you wait until I finished."

Her accusation stung. Edelson didn't really remember making that promise, but he must have, or she wouldn't keep throwing it in his face. Robin seemed to hold everything he said as some brand of solemn oath. He couldn't say a damn thing anymore without it being construed as a binding contract.

"Besides, I can get financial aid."

Great, more debt, he thought.

Edelson awoke in the middle of the night to the wet nose of Robin's cat nudging its way down the length of him, burrowing between the sheets. He flung the covers back. "Get out of here," he roared.

The cat skittered off the end of the bed, and Robin came awake laughing.

"I hate that cat!" he seethed.

She slid out of bed. "C'mon, Peachy, you woke the ogre." And put the cat out of the bedroom. The arc of her hip shone smooth in the moonlight as she bent to push the creature away from the door. When she turned, her breasts were illuminated like twin moons of her own. Edelson greeted her return to bed with a full-on grope.

"I'm still mad at you," she said, pulling away from him.

He caressed her, but she turned her back to him. He pressed his groin against the small of her back. Reached a hand and cupped her breast. She dropped her head forward — a gesture Edelson read as surrender. He kissed her neck.

"I hate you," she sighed.

"I know, but I can fix that."

Gray sat up in the black night, taking in a sharp gasp of air. He looked down at his hands, but couldn't make them out in the dark. He pressed them to his nose and smelled them. The dirt and grime gave them a rubbery scent, like a school eraser. He held them there against his face. The revolting odor of the corpse seemed to have followed him to his room. His eyes went to the window.

When he'd gathered his courage, he swung his legs off the bed, shuffling through cast-off clothes. He stepped on a sharp plastic toy with his bare foot and gasped. "Fuck!" He fumbled toward the light, which stung his eyes. He inspected the tender skin, but there was no blood. He rummaged for his book, pulled his bedspread around him like a shroud, and returned to bed, where he began to read. He figured his dad was too drunk to see the light under his door.

3

EDELSON SAT AT THE SILVER DOG BAR waiting for McHugh, the bartender-owner, to make his way down to him. Edelson admired the massive, oak bar in what he believed was the best building in Magda. It was a manly building — stout — constructed of brick with ornate cornice work, a rare specimen of nineteenth-century old-west architecture. Edelson had spotted its red façade from the Interstate where it stood in high relief against the forested backdrop. He had taken an instant liking to it.

"What can I get ya?" McHugh said, placing a cocktail napkin on the grease-smoothed counter. The beer and liquor were already flowing freely at the tavern, despite the fact it was only one-thirty in the afternoon.

"I'll have a bacon burger and a mineral water."

"Mineral water?" McHugh frowned.

"Yeah. Perrier, if you've got it. With lime."

"Sorry, don't stock that French shit. How 'bout a tonic water instead?"

Edelson grimaced. "If it's all you've got, I guess."

"Last sheriff preferred his with Seven Crown. How 'bout you?"

"I don't drink."

"At all? Or just on the job?"

"I'd have eaten at the diner if I'd known it was going to be twenty questions here."

"Fine." McHugh threw his hands up in mock surrender. "Bacon burger and a tonic water."

Edelson glanced around, trying not to attract too much attention. But he'd put a hush over the place just by walking in. He had hoped to overhear some nugget of information, some bit of speculation or gossip that would turn up a clue about the skeleton. Someone long missing. A sordid rumor of murder. People were notoriously loose with their opinions and extrapolations in the wake of sensational discoveries. And even though Edelson found this type of information largely unreliable, it was freighted with some third-hand truth, no matter how warped or twisted it'd become in the retelling.

"Hey Clint, you forget your spurs this mornin'?"

Edelson swiveled on his stool and faced the man who'd addressed him, a swarthy looking fellow with a greasy ponytail and a collage of tattoos from his wrists to his shoulders. Snakes and skulls. Scimitars and bare-chested women. Edelson peered down at his boots. Looked them over thoroughly, then shook his head. "No . . . I don't care much for spurs. They make too much noise. Jingle like Christmas elves."

The crowd got a mild charge out of the new sheriff's wit, as if he'd passed some secret initiation with his good-humored response, and the conversational hum picked up again. The man's companion, another extravagant expression of needle art, said, "What d'ya thinka that little present somebody left ya down at the river?"

"Still forming my opinion. Nothing I haven't seen before, just wish it wasn't a kid that found it."

Both men nodded in agreement. "Jim's kid is a tough little cowboy. He'll survive," the first man said and straightened himself in the booth, a signal the conversation was over.

Jim Dausman, Gray's father. Kip Edelson had gathered all the pertinent information on him, simply because his son found the body. Nothing much to set him apart. A misdemeanor arrest when he was twenty-one for whacking down mailboxes with a baseball bat while hanging out of a speeding pickup. A common enough sport in these parts, forcing residents to invest in reinforced steel boxes set deep into concrete. A cottage industry had sprung up around the problem.

Dausman worked at the paper mill as a warehouseman, licensed to operate the forklift. Shift work, there long enough to be working days. Married and divorced, but Gray wasn't the product of that relationship.

The sheriff swiveled back to the bar and sipped his drink. Too sweet — like candy dissolved in carbonated water. He liked the bitterness of mineral water. Bitter and tart with the added lime. He pushed it away, and thought about Gray's determination to go to jail rather than face his father. Edelson spied the two men in the mirror over the bar, amidst the vermouth and brandy bottles. If Jim was anything like these two appeared, Gray might have good reason to avoid a reckoning.

McHugh plopped an enormous burger down in front of Edelson. Homemade fries with the skins still on piled to one side, two wide strips of bacon hanging out of the bun. The Silver Dog didn't mess around with ready-made products like the warehouse store off I-90 near Missoula. Everything at the Silver Dog was fresh, prepared on the spot and to order. Known for their gargantuan portions. A meal in this place would serve a diner for a day or better. Edelson squeezed out a glob of ketchup from a plastic refillable bottle. It was the ketchup bottles that had brought him here this afternoon. He liked that the Silver Dog hadn't given over to the trendy notion of small cups of ketchup on the side, or glass bottles like at home—waiting for the damn stuff to come out while his food got cold.

"Anything else?" McHugh said.

"No. Thanks." Edelson dipped a fry and shoved it in his mouth. "Just the check."

"On the house."

Edelson looked up with a suspicious squint.

"My civic contribution."

"I'm sure you can put it to better use. I'll take the check, thanks."

McHugh stood opposite the bar and stared Edelson in the face. They were eye to eye, and the sheriff realized the floor was higher behind the bar. Apparently, it was important for the bar-man not to appear vulnerable. McHugh had a quizzical look about him as he teetered from foot to foot, as if he were wondering if this sheriff was from a different planet. "Now how are we gonna get along if you don't play the game?"

"We'll get along just fine."

McHugh nodded to himself and made his way back down the bar toward the register, querying customers about their refreshment needs.

Edelson turned his attention back to his lunch and the woman sitting to his left, chewing her straw and running her fingers through the graying hair of the man next to her. She was going on at length about her sister, who she believed to be a shameless whore because she'd managed to secure a live-in arrangement with one of the Reed twins who owned the Gas'n'Go up in St. John's. The woman had recently visited her sibling to look upon her fortune in the form of cherrywood cabinetry and slab-granite countertops, double ovens and a walk-in pantry. Not to mention the garden tub a tall girl could lie down in.

The man was not as impressed with her story as he was with her thigh, which he inched up until his hand disappeared.

McHugh had watched the sheriff carefully from his post near the cash register. He studied the way the man ate his burger, cutting it into two pieces and wrapping a napkin under it to catch the grease. McHugh was a meticulous man himself, and Edelson's uncommon behavior both intrigued and repulsed him. He didn't like this new sheriff. Edelson obviously didn't understand the order of things in this town, or he would've worked harder to garner McHugh's support. When Edelson came through on his campaign for office, he'd simply shrugged and moved on when McHugh told him he didn't vote. McHugh didn't have to vote to get what he wanted.

McHugh filled a beer glass from the tap and set it on the counter for a grizzled and surly regular who had just drunk down the last suds of his previous beer.

"What d'ya makea the new sheriff?" the regular said, rolling his head toward Edelson.

McHugh glanced at the sheriff and away. The bar patron spoke too loud, and McHugh was tired of the question, asked by everyone who sat down. He shrugged it off. McHugh glanced again as Edelson made a face at his glass of tonic water, then shoved it away. "Guess I'll have to start ordering mineral water," McHugh said, mostly to himself. And the more he thought about it, the more he imagined the sheriff was just feeling him out before making any demands. He hoped they weren't too steep, that they could come to a gentlemanly agreement. After all, if Edelson was truly as straight-laced as he came off, why would he have come to the Silver Dog for lunch?

Edelson spent the remainder of the day at his office, studying the coroner's report as the waning afternoon rays filtered through the dirty window. Female. Late thirties to mid-forties. Cause of death unknown, but deceased a year or more. What bones had been recovered were mostly intact, save for the gnawing of animals. No sign of foul play. In short, the body was too far gone to yield much in the way of evidence. The forensic team had compared dental records to all known missing persons in western Montana, northern Idaho, and parts of eastern Washington, but no match turned up.

He pushed back in his swivel chair, rattling across the painted cement floor until he bumped against the metal file cabinet. Now what? He'd hoped for a little more information to start the investigation. And for a moment he wondered if he was up for the job ahead of him. Despite what he'd told McHugh that evening overlooking the river bank, there was more than a small part of Edelson that had believed he could coast a little here, recover his bearings again. Remember why he became a lawman to begin with, and hopefully draw enough reason from it to remain a lawman.

Gray Dausman stumbled out of bed and into the kitchen, trying to get to the phone. His hair stood up in the back where he'd slept on it, and his eyes stung from his abrupt awakening. It was eight-forty-five; his father had left for work two hours ago. "Hello?"

"Is this Gray?"

"Yeah," he rubbed a hand over the indentation of his belly, wishing for a glass of water to stave off the hunger pangs.

"Gray, this is the school secretary calling. Why didn't you report for class this morning?"

"Uh . . . I didn't know it was the first day of school." He looked out the front window, as if he'd missed a sign.

"What do you mean you didn't know? Didn't your mom get the information in the mail?"

". . . she doesn't live here."

"Then your dad?"

"I don't know."

"Is he there? Can I speak to him please?"

"No. He's at work. But I can come now."

There was a pause on the line. Then, "Okay."

Gray ran to his bedroom, rooted through his dresser for a

clean pair of jeans, gave it up, then went to the hamper in the hallway and dug until he found a pair of wrinkled, canvas pants with cargo pockets. In the bathroom he brushed his teeth and combed his hair down in the front, entirely unaware of the matted back.

He paused at the door, thinking he needed something. Pencils maybe. Or paper. But he didn't have any of those things. He knew they would give him what he needed from the teacher's supply. Leftover stuff. He wanted to go to school. But he didn't. Didn't want to see Jordan's new notebook with all the cool pockets that he was bragging about last week when they were watching the police dig up the skeleton. Or Madison's colored pencil set she brought out to show everybody. Or he did want to see them. Wanted to have them, too. He went back to his room and dug through a shoebox until he found a small metal airplane. It was heavy and painted like a real one, only miniature. He shoved it in his pants pocket. Maybe Jordan would trade.

Edelson was cruising through Magda on his way to the Interstate when he spied Gray walking down the middle of the street. He glanced at his watch and pulled up alongside the boy. "Shouldn't you be in school?"

"That's where I'm going," Gray said, pointing up the street at a rambling brick building with a weedy yellow lawn. It housed all twelve grades. A faded sign out front sported a snarling bear and the words *Go Griz!*

"How come you're late?"

"I didn't know it was today."

The sheriff tipped his chin back and contemplated the boy a moment. "Go on then."

Gray broke into a run.

Edelson watched the boy until he disappeared through

the school's double doors. Gray was empty-handed, in rumpled clothes, and a cowlick bounced wildly at the back of his head. The sheriff pulled onto I-90 and headed not to Peerless as planned, but down Frenchtown way.

An imposing industrial complex of metal and steam, the pulp mill gave the appearance of something assembled by a five-year-old. Pipes jutting out of nowhere, aerial catwalks, chain-link fencing. Peeling, putty-colored paint. Edelson parked in one of two visitor spaces in front of the barren office entrance. He hadn't imagined buildings around here could get bleaker than his own little jailhouse, but he was wrong. A shrub of any sort around the mill office would be a vast improvement. He paused to wonder what manner of chemical destruction was spewing from the stack overhead. It hadn't taken but a day in Magda to understand the proximity of the mill and the natural tendency of the wind. Rotten eggs. Some mornings the smell seemed to just hang in the air. He strode into the building.

"Can I help you?" The receptionist had seen him coming and wasted no time.

"I'm looking for Jim Dausman."

She nodded, started to ask a question, then changed her mind. He was accustomed to that. As if the ritual of asking who's calling took a moment to stopper when the obvious stands before them. "One moment, Sheriff." She picked up the phone and called the warehouse. "Jim has a visitor. It looks important."

Jim Dausman was not what Edelson had expected. True, he looked unkempt, and appeared to have left off shaving some days ago, as if he intended to grow a regular beard. His hair was short and greasy. His gut could pass for a woman's in her third trimester. He had a sleepy look about him, like a big lazy hound.

"Mr. Dausman?"

27

"Yeah?"

"I'd like to ask you a couple of questions. Would you like to step outside?"

Dausman glanced briefly at the receptionist, then nodded. The two men stepped out onto the cement entryway. "This about Gray findin' that body?"

Edelson was silent a moment. He'd learned as a rookie to let people ramble a bit out of nervousness, a tactic that could reveal leads that driving the conversation would never bring about.

"He told me about it. I was working when he found it. Didn't get home until after dark. By then it was too hard to see."

Edelson waited. It was true that he hadn't recalled seeing Dausman's face among the onlookers.

"I came to ask about your boy," Edelson said.

"Gray?"

"Do you have more than one?"

Dausman shook his head, and the sheriff concluded that the man wasn't very bright.

"Did you know today is the first day of school, Mr. Dausman?"

"Shit!" He rubbed the back of his neck hard with his flattened palm. "No. Did he get off all right?"

The sheriff studied the man. "He was late, but he made it."

He spit on the concrete. "I got a letter from the school, but I didn't get around to reading it."

"If you want, I can have a social worker come by and help you get things organized for the boy."

Dausman's eyes went hard, like frozen little ponds of blue. "I don't need a goddamn social worker!"

"Okay, but consider yourself on notice."

Dausman went red and tense, but kept his lips firmly creased.

"I guess you'll go by the school and find out what the boy needs, won't you?"

Dausman gave a curt nod.

"Good." Edelson strode to his cruiser and pulled away, leaving Dausman red-faced.

The house sat empty and forlorn when Edelson got home, lonely on the knob over the river, its windows dark. It was well past seven, and his stomach had been rumbling for hours. He'd hoped Robin was cooking spaghetti or tacos — her favorites. His, too. But it was obvious she was not there. Only his nemesis, Peachy, sat on the bottom-most tread of the porch steps, waiting for him.

Inside, he found a terse note from Robin stuck to the refrigerator about getting a last-minute class on Monday and Wednesday evenings and not to wait up. He crumpled it and tossed it in the trash. Then he pawed through the freezer for a rock-hard burrito, which he warmed in the microwave oven and ate on the porch with a cup of reheated coffee, waving his sock feet at the cat to keep it at bay. Listening to the drone of eighteen-wheelers coming down the pass.

Gray Dausman finished reading *The Thief Lord* and closed it, feeling a sense of loss that the story was over. He looked up at the clock. Eight-thirty. He wondered where his father was. He got up and peeked into the refrigerator. Amid the jars of relish and mayonnaise, behind the loaf of moldy bread, he found a hard little orange. He spun it between his fingers. It felt more like a rock than a piece of fruit, but he dug his grimy, chewed-off fingernails under its peel. It was dry and tasted like cardboard.

He returned to his chair, picked up the book and opened it to page one. Gray studied the crisp letters, the chapter title, and the opening line, which led to the next, and to the next after that.

He'd finished the second chapter again when his father

walked in and dropped a plastic sack on the floor in front of his chair.

Gray stared up at Jim, bewildered.

"School supplies. You went today, didn't you?"

He nodded. "Yeah."

"Sorry. I should've taken you shopping. But I got what you need." His father turned on the television, then stalked to the kitchen where he unpacked another small sack of groceries. He pulled a bag of corn chips out, paused and looked at Gray. "These aren't for you." Then opened the refrigerator and put away the beer, holding out the first bottle and tossing the twist-cap on the counter.

Gray's stomach ached at the sight of the corn chips bag. He could usually ignore his hunger, but there were times when it sprang up unexpected and took hold of him. It would be a long wait for school lunch tomorrow. He wanted to ask his dad if he could just have a few chips. He wouldn't eat the whole bag — just a couple of chips. But he knew better.

He took the bag of school supplies to his room where he could examine the contents in privacy. He pulled out the packet of number two yellow pencils, the white plastic binder without pockets, the packet of lined three-hole paper. He found a cheap tray of watercolor paints in the bottom of the sack. An item for the younger grades. Not the colored pencils required for fifth grade. He slipped it under his bed. The school would give him the colored pencils if he had nothing, but if he showed up with something close, but not quite right, he'd be stuck with it. His dad was an asshole.

4

EDELSON STUDIED THE GLOSSY PHOTO opposite
September in the *Playboy* calendar left behind by the previous
sheriff. He ultimately concluded that the woman's breasts were
silicone. They couldn't be that big naturally on someone with a
waist that small. Could they? The phone rang, startling him.
He tossed the calendar face down on his desk. "Sheriff's office."

"Chris," the voice rasped.

"You have the wrong number."

"The body at the river . . . was Chris."

"Who?" Edelson popped out of his chair like a startled
bird. "Who's calling?"

Click.

He pulled the receiver away from his head and stared at
the ear piece, as if he might divine the caller. Then pressed it
back to his ear. "Hello?"

"Chris," he spoke aloud, digging in his pocket for his notebook. He jotted the name down. Not that he'd likely forget it.
"Chris."

He sat in his cruiser outside the residence of record for the first
Chris on the list he'd assembled from census records. For a
county with only a few thousand residents, Chris, and all its
variations, proved a highly popular name. Christine, Christina,
Kristen, Krista, Kristi, Crystal, and of course Christopher,

which he'd promptly ruled out on account of the coroner determining that the skeleton had been a woman. Had it been a man, his job would've been considerably easier as there were only six Christophers to the 114 females sharing some variety of that name. Edelson focused first on the slim I-90 corridor of Magda, Peerless, and St. John's, which narrowed the field to eighteen. Then he eliminated those under the age of twenty and over the age of sixty, bringing his list down to ten.

Christine Rybloom's home was in Magda proper, a three-block stretch of narrow, elm-lined lanes. Small but well preserved bungalows from the 1920s and 1930s, meticulously painted in pale lemon, sky, or sage, and sprawling porches with heavy, angular pillars and low overhanging eaves. The neighborhood was flanked on one end by the Catholic church with its neatly trimmed hedge and leaded-glass windows, and the Silver Dog on the other, with its diagonal row of backed-in choppers — Harleys mostly.

The sheriff squinted up at the yellow house, knowing before he got out of his car this would be a dead end. But the visit would tick one name off the list, so it was worth the effort. Leaves blanketed the woman's lawn, but they were fresh — within the week. The grass was recently mowed and the flower beds were churned and mulched and prepped for winter. He used the brass knocker to announce his visit.

A frail woman opened the door. "Yes?"

"Mrs. Rybloom?"

"No, that's my daughter. I'm Mrs. Sherwood."

Edelson looked at his list, as if it held some detail he'd missed, then back to the elderly woman. "Is she in?"

She peered at him curiously. "You're not from around here, are you?"

He followed her inside, pausing a moment in the foyer to give his eyes time to adjust to the darkness. The shades were drawn, giving the place the feel of a genteel cave. She mo-

tioned him to an ornate Victorian settee and disappeared to return promptly, teetering beneath a tray of teacups, a porcelain
kettle with matching sugar and cream dispensers. Her gait just
a slow shuffle, her arthritic knuckles white. Edelson stood and
relieved her of the burden, setting it on the coffee table.

"You're so kind," she said.

"About your daughter . . ."

She patted his arm and poured the tea, leaving him to
wait, then handed him a delicate little cup that he cradled in
both hands like a chalice, burning his hands rather than worry
about breaking the handle off.

The old woman sat down and situated herself. Sugared
her tea and sipped. "Christine's been gone for eighteen months
last Thursday."

"Gone?"

She looked toward the window. A gravely sad expression.
"Ran away."

"Ran away?" He felt like a parrot.

"From her husband."

"Oh." He nodded. "You don't know where she went?"

"New York."

The sheriff waited for her to go on. Had the urge to get up
and shake the information loose from her. Imagined one-and-
two-word phrases raining onto the Chinese carpet. "New
York?"

She nodded.

He sighed. "Is there anything more you can tell me?"

She thought a moment, then began to tell him the story
from the beginning — when she was pregnant with Christine
— through all the milestones. First lost tooth, eighth grade
graduation, the prom, going off to college. Then on to the birth
of her grandsons.

It didn't take ten minutes for the sheriff to understand that
he was the first living, breathing person to happen into this

33

woman's desperately lonely world in a long while. He nodded and smiled, and made expressions of sympathy, all the while searching frantically for some not too obvious reason to extract himself.

"Well, I've got some police business to attend . . ."

But the old woman went on. And on — all the way through the details of her daughter's mid-life crisis. Her decision to leave Eddy and their three boys, at first moving back home, and finally her pursuit of an acting career in New York City.

It was dusk before Edelson could say, "Thank you, ma'am. You've been very helpful," and get to his feet, his knees aching from the cramped space between the settee and the walnut coffee table.

"You're leaving?" Mrs. Sherwood stood, also. "I can fix you something to eat."

"No thank you. My wife will be waiting for me."

"Oh." She nodded sadly. "Okay, then. But if I can answer any more questions, please do come back."

He smiled politely, realizing she had no idea why he'd come in the first place. "I'll do that. I promise."

At home, while his frozen burrito heated, Edelson poured the dead woman's effects from an envelope onto the dinette table. Two thin abalone buttons, one still clinging to a scrap of stained blouse, the faint blue or pale green of plaid still evident. A rusted Levi Strauss button from a pair of 505 jeans. And a stainless steel stud — long and thick, the sort one might use to adorn a tongue, or a navel. He rolled it between his fingers while trying to imagine the woman whose bones he'd become so well acquainted with as a living, breathing creature. Wearing this ornament. It held a certain sexual allure, anti-establishment sentiment. Edelson considered himself the establishment, yet the stud piqued his interest.

34

Finding a woman in Montana based on her affinity for Levi 505 jeans was tantamount to locating a dairy cow based on her possessing an udder. The same was almost as true for the abalone buttons. What closet didn't have at least one article made in China? The stud, however, seemed to point to a younger woman.

The microwave beeped and he carried his supper outside, overlooking the river. The sun warmed the side of his face as it perched on the topmost spine of the mountain, preparing to sink into the night. He'd taken the time to fix fresh coffee, and drank it with his burrito, the steam blowing off the cup, westward, toward the pass. He thought about Mrs. Sherwood. Should he have stayed for supper? Why the hell not? She was probably a pretty fair cook.

Gray Dausman threw his school books down in the entryway and went to the kitchen. He gulped down a glass of tap water, then soundlessly unrolled the crumpled corn chips bag even though his father was not there to hear the noise. Peeking inside the half-empty bag, Gray scooped out a small handful. He counted them — nine — then reached in for one more chip, gauging the amount left in the bag. He lined them out on the counter about three inches apart, then rolled the top back down on the bag, exactly as he'd found it, placing it back in its precise location. He lingered over the first chip, touched it, licked the salt from his fingertip. Finally, he put it in his mouth. Crunched it slowly, savoring it.

He went back to the entryway for his books, paused a moment to watch the neighborhood kids taking turns racing their bikes up a plywood ramp in the street to see who could jump the highest. They rotated through the group and started over, a big, grungy kid named Brady the clear winner. Sadly, Gray brought his books to the table. He had math homework and a report to do on the explorer of his choice. Shoving the math aside, he opened a school library book about Vasco da Gama, an old explorer, but one the other kids didn't care enough about to fight over. He studied the angry looking man in what appeared to him to be women's clothes, a lacy white blouse and embroidered jacket with puffy sleeves. Then Gray traced his finger over the map on the opposite page.

He watched the clock as he read. At ten after three he got up and savored one more corn chip. At precisely three-twenty he repeated the ritual. Then again at three-thirty. And so on, until the ten chips were gone.

The Magda Diner was a dingy, flat-roofed shack in sad contrast to the Silver Dog, and was set too close to the road. A greasy spoon sort of place, decked out in orange and brown plastic. It seemed to have a loyal, aging patronage. Kip Edelson was meeting his wife, Robin, inside. She sat in the middle of the room, papers and books stacked on the cracked formica table in front of her. Whatever she had to say, it couldn't be good. When she had something on her mind, she liked public meetings, and this choice of a highly visible table only deepened his anxiety.

"Hello." Her eyebrows arched in accusation, her tone terse.

"Hi."

"What's the matter? I'm not going to serve you divorce papers."

He squinted at her, the way he squinted at people when he didn't want to reveal his thoughts. Or sometimes when he wanted to intimidate. But now it was reflexive; her comment had cut him to the toes. "Never quite know what to expect anymore. Robin, what do you want? Why couldn't we have discussed whatever it is at home, or at my office?" He glanced around at the patrons, felt their ears straining the dense air to overhear.

"What? We can't just have lunch together?"

"I'm the sheriff. What do you think?"

She sat back in her chair and looked at him. "I have decided to move into Missoula. To be near the University."

She may as well have brained him with one of her school books. His mind stuttered to a halt as he tried to think of something to say.

"I think the separation will be good for us. I mean, I need some space. I need to think some things through."

"Like what?" He struggled to keep his composure.

She let out a long, contemplative sigh. "Things haven't been right with us for a long time. You know that."

"No, I don't know that. Things were fine."

The waitress appeared at his elbow. "What can I get you?"

"Nothing," he snapped, jerking the flat of his palm up.

The woman took a step back and looked at Robin.

"Just coffee," Robin said. She turned back to Edelson. "Look, I didn't come here to fight."

He snorted, then homed in on her with a scrutinizing glare. "You're not seeing another man, are you?"

"You're such an ass. Of course not."

"I'm not supporting you while you *think things through*. You're on your own."

"Jeez, Kip. Will you listen to yourself?"

He looked over his shoulder at a couple in the booth next to them. Stared them into looking away. "Just tell me what's wrong. We'll fix it."

She shook her head. "I have. So many times."

Later, on the Interstate heading west, Edelson felt the pull of the engine as he accelerated to fifty, sixty, seventy. He came up on a Ford Torino in the left lane, passing a silver truck heavy and slow with milk. He flipped his lights on and the Ford moved over. He passed it and sped up. Eighty, ninety, ninety-five. The curves came fast and sweeping. Left, then right, then left. Like a lateral roller coaster. His hands gripped the wheel, pulling the cruiser smoothly and precisely, leaving a long trail of right-laned cars and trucks in his wake. They all moved frantically out of his way, responding to his urgency.

It was dark when he stopped at the rest area on the other side of Coeur d'Alene. He laid the seat back and tried to catch a nap, but all he could see were Robin's defiant eyes. He tried to imagine how he could've not known she was so unhappy, but it escaped him. What was so terrible about their life? Things were fine. How could she not be happy?

Gray Dausman heard a low moan coming from his father's room. He sat up and listened hard. Something was wrong. He tiptoed into the dark hallway and pressed his ear to his father's door. There it was again. Was he sick? He pushed it open. "Dad?"

"Goddamn it, Gray! Get out of here." A pillow flew at the door and Gray slammed it, stunned by the image of his father having sex — a strange woman on top, leaning over his father's doughy belly, her sagging breasts flopping as she moved. The woman laughed, and Jim Dausman let off a pirate's volley of cussing.

Gray went back to his bed and tried to forget the tangled limbs. The arched back. The painted toes. Her breasts were bare and hanging. Like nothing he'd ever witnessed before in his life. Large purple saucers staring at him. Holy shit!

The asphalt steamed in the sun, emitting a rubbery scent. Edelson pulled the visor down to shield his crusty eyes as he came down the pass into the morning, zipping through the curves. Semis to the right. Motorists moving blandly out of his way and hanging back, no one brave enough to pass him. He didn't care; he wouldn't have pursued even the most audacious speeder today.

He wished Robin had called his mother before she rashly decided to go live in Missoula. A sensible woman who could offer some advice, his mother had stuck with his father through thick and thin. And it was pretty damn thin in the end. But she never complained, raised two teenage boys alone too. Some part of Edelson understood his expectations of marriage were dated. From another era entirely. But still . . .

Maybe it was the baby thing. He had never really told Robin that he didn't want kids — not in so many words. She wasn't getting any younger, though. He winced as he recalled the persistence with which he confirmed she'd taken her birth control pills. He sped up, descending into the lowland curves outside Magda at eighty-five.

In his office, he picked up messages. Then, responding to a call from his dispatcher, he drove in to St. John's to question a man accused of stealing a pack of cigarettes from the Gas'n'Go. The toothless derelict sat on the curb in a rank-smelling tee shirt, smoking the contraband and denying that he'd walked within a hundred feet of the place.

The store manager paced the sidewalk near the pumps, watching, straining to hear. Finally, he shouted, "Just get the bastard off my lot and make sure he never comes back."

"You hear that?" Edelson asked the man who shoved the butt in his mouth and staggered to his feet. Appearing to have been through the routine before, he wandered a crooked path across the street to the Cherry Tree Motel, a sprawl of boxy little cabins painted eye-stinging white.

"Don't come back. I'll arrest you next time, even if the manager doesn't want me to."

The man mumbled as he went, not bothering to look back or acknowledge the sheriff's order.

Edelson watched him go, thinking he should have arrested the bum. He'd always taken the tough-cop role, believing his reputation alone could deter most people from petty crime. But he just didn't care today. It worried him a little, this new apathy.

Since he was already in St. John's, Edelson scanned his list of Chrises for the ones in town. There were only two. Kristen Hogarth he found at the school, where she served as principal. She assured him she was quite alive and never went by the name Chris. Christina Samuelson's last known residence, however, he found long abandoned, attached at the roof to a still-thriving and raucous saloon. Edelson poked his head in the empty cabin, assessed the vagrant squalor piled and rotting in the corners of the room.

"Place ought to be burned," he said aloud.

"Help ya, Sheriff?"

Edelson turned. A stout man wearing a stained cook's apron and holding a large bucket of soapy water stood in the side door of the saloon. His bald scalp appeared waxed under the winter-white sky.

Edelson glanced at his note. "Christina Samuelson?"

The cook tipped his chin up and thought. From his face, it did not appear to be a wondering sort of thought, as if accessing a vast database of names and faces, but a suspicious sort of thought. A *should I tell you?* sort of thought. So it appeared to Edelson, anyway.

"This is her residence of record." Edelson gestured a hand at the cabin.

"She's up the Flathead these days."

"Flathead Lake?"

"No. Flathead River. Up Montana 200."

"Any idea why she moved?"

The cook frowned. "Yeah."

Edelson squinted at him, waited for him to continue.

"Git away from me, I imagine."

* * *

There was a satisfaction in making a trip up to the Flathead. He'd been there before, years ago with his father, and its beauty was still bright in his memory. Rugged peaks, sloughing shale from their vertical upshot into shimmering green piles. Lodgepole pines gathered along the hem like children. And a turquoise river, placid and reedy — brimming with some subtle and untapped potential that he would be hard pressed to articulate. But the trip was also welcomed because Edelson liked to drive when he had a problem to think through. Wandering through wilderness would take up the better part of the day.

He found Christina Samuelson's place by the cook's description, a squat stone house on the opposite shore of the river. He could see it there, nestled in tight to the slope — absolutely no way to reach it. Her pickup, a mid-1960s Ford in duo-tone red and white, was parked at the ramp, locked. The flat-bottom cable ferry she used sat idle on the other side, and he couldn't see how to retrieve it. A black and white collie raced circles on her ragged lawn, barking across the river at him.

Edelson skipped stones across the glassy surface of the river for a while, rousted a pair of cinnamon teal ducks from their marshy home, discovered a damp little path running along the edgewater, under the locust trees, which he followed for no other reason than he didn't feel like returning to his own county yet. And that was where he found the canoe, bottom up in the shade.

Starting off slowly, he worked the paddle from side to side, pulling too hard and twisting the canoe first upriver, then down. But he shortly found his rhythm and brought a smooth stroke to his paddling, pointing the craft at the house and gliding silently over the serene water. Official business and his sense of duty pushed him forward until the wooden boat scraped the gravel launch on the other side.

The collie greeted him with a thunderous bark for such a small creature.

"Down," he commanded, and the dog dropped submissively at his heels.

A woman stood in the doorway of the cottage. "That's a private boat," she informed him.

"That's the only boat," he said, as he gained the yard proper.

"I know. I like it that way." She folded her arms across her chest.

The sheriff paused to take the place in from this side of the river. She had a sweeping vista of the milky green water. Montana 200 curled narrowly along the far bank, too far away to hear the cars. It would've made the perfect military encampment, he thought.

"To what do I owe a visit from the law?"

Edelson turned back to her. She was a handsome woman in her late thirties, fit. Weathered in the face, but tanned and natural. She wore her hair in a long braid that swept the length of her back. Thick and dark blonde. "Are you Christina Samuelson?"

"Chris. I go by Chris."

"Well, Chris, I'm just checking to see that you're alive and well."

"Is this some new service of the government? Couldn't think of anything better to spend my tax dollars on?" Then she cocked her hip. "What's the real reason you're here?"

He looked back at her and squinted. "Is there some other reason I should be here?"

She pressed her lips tight.

"The cook down at Shank's told me where you were."

A look of disdain crossed her face. "Pete?"

"Yeah, I think that's what he called himself." He scanned the trees and thought of the certainty of bears. "Dangerous place for a woman."

She stared at him a moment. "The *world* is a dangerous

42

place for a woman. I'll remember to keep my canoe on this side of the river from now on."

"I'm investigating a lead on a body we turned up down in Magda. Her name apparently was Chris."

"Well, I'm not who you're looking for."

"Indeed not." He looked up river. Took in the view one more time. The sun glittered white and topaz across the water. "Well, I guess I have my answer." He started back toward the canoe.

"Wait. I'll run you over on the ferry. I have to go to town anyway. That is . . . if you can wait a few minutes while I get ready."

Edelson dragged the craft onto the bank and turned it over, laying the paddle along its side. It was exquisite, a cedar-strip canoe, handmade. He ran his palm over the wet bow to get a sense of the craftsmanship, and wondered what this Chris would look like wearing the other Chris's bellybutton stud. A surge of masculine admiration for the idea coursed through him, culminating in his crotch before he could halt it.

5

It was still there — the smell, hanging in the windless air. Gray stood overlooking the river. Leaves had obscured the grave, like a golden carpet. But the smell was still there. Not that he could readily say to someone, "Do you smell that?" It wasn't that obvious. But somehow, mysteriously, it lingered.

He tossed a stick down into the leaves where they'd unearthed the skeleton. Then a stone. He waited, hopeful, for the sheriff, whom he hadn't seen in a while. Maybe he might come down here again. Gray wished Edelson *would* come back.

"Hey, Graaaay." It was Brady, from the neighborhood, dragging out his name the way one might call a dog. He approached with a small tribe of boys, four in all. On bicycles.

"Lookin' for your girlfriend?" Brady said. The others snickered.

Gray looked for an escape route. Down the sun-bleached fence, around the far end of the housing tract maybe? But they'd follow.

"Maybe it was your mother they dug up."

"Bet she killed herself to get away from you, another boy added."

Gray scuffed his toe in the soft dirt and avoided their stares.

"What's the matter with you?" Brady said, shoving Gray's shoulder. "Can't talk?"

"Leave me alone," Gray said.

"Leave me alone," Brady mimicked. "Whatcha gonna do? Tell on me?"

"I didn't do anything to you."

"You were born," he sneered. Brady was three years older, but only two grades ahead in school. A big kid with a fat gut that hung out of his tee shirt, and pudgy arms. Little black eyes that looked like they were poked with a pencil tip into leavened dough. He sat astride his bike, scanning the river. "How'd you get a stupid name like Gray, anyhow?"

Gray didn't answer.

"Maybe he's looking for more bodies," Brady said to the others. "Go look, then." He shoved Gray savagely, sending him tumbling over the bank.

Before he rolled to a stop, Gray popped up like a spring and darted down to the river's edge. He stood ankle deep in the icy water and gasped, staring back at where he'd landed. Where the body had rotted to bones. The boys were laughing above him. Gray brushed at his clothes, muddy now, trying to catch his breath.

"You get any brains on ya?" Brady called down.

Gray picked up a fist-sized rock, muddy and encrusted with periwinkles, and held it, ready to launch it at the bully if he came down after him. But the boys disappeared. Gray could hear them laughing and joking a long way off.

Robin's cat, Peachy, waited on the step once more as Edelson pulled in. He hadn't been home since he'd met Robin at the diner. But the cat gave him hope. Maybe she hadn't really moved out. Maybe she was just at class.

But her things were gone — the things that mattered anyway. Clothes, jewelry, shoes. She left a note with a number. Said she'd call him in a few days. He read it four times. Peachy rubbed against his leg and made a racket to be fed. Edelson looked at the animal.

"Guess she doesn't care that much about you either," he said, "to leave you here with me."

He fed the cat, showered, and started for town. Not in his cruiser, but in his pickup, dressed like a cowboy. A civilian. As much as the sheriff in a one-sheriff county can ever really be a civilian.

The Silver Dog was nearly packed. Friday night. The jukebox wailed out Hank Williams Jr. on the heels of Pink Floyd's *Dark Side of the Moon*. Edelson sat at the bar and waited for McHugh to make his way down to him.

"Sheriff, what can I get ya?" He chirped it like a bird. A little happy finch.

"Get any mineral water yet?"

"Californian. Just for you. But I ain't orderin' that French shit."

"Good enough. And a bacon burger."

"Comin' up." McHugh hopped along the bar, snapping empty glasses up and offering refills. When he returned, he set a bottle down with a glass of ice and a lime wedge. "Top it off with somethin' interesting?"

"It's interesting enough, thanks."

"Okay, then."

Edelson scanned the crowd from the mirror over the bar. A pair of teenage boys played pool, two more leaned against the wall watching, waiting their turn, all engaged in their own contest of colorful and inventive uses of profanity. So much so that Edelson couldn't find a common subject-line in their banter of fuckin'-this and fuckin'-that. A half empty glass of draft beer was perched on the edge of the pool table. He gauged the two against the wall, sipping the foam from newly-poured pints.

46

When McHugh brought him his burger, Edelson gestured over his shoulder with his chin. "Don't look twenty-one to me."

McHugh surveyed the boys, his jaw tense. "Oughta be pretty close. That's the Martin boy and his cousin."

"Close doesn't count. You know that."

McHugh's gray eyes landed on Edelson like two hard pebbles. "Draw too tight a line in a town like this and a man just might find himself out of business."

"You don't draw a tight enough line and you might find yourself out of business anyway."

The two stared at each other until finally McHugh stepped back. "I won't refill."

Edelson nodded, satisfied with the compromise. McHugh returned to the bar to lean in close to Edelson's ear. "You're in Montana now, Sheriff. Might behoove you to learn a little something about the culture in a place like this. If you get my meaning." He paused and gave the sheriff a meaningful stare, then hopped to the next patron, chirping like a bird again.

Edelson's stomach lurched. He lifted the bun and inspected his burger, a long-standing habit that suddenly took on new context.

"*Jackass,*" McHugh said under his breath. He'd lose enough money to feel it if he started carding kids. It wasn't just tonight, either. He had a reputation for looking the other way, and he was rewarded with lifelong patronage. These teenagers were tomorrow's adults. If he stopped serving them, they'd only head up to Shank's instead.

When Edelson took up conversation with the man sitting next to him at the bar, McHugh wandered out into the room, checking to see if anyone needed a refill. He slid alongside the Martin kid and said, "Sheriff's here, and he's got his eye on you boys. Can't refill until he leaves."

47

Martin cut his eyes over at the sheriff and sneered.

"Hang tight. He won't stay long."

Martin nodded and bent over the pool table to take his shot.

McHugh returned to the bar, satisfied for now, but what did this new sheriff really want? To put him out of business? McHugh had been waiting for Edelson to return to the Silver Dog, to set the ground rules, figure out what McHugh was doing and get his piece of the action. Unfortunately, the bartender was coming to believe this sheriff was clean and straight. A costlier prospect.

Edelson didn't actually think his plan through. Not with a decisiveness he could later recall anyway. But when he reached the Flathead River and unloaded the new canoe he'd bought that morning, he had some inkling of how quickly a man can go wrong.

A thin mist floated down the middle of the river, apparition-like. Autumn-red trees reflected in the glassy surface. The boat was stiff at first, not like Chris Samuelson's cedar canoe. This one was plastic and too wide in the center, giving it a buoyancy that constipated its speed. He knocked the paddle on the bow as he switched sides and wondered if he'd made the wrong selection. His choice had been driven entirely by price. Had Robin been with him it would've culminated in her accusing him of being cheap.

Robin. He pushed her from his mind. He would go nuts if he didn't.

Edelson paddled the highway side of the river, down past the rotted-out train depot at Perma. He didn't look at Chris Samuelson's house directly as he passed, but noted that her ferry was across the river on the far shore, her truck at the ramp, her canoe bottom-up where he had left it. A curl of smoke floated into the morning sky from her cobblestone chimney.

This unusual creature, this woman, had taken up residence in his thoughts. Moved right in, uninvited, with an appalling demand on his attention. He'd driven back to Magda the previous day with the idea Chris Samuelson was sitting in the passenger seat. Not saying anything in particular, just with him in a general sort of way. He'd drifted off to sleep the previous night filled with curiosity, wondering how she came to this hermit life. How she'd managed to set it up so brilliantly. Unreachable — unless she wanted to be reached.

He crossed to the far side of the river and turned back, paddling along a marshy edge in a stretch where he no longer had full view of the river lying hidden beyond a sharp bend ahead. And as he rounded the point, he found himself face to face with a black bear the size of a Volkswagen wading in the shallows. It paused, one large paw drawn up, and stared at him. He paused in turn, mid-stroke, and stared back. The animal abruptly turned and bounded up the shoreline a way, splashing wildly, then galloped up the bank and into the trees. Kip pulled his paddle across his lap and drew a sharp breath. "Shit! Shit-shit-shit."

After a moment to reflect on his life and how quickly it might have been stolen from him if that bear had been ill-tempered, he got underway again, a little farther from the shore this time, his arms and legs rubbery and uncooperative.

She was sitting in a lawn chair with a steaming mug in her lap. "Spying on me?" she called while he was still some distance away.

He didn't answer straight away, but paddled a steady line toward her. "A man can't go for a paddle down the river?"

"Why this river? Don't you have one in your own county?"

He let his canoe skim into the weeds where he bobbed in place. He turned and looked downriver, then up, then at her. "This one's a lot prettier."

She studied his canoe.

"Aren't you going to invite me up for a cup of coffee?"

"No."

He hid his disappointment and pressed the end of his paddle into the mud, pushing away from the weeds.

"I don't drink coffee. But you're welcome to a cup of tea."

He twisted around to look at the ferry launch on the other side of the river, as if it silently beckoned home. "I don't drink tea." He swished the paddle backward, inching out into the river, righting his craft. He took a slow stroke, faced upriver.

"Fine, I'll make you a cup of coffee then."

He smiled benignly and paddled toward her shore again. He pulled his boat up onto the ramp, her dog sniffing his ankles. He followed her to the door of the cottage. It was barely that, really only a square stone structure with a low beamed ceiling. One room.

"Nice place," he said.

"It was built by a Chinese immigrant. It's been here since the mid-nineteenth century. I had to reroof it. But it's as sturdy as anything you can build today."

Edelson ran his hand over the stacked river-rock wall. The stones were green, red and purple. An occasional yellow in the mix, a few gray. That natural rainbow of colors Montana was famous for. "How'd you get a roofing crew to come all the way out here?"

She turned to him. "I didn't. I roofed it myself."

He laughed.

"You think I'm lying?"

"No. No, of course not. But you had some help, I'm sure."

Chris poured the coffee from a small French press into a mug and handed it to him. "No. I didn't. Milk and sugar?"

"Milk, please."

"Goat okay?" He grimaced, and she put the creamer back in the refrigerator. She led him down to the lawn chairs overlooking the river, but before sitting, she kicked the bow of his canoe. "Where'd you get this?"

"Rod's Sport. Down in St. John's."

She turned and looked squarely at him. "Why are you here, anyway?"

Edelson didn't have an answer. Not even an answer he didn't want to share. "I don't know," he admitted.

Chris looked him over more carefully. "You're married." She pointed at his ring.

"She moved out."

"Oh." Chris nodded. "That's why you're here."

Her comment annoyed him. As if he was simply out to find a replacement for his wife of fifteen years. As if just anyone could take Robin's place. "I still love my wife."

Chris sipped her tea, leaving a silence between them.

"Don't you like my canoe?" he finally said.

She laughed, blowing bubbles in her cup. "Well, in fact, it's possibly the ugliest canoe I've ever seen. Why red?"

"It was on sale."

"Ah. Well, there you have it."

"I think I'll take it back and get a different one," Edelson conceded. "Do you want to come?"

Saturday mornings were fine with Gray. Cartoons from the time he awoke until noon. He especially liked Jackie Chan and the talismans Jackie's niece always managed to find that did cool things like make her invisible. He was old enough to know there were no such things, but he still indulged in a spot of fantasy when he watched. What if he could turn invisible? What would he do? Well, for one, he'd go to the diner and eat all their pies. Or maybe just sit in the corner of the kitchen and sneak food from the grill when the cook wasn't looking. He'd put a tack on his fourth-grade teacher's chair — a really long one. And he'd go to the store to get a binder with pockets. Gray paused over the idea. That would be stealing. He puzzled it out for a moment, then shrugged it off. One thing he'd do for sure is trip Brady coming down the concrete steps at the school. He'd wait for the perfect opportunity, when he was going fast enough to knock his teeth out.

Gray's father worked Saturdays and Sundays — his days off Tuesday and Wednesday. But the woman, Andrea, was still there this morning. Sleeping. She'd yelled at Gray twice to turn down the volume on the television. He hadn't gotten a look at her, except the initial meeting, which was all he could think of when he thought of her at all. Her breasts blazing in his face like gun-barrels. So when she slunk from the bedroom in his father's tee shirt, her legs bare and her hair whipped up like she'd come in from a terrible storm, Gray pretended not to notice.

The woman banged around in the kitchen, looking through cupboards, then appeared over his shoulder. "Don't you have any cereal or anything?"

He shook his head.

"What did you eat?"

"Nothing."

She went back to the kitchen and stood with her face in the refrigerator.

Gray sneaked a peek at her. She was old. Her hair was mostly gray, but long, like a schoolgirl's. She gave up on breakfast and lit a cigarette instead. Then she joined Gray in the living room and watched an episode of Scooby Doo with him.

"What time does your dad get home on Saturdays?" she asked.

He shrugged.

"I have a little boy like you."

He ignored her. He wasn't a little boy.

"He lives in Ohio with his grandma. Jason is his name. He's twelve." She lit another cigarette. "How old are you, Gary?"

"Gray."

"Sorry, Gray."

"Ten."

She threw one knee over the sofa arm, giving Gray from his place on the floor a fine perspective of her bare bottom. His face went hot upon seeing the mat of black hair and ruby flesh, and he turned his back to her. She watched a show about a crocodile hunter with him, then went back to the kitchen for another look.

6

CHRIS SAMUELSON HAD DECLINED Edelson's invitation, but the reason she supplied left the distinct possibility of future endeavors.

"You can't just paddle up here and expect me to drop everything to go shopping for canoes," she'd said. Then added, "I don't even know you."

So Edelson wandered solo through the sporting goods store, pondering the canoes suspended overhead, his criteria for another boat simply whether or not Chris Samuelson would approve of it. But not without a persistent nagging that he'd never cared so much about what Robin thought of canoes. In fact, knowing if it was Robin he was trying to please, he wouldn't be trying this hard. He wondered if his fascination with Chris Samuelson was simply a diversion from his floundering murder investigation. Three Chrises down and not a single lead. Would he focus on his marriage and not Chris Samuelson if the murderer were behind bars? He didn't think so. He paused in the aisle, between the sleeping bags and a row of erect fishing rods, standing at attention like soldiers, and asked himself most directly if he really loved his wife as he'd attested to that morning. The answer wasn't readily apparent. Of course he did, he assured himself. But then why . . . he peered up at a superbly varnished cedar strip craft with a sleek narrow hull. It was three times the price of his red, plastic boat, but he hailed the clerk and said, "This one."

Gray saw the canoe before he recognized the sheriff. It was perched on his pickup rack like a trophy, the shiny hull sparkling in the sun. Gray's father had promised to take him out in a boat someday, had been promising it since Gray could remember. A grand day in the future when they would catch giant fish and be happy, like other people. A day that proved ever-elusive. Gray had left off asking about it some years ago.

The sheriff didn't look like himself without his uniform and badge. He looked like he was going down to the Flying W to help out with cattle branding. All the men, at least all the men who didn't live in Gray's neighborhood, went. Branding at the W was like a holiday in Magda — the way some towns have onion festivals, or turkey shoots. He'd heard a lot of stories, but he'd never been invited to go. The boys from school would come back after branding, bruised or stitched, spilling stories about Rocky Mountain oysters, the smell of singed hair and burning flesh, or the drunken brawls at night. Boys who carried themselves like men now that they'd been allowed to participate. They were part of a secret club after the event, and they got more respect from everyone. Not just other kids, but teachers and parents too. It cut a sharp line through the boys at school: the included and the excluded. Or, the poor kids and everyone else, Gray decided. But that didn't serve to create a bond among the kids in his neighborhood; it intensified the pecking order instead, deepening Brady and his gang's mean-streak.

Gray sighed, and then called out to Edelson.

Edelson nodded sternly. "You keeping out of trouble, kid?"

"Yeah." Gray crossed the street and gazed up at the new canoe. "Cool."

Edelson looked at the canoe too. "Like it?"

"Yeah."

"Just bought her this morning." The sheriff started into the post office.

"Did you find out about the skeleton?" Gray asked quickly.

Edelson turned back. "A little. But not enough to know who it was."

"What did you find out?"

"It was a woman."

Gray looked at his feet. "Oh," and tried to think of something else to say so the sheriff wouldn't go.

Edelson waited expectantly, then drew out his wallet and extracted a crisp five-dollar bill. "Here. Buy yourself a treat."

Gray just stared at it, unbelieving.

"Consider it a reward." He thrust the money into Gray's hand and went inside without looking back.

"Thanks," Gray said too late. He headed straight for the Mini-Mart at the east end of town, where he bought himself two corndogs with mustard and catsup, a bag of barbequed potato chips, and a huge Pepsi from the fountain. He sat on the curb outside the store and tore into the food, devouring the corndogs in seconds. He sat back against the cinderblock wall to sip on the Pepsi and savor the chips, thinking about what he'd do with the two dollars he still had. He could go back for more food, or he could go to Rowena's Secondhand Store. The idea made him smile and gulp down the last of his Pepsi.

A bell on the door signaled his arrival. He stood in Rowena's entryway a moment, accosted by the musty stench of cast-off housewares and stale smoke, scanning the piles of junk. Pots and pans, racks of unwashed clothing, a shelf crammed with old radio alarm clocks in fake wood veneer, their unruly cords spilling out like snakes. The floor was rotting, its tongue and groove planks gaping in places wide enough to swallow a marble.

56

"What d'ya want?" the old woman hollered from behind the counter, eyeing him suspiciously.

He took a tentative step forward. "I just came to see what books you got."

"You have money?" Her voice popped and ground like a rock crusher.

"Yes, ma'am. A little."

"A little? How little?" She got to her feet and leaned over the glass counter, her cigarette ash dropping to the floor in front of him.

"Two dollars."

She nodded. "You'll find a couple books for that."

Gray stepped past her and down the narrow aisle to the bookshelf at the far end of the store. Next to the stinking bathroom with the mean black cat that hissed at people. He started on the highest shelf he could reach and read the title of each book. Occasionally he pulled one down and read the jacket, or if it was missing, the first page. If it looked interesting, he'd check the price, penciled on the inside of the cover. Most hardbacks were marked three dollars, so he focused on the paperbacks, which were mostly marked one dollar.

The old woman watched him like an already fed lion. Lazy and half-interested. "Don't make a mess of those books," she said.

"I won't." He was careful to put them back in the exact same place, even though he couldn't see any order to them. Some were crammed in sideways and on top of each other, wherever there was room.

He'd almost settled on a book about the plight of a morbidly obese boy whose guardian uncle gives him to a traveling circus, when he happened on a small book on the very bottom shelf about a Cherokee Indian girl. He read the back, then checked the inner flap. Two dollars. He held it up. "How come this one is two dollars and the others are only a dollar?"

Rowena held her hand out for the book and examined it. "It was printed in 1945. It's an antique."

Gray considered it a moment. He could get two books if he picked different ones, but this was the book he wanted. His mother was part Indian and she had talked about that a lot. About growing up on the reservation. How the white man had screwed her people. Gray knew what that meant now, but not when she was telling him. She wore beaded jewelry and feathers in her hair. No one ever believed him when he said she was an Indian. She didn't look that much like an Indian. But he believed her.

"Okay," he said, and handed over his bills.

Rowena shoved the book back at him and put the money in her cash box. "Have you been in here before?"

"Yes, ma'am."

"You ain't the kid that keeps stealing my stuff, are ya?"

"No." He shook his head and took a step toward the door. "I never stole anything."

"You live over in that housing tract by the river?" She threw her chin grimly in the direction of Gray's house.

"Yeah, but I never stole anything. I swear."

She looked him up and down, as if trying to determine if he was lying. Then a dawning expression crossed her face. "You're the kid found that body, ain't ya?"

Gray nodded and pushed the door open. Didn't want to talk about the skeleton. Not to anybody except the sheriff.

She watched him go. Gray felt her eyes boring into the back of his head. He hated going in there. Rowena always made him feel lousy. Like he shouldn't be in her store. Or anywhere.

He tucked the book under his arm and started toward home, breaking into a run.

Edelson hesitated before answering the phone. It might be Robin. She had said she would call, but four days had passed.

He hadn't called the number she left, either. What would he say? Beg her to come home? But it also might be his anonymous Chris-tipper.

"Hello?"

"Kip, it's me."

"Hi, Baby."

"How're you doing?" Her tone was gentle — almost sweet.

"Getting by, I guess."

There was an awkward pause.

"You?"

"Good. I'm really good." She sucked her breath in. "I found a nice little place on Third Street. It's not too far from campus. I can walk most days . . . until it snows anyway."

Another silence.

"Well, I just wanted to make sure you were okay," she said.

"Wait. Don't hang up."

She listened.

"I don't get it. I don't get why you can't go to school and still be here with me."

"I just need to think, that's all. I'm not closing the door on our marriage."

"Well that's good to hear." He failed to hide the bitterness in his tone. The idea that she *might* close the door so much more real now that she'd said it.

She didn't respond.

"I thought I provided a good life for you," he said, trying to get the conversation back.

"You know, Kip, you should try being a woman for just one day."

"What? Where do you come up with this shit? How am I supposed to be a woman for a day? And why in God's name would I want to?" There, he'd said it. And he knew it. *Shit*. "I mean . . . I don't mean there's anything wrong with it." He shook his head and pinched the bridge of his nose.

Robin was silent, but he could feel the heat of her temper through the phone line.

"I'm sorry. I didn't mean it the way it sounded. I just don't understand what you're talking about."

"I think you said exactly what you meant."

"Robin, please."

"You haven't got any idea do you? The next thing you'll do is suggest I call your mother or something. Go talk to a nice role model who slaved for her family and never complained."

Edelson's ears burned. "I never said that."

"I don't want to be like your mother, Kip."

"Better than yours."

Click.

He immediately regretted the barb. Knew it would hurt her. Said it to hurt her. He slammed the phone back in its cradle and ran his fingers wildly through his hair. Peachy rubbed against his ankle and he set the cat to flight. It landed smoothly on its feet and darted through the open door and into the yard. Edelson stared after it, wondering when he'd become so mean.

"Here, kitty-kitty-kitty. Here, kitty." Edelson crouched at the back porch, an open can of expensive cat food in one hand, a flashlight in the other, and strained to see under the planking. "Here, kitty-kitty."

Peachy moved cautiously to the front, sniffing.

"C'mon, kitty." Edelson pushed the can toward the animal, stretching his arm until his shoulder joint popped. "C'mon out, kitty."

The cat followed him out, but stood his distance. Edelson backed up the steps into the house, holding the can in front of him. Inside, he set it down on the linoleum and watched the cat devour it. He wished Robin was there to witness the gesture, choosing not to recall why he needed to coax her cat back to the house in the first place.

He made himself a bologna sandwich and settled into his reclining chair, where he numbly gazed at the TV, not comprehending the content of any show, but sifting through people in his mind: Robin, Chris Samuelson, and the dead woman. He'd crossed two more Chrises off his list that afternoon and was no closer to identifying the skeleton. He wished his anonymous tipper would call again. He needed more information. He was running out of leads.

Edelson thought of the kid, too. Why? He was just a poor kid from a neighborhood like many others. But he had discovered the skeleton, a horrendous act for a youngster.

Edelson left off thinking of Gray Dausman to consider Robin's assertion that her husband should try being a woman for a day. It wasn't the first time she'd said that, which is why he had reacted the way he had. He leaned back now and fantasized about having large, voluptuous breasts to suds up in the shower. Not a bad way to start the day, he thought, and got a little excited by his fantasy. He never could figure a pattern to Robin's moods, but she always had supper waiting for him when he got home. Sometimes he was late, and he was bad about calling. Edelson resolved to be better if he could get her back.

"Enough of this shit!" he spat, getting up to start a pot of coffee.

Wonder if I should warn her, McHugh thought. He wished he'd gotten a better look at that list the sheriff was poring over at the bar while he ate his lunch. It was all everyone talked about now — the sheriff and his list of Chrises. The man had been all over the county tracking down women named Chris. But Edelson kept his information to himself. Nobody knew what the connection was. Did he think the body belonged to someone named Chris? Or was it the suspect? McHugh almost asked to see the list — to check for his sister's name. But what would Edelson want with his sister?

McHugh glanced down the bar at his brother-in-law, Russell Vining, who now sat where the sheriff had been. He pulled a clean glass from the beneath the counter and filled it from the tap with Budweiser, then carried it down to the man, wishing his brother-in-law would take off, leave town, or die. Anything, to keep his filthy hands off McHugh's sister.

Crystal O'Shea lived in Peerless, next to the County Historical Museum, in a turquoise trailer adorned with a white stripe and wedged between two giant locust trees. Edelson banged on the dented metal door.

"Who is it?" a woman called in a ragged voice.

"County Sheriff. I have some questions for you, ma'am."

After a moment, the woman cracked the door and peeked out with one eye.

"Are you Crystal O'Shea?"

"Yeah."

"Can you prove it? I'm following up on a lead, ma'am. And as long as you can prove you're Crystal O'Shea, I'll be satisfied and you can get back to whatever you were doing."

"I can prove it," she said and shut the door in his face. After a minute, she opened the door again and thrust her driver's license at him. He examined it. It belonged to Crystal O'Shea. But the woman in the picture didn't resemble the woman in the trailer. He pushed the door open a little wider to see her in the light.

"You don't look five-eight to me."

She stood a little taller. "No one tells the truth on their license. Everybody knows that." She held her hand out for the license.

"Says here you have brown hair." He looked at her again. "Your hair looks blonde to me."

"You never heard of hair dye?"

He twisted his mouth. "You have any other ID?"

"Nope. That's it." She took the license from him and started to shut the door.

"Hey, Sugar, who is it?" a man called from the back of the trailer. "Tell him to wait his turn. Unless it's another woman, then bring her on back."

Edelson rested his hands on his belt. "If I have any more questions, I'll stop back."

"You do that," Crystal O'Shea said and shut the door with a tinny pop.

He stood on the stoop for a time, listening. The door flew open and a balding man sprang out, his shirt cuffs still unbuttoned.

"She takes in laundry," the man said, gesturing back at the trailer.

Crystal O'Shea leaned against the jamb of the open door and lit a cigarette.

"Laundry?" Edelson inquired.

"Yeah. How 'bout you, Sheriff. You need any washin' done? I used to do a little laundry for the last sheriff."

"No, I don't need any washing done." He stepped off the porch and started away. "I don't think this town's big enough to support a washerwoman. If you know what I mean."

The woman gave Edelson a hateful glare.

As he walked, he took out his list and drew a line through Crystal O'Shea.

Gray gazed out his classroom window at the coming fall, soft with yellow and fading orange, thinking about the sheriff and how he had combed the ground that night at the river, slow and methodical. How he had snapped at the others when they packed up the body. The way he told them the area hadn't been thoroughly searched. And how he stood his ground, bringing them all back down to the place where the skeleton had been, and how they got down and searched with the sheriff until he was satisfied.

"Gray?"

Gray focused on his teacher, a white-haired man with a perpetually cross expression.

"Can I trouble you to give your work some attention?"

Gray looked down at his math worksheet, a jumble of numbers that made no sense to him. He'd tried to listen and unravel the mystery that his classmates seemed to already understand. But he couldn't stay tuned to the drone of the teacher's voice. Couldn't make sense of the overhead projector demonstration the teacher had given at the start of math period.

"You're failing math, Gray. You do realize that, don't you?"

The girl who shared his table giggled. She always finished her assignments early and laid her papers out on her desk when the teacher handed them back with "Good job" scribbled across the top, next to the giant A.

Gray dipped his chin. The teacher turned his attention to another derelict student, suggesting he'd better get busy or fail along with Gray Dausman.

When school let out, Gray gathered his books and walked down to the river. He scouted the site the way the sheriff had, looking for something left unfound, some small thing they'd missed that he could report to the sheriff.

It had been the white swell of the skull that had drawn him down to the riverbank. The way it lay in the leaves, it looked like a baseball. He spotted it from the bank and came after it with a large stick that he whacked like a club at an oversized golf ball, expecting the object to skip and roll into the river. But it was rooted in — still attached. It twisted up out of the mud enough to bare its teeth at Gray, the jaw gaping, as if it meant to cry out from his assault.

What visited Gray again and again was the slight movement his stick caused and the awful stench of the corpse. The sight and smell came to him at the oddest times, like when he opened the refrigerator, or turned back his bed covers, or caught any flash of white in an otherwise colored world. But most particularly when he ventured near the river.

Gray thought the sheriff had probably seen worse, though. A policeman's job would be full of so many dead people it wouldn't really bother him anymore. And Gray wanted that — to not be scared by terrible things. That was why he had come to the river today, and why he forced himself to scour the leaves searching for some missing clue.

7

Edelson propped his boots on his desk and examined the arrowhead he had found at the crime scene again, having confirmed the curator's story that Indians had never inhabited the area.

He pinched the stone between his thumb and index finger — point to tail — and held it against the bright backdrop of the window. The downward pitch was markedly longer on one side than on the other. He turned it, felt the fine sharp edges that had been chiseled by a precise hand. His father would have admired it, would have placed it in a glass display frame, labeled, with an approximate date. Would even have tried to pinpoint the specific tribal branch it came from. Edelson wondered where all those artifacts were that his father had collected and cataloged over the years.

He spun the arrowhead, which came to rest pointing at the phone, reminding him of his anonymous caller who had fingered someone named Chris. He wished she would contact him again. He had a host of questions — her involvement, her relationship to the deceased. She was scared. That much he could tell from the sound of her voice.

He scanned his list of Chrises. "Who's next?" he said aloud. "Kristi Blackhorse." The name was last on the list, but it stood out. Could be an Indian name, he thought.

*   *   *

Edelson wove his way through the housing tract outside Magda, looking for Kristi Blackhorse's address: 828 Big Sky Court. But the moment he laid eyes on the house, he knew she wasn't there. It was Gray Dausman's house. He made an arching turn in the street and headed out toward the pulp mill.

Jim Dausman greeted the sheriff with, "What is it now? I've got a job to do. You keep comin' down here to see me, my foreman's gonna get the wrong idea."

Edelson squinted at the man. It didn't take all that much to get his dander up. The sheriff motioned toward the door and both men stepped out onto the ugly concrete walkway.

"How are you acquainted with Kristi Blackhorse?" Edelson asked.

Dausman loosed a wad of spit and shot it near the sheriff's boot. "That's Gray's mom."

"When was the last time you saw her?"

Dausman held his fists at his sides, clenched tight. "If you know where that bitch is, you tell her to get her ass back here and take care of her kid."

"When did you last see her?"

"Shit, more than a year ago probably. She run off with some asshole from down around St. John's. Big guy — a trucker. Took everything but her kid. Cleaned out my account. Took everything."

"Do you know if she's Indian?"

"She ain't no goddamn Indian. She's as light as you or me." Dausman pinched his cheek, raising a red welt. "Maybe she had some distant ancestor. She was always tryin' to git the BIA to recognize her."

Edelson nodded. He'd come across people claiming to be Indian simply to collect money from the Bureau of Indian Affairs. "She collected a Bureau check?"

"No, but she was just tryin' to scam the government." Dausman paused and thought. "What's she done to git the law on her trail?"

"Who said she's done anything?"

Dausman scrutinized the sheriff. "She has a sister down in California. That's where she was headed the last I heard from her. Anita Jossey. Lives in Susanville."

"Thank you. That's all I need." The sheriff started for his cruiser but stopped short and turned. "How's your boy doing in school these days?"

Dausman set another wad to flight. "He's doin' fine." His tone had flattened.

"You been down there to find out?"

Dausman didn't respond, and the sheriff accepted the silence as an invitation to follow up on Gray himself.

Perusing his list of Chrises and those he knew so far: a mid-life-crisis runaway, a school principal, a self-appointed hermit, a whore, and the mother of the boy who found the body, Edelson ran his fingers through his graying hair. There were still several names left on the short list. More women to hunt down. The very idea that Gray might've dug up his own mother made Edelson want to puke. He had to keep on questioning.

The evening was early yet. He changed from his uniform and prepared to drive up to the Flathead, thinking he might enjoy an outing in his new canoe. But even as he loaded it onto his pickup, he was already talking himself out of going. If he wanted to go canoeing on the Flathead, he had to at least admit his intent was to see Chris Samuelson. And if he wasn't ready to accept the truth, he'd best just stay away. But he was hungry.

He drove back to Magda, turned at the Catholic Church and pulled up in front of the pale yellow house with the well-tended flower beds.

"Do you have some time for a couple more questions?" he

asked Mrs. Sherwood, his hat in his hand. He knew she had time for him or anyone else.

She escorted him through the parlor and into the bright kitchen and dished him a bowl of spaghetti without asking if he wanted some, then set about warming some toast.

"How old is your daughter?"

"Forty-two," she said, without turning from the stove. "Christine got a scholarship at the university for speech and debate. But she didn't finish. She met her husband, Eddy, who was two years older, and when Eddy graduated they went to Portland, Oregon." The story was familiar to Edelson and, seemingly, one that Mrs. Sherwood wanted to tell.

"Did she ever go back to college?"

The old woman turned with a surprised look. "Why would she run away if she had?" She shook her head.

Edelson twirled the noodles onto his fork and stuffed them into his mouth. Finally, he said, "Did Christine have her bellybutton pierced?"

The old woman dropped the salt shaker. It bounced off the stove and landed in the middle of the kitchen, sprinkling the linoleum. "Oh, my goodness, I hope not." Her face went scarlet.

After supper they shared a pot of coffee. Edelson listened to one of the old woman's stories and told a couple of his own about growing up in Idaho with his forest ranger father and his little brother, Monty.

"He lives in Saudi Arabia now," he said. "He's a real big shot."

Mrs. Sherwood smiled and glanced at the clock. It was ten-forty-five. "Won't your wife be wondering where you are?"

He quickly replied, with no comment, "Yes. Thanks," he said. "For the information and the supper. It was delicious."

She told him to come again.

*　　*　　*

The next Chris on the list was Christen Vining. Immediately after he called the Susanville, California, police department and explained about the skeleton, his anonymous tip, the list of Chrises, and asked them to locate Anita Jossey and her sister, Kristi Blackhorse, he headed for Vining at Nine Mile Creek. The creek intersected I-90, halfway between Magda and St. John's, not too far from his own house. He followed a rutted gravel track deep into the mountains, hoping he was on the right path, even though no mile markers or other residences appeared to check the address against. But he felt no sense of urgency. After all, it wouldn't bring the woman back from the dead to know if it was Gray's mom they had unearthed. He had a keener interest in whether the Susanville authorities could substantiate Jim Dausman's story.

Dust roiled up behind the cruiser as he drove deeper into the alpine forest. The grade climbed steadily and Edelson found himself flexing his jaw, trying to get his ears to pop. He thought briefly about whether it was wise to venture this far into the wilderness without backup and radioed his dispatcher to let her know where he was.

"Okay," she said, as if she didn't know what to make of the information.

"If you don't hear from me by . . ." He looked at his watch. ". . . by, say, two o'clock, send someone in looking for me."

"Who am I gonna send?"

"I don't know. Don't we have a volunteer fire crew or something?"

"Okay," she said again, her uncertainty still apparent.

He pulled to the side of the road and got out to piss in the bushes. The ditch was littered with broken bottles and beer cans, many faded to white. He sent a sixteen-ounce Bud can sailing with his boot and craned up at the lodgepole pines. Nine Mile Creek babbled along the downhill side, at the base of a rocky slope. He took in the cold mountain air, pine-sweetened. The place seemed close to the edge of the world. Edelson retrieved his jacket from the trunk. He drove slowly, gravel crunching beneath his tires, rambling along another ten miles before he crested the summit. He came into a clearing at the peak, and he could see east for fifty miles or more. The pulp mill where Dausman worked was just a dull speck beneath billows of white steam. The Clark Fork snaked its way into the haze of the far horizon. The road ran along the ridge a way before dipping back into the trees on the other side of the slope. He might now be in Sanders County, or Lake. The two bumped into Mineral County somewhere in this no-man's-land.

At last he found a mailbox, at the end of the road and civilization. Edelson squinted at the rusted metal numbers nailed on the post, compared them to the numbers on his list, and pulled into a driveway — two parallel ruts in the hardpan. His cruiser bottomed out in places, but he ventured on, knowing he was on the right trail. He emerged from the forest suddenly, into the dirt yard of a mobile home. A single-wide, white and brown, without skirting. It was battered so profoundly it might have been left to die.

Through his dusty windshield, he peered at the scattering of derelict car bodies. A mid-1950s sedan in faded aqua sat at the center of the yard with a sapling growing through its broken-out rear window.

A violent barking reverberated over the stillness, but Edelson couldn't see where it came from. The animal sounded vicious and big. He climbed out slowly and scanned the area. He realized, with some relief, that the dog was inside.

Only twice had a sequence of events come at him so rapidly that thinking never figured into the equation. Once, when his younger brother had slipped through the trapdoor at Gravepoint Lookout and Edelson caught him by the forearm and yanked him back up from the rocks forty feet below. The

71

other was on an icy highway when a pickup in his oncoming lane went into a frantic spin and careened straight at him. He could not recall deciding on the path he took. Across traffic. Steering into it. And how he waited for the crushing impact that never came.

So it was, in the remotest mountains of Mineral County or Sanders or Lake, that a man stepped out from behind the trailer and leveled a shotgun at Kip Edelson's head. Cool and smooth and with no recognizable fear. A sharp crack broke across the day, assaulting the deepest region of Kip's inner ear. And a sulfurous smoke sifted away in the late morning light.

His wrist burned and his head swam. His pistol was drawn, but already loose at his side. And the man before him lay dead, a bullet in his skull.

Edelson could not recall a conscious decision to fire.

He crouched behind the door of his cruiser. Waited. The dog snarled and scratched viciously to get out. A curtain moved, and inside the trailer, Christen Vining shrieked and wailed. Edelson reached for his radio. "Send the backup fire department. Send them *now!*"

Christen Vining claimed no knowledge of the finely cultivated, well-watered marijuana crop that flourished in the clearing behind her trailer. And though he'd been an officer of the law for fourteen years, Kip Edelson's stomach jellied and his limbs quivered when he recounted the sequence of events to the federal investigator, who never questioned his story, never asked for details beyond those Edelson provided. He'd been on the Vinings' trail for some time, but had declined to share that fact with local authorities, arrogantly so, in Edelson's estimation. And Vining, for his part, was onto the Feds. Edelson guessed that Vining was prepared to blow the investigator's head off and the Fed was relieved that it was a bumbling local sheriff who finally put Vining to the test.

But knowing these things didn't dampen the image of Russell Vining laid out in the pine needles, limbs askew, mouth pursed as if to speak, eyes directed blankly skyward. Or the wailing of his wife. No amount of official police description could hold those recollections at bay when Kip sat in his Adirondack chair of an evening, listening to the elk whistle.

Gray Dausman didn't much enjoy the book about the Cherokee girl. Its language was old-fashioned and hard to understand. The girl in the book didn't in any way resemble his mother. And looking for some connection to her in those pages only served to underline her absence. She'd been gone since the end of his third-grade year.

He wrote his mother often, carefully addressing his envelopes to Kristi Blackhorse, and in capital letters CALIFORNIA. He used his best handwriting. He gave them to his father, who agreed to take them to the post office. But it seemed forever since he'd mailed the first one, and he hadn't heard one word from her.

He sat on the edge of his bed, the onset of evening casting a chalky haze beyond his window, and started a new letter.

> *Dear mom,*
>   *How are you in California? I hope you are ok. We found a skelatan down by the river. It was grose. Scool is ok. I got Mr. Allen this year. He is meen. Please rite or call me. I realy miss you.*
> *Love,*
>   *Gray*

Andrea, his father's girlfriend, was in the kitchen stirring a skillet of Hamburger Helper when Gray brought his letter out to be mailed. He didn't mind so much anymore that Andrea was there because most evenings she cooked. And that amounted to two meals a day for him now that school had begun again and they gave him a free, hot lunch. His father never cooked and forbade Gray to use the stove.

"What's that?" she asked, picking up his letter.

Gray immediately wanted to grab it back. "Just a letter."

"Who's Kristi Blackhorse? Is that your girlfriend?" She flashed him a teasing smile.

"That's my mom."

"Oh." Andrea examined the envelope more closely. "Well, it won't get to her without a street address."

"Yes, it will." Gray stood with his arms folded across his chest.

"No, it won't." She looked at him pensively. "Do you ever think about living with your mom?"

Gray didn't answer. He knew better, even though he thought about living with his mom every single day.

"How long has she been gone, anyway?"

"She's looking for a house. Then I can go see her."

Andrea rolled her eyes and turned back to the sizzling macaroni noodles. Gray took his letter and sat in the living room, listening to the news. The sheriff was on TV. A reporter was talking about how he shot a man and people in pale blue uniforms were cutting down giant plants on the hillside and talking about how they were worth hundreds of thousands of dollars.

Andrea came in and stood behind the couch clucking her tongue. "Those pigs don't have anything better to do than kill people because they're smoking a little weed?"

When Gray's father got home, Gray met him at the door and thrust the envelope at him. "Will you mail this tomorrow?"

Jim took it and shoved it into his breast pocket without comment.

Gray followed him through the clutter to the kitchen. "It'll get to her, won't it?"

74

"Yeah, sure it will," his father said, opening a bottle of beer. He paused to kiss Andrea, and she wrapped herself around him like a mink stole.

"Are you sure?" Gray said, watching the spectacle in dismay.

Randy McHugh didn't open the Silver Dog the day after the sheriff wasted Russell Vining. He drove down to Missoula instead, to see if he could find his sister a defense attorney. His cook offered that he and the waitress might probably be able to run the place in his absence. But McHugh declined, knowing they'd get a blood-thirsty crowd that day. And he wasn't keen to have his tavern destroyed while he was gone.

He reminded himself to be patient with his sister, though he could hardly understand how she mourned Russell at all. She was a mess, unable to talk about what had happened or the trouble she faced. McHugh tried to help her see that placing all the blame on Russell was her only hope, but she was reluctant to betray him. She seemed afraid of her dead husband, making McHugh wonder if Russell had hurt her in ways he wasn't aware of. The idea made McHugh's blood boil. Russell was better off dead.

McHugh was glad he'd have his sister under his roof where he could protect her. She needed him now, and he'd show her that he'd always been the one she could count on — the one who truly cared for her.

Edelson glided along the edgewater of the Flathead in his new canoe. The sky was flinty, and the water dull. A cold breeze twirled leaves into the air, and he recognized that moment on the cusp of changing seasons when summer simply ceases to be present. It was a short, downhill sprint to winter from here. His reddened hands ached with cold, but he paddled along in silence.

Chris Samuelson's ferry was on the highway side, her pickup gone, as well as her dog. He paddled past her house as if not noticing and crossed over at Perma, coming up the center of the river, not keeping his eye out for bears, or paying attention to much of anything at all. He didn't know what he'd come for, but was bitterly disappointed by its absence.

When Edelson arrived home Robin's car sat in the driveway. She was waiting in the kitchen, stewing a pot of chili.

"This is a surprise," he said.

She poured him a cup of coffee and set it on the table. "I saw the news. Are you okay?"

He just looked at her. "Well . . . I was faster than he was."

"That was my worst nightmare come true, Kip. It was everything I never wanted to think about. A lone sheriff, chasing a maniac into the woods."

He winced. "I wasn't chasing a maniac. I was looking for his wife. She was on my list of people to find after we dug up that skeleton."

They sat across the table watching each other silently for a time, until Robin started to cry. Edelson moved to her side of the table and put his arm around her. He whispered in her ear, telling her he was fine, but her tears only came faster.

"This is the one thing I've feared the most," she sobbed. He pulled her closer and kissed her temples, but she pulled away. "Stop. I can't do this." She got to her feet and wiped her eyes.

"Please," he said, grasping the tips of her fingers.

She gathered her things. "I can't do this." And slipped away.

It had been seven and half years since Kip Edelson had taken his last drink. He could never really put his finger on why he'd become an alcoholic in the first place. He hadn't experienced any horrible childhood tragedies, hadn't lost a lover so dear he couldn't go on, hadn't been the target of schoolyard bullies. That was the shameful part of it, that he'd drowned himself in gin without even having a decent reason for doing so.

The epiphany — that clarifying moment when an alcoholic recognizes the true, honest-to-God state of affairs — came at eleven o'clock on a Sunday morning. Robin had been listening to Mozart while she painted horse portraits — one of her many short-lived careers. It required a certain frame of mind she told him, which classical music inspired. Edelson decided to give up gin and, instead, cultivate an appreciation for red wines to accompany her music. He'd focused his attention on a small microcosm of Willamette Valley vintners, primarily because they were still affordable on his law enforcement salary.

He'd spent the better part of the morning sucking down a bottle of Pinot Noir, light and fruity with a raspberry bouquet, blissfully convinced he wasn't really drinking because, after all, it was only wine. When the bottle was empty and he looked hazily ahead at the remainder of the day, somewhere in his mind he understood the greater reality. But it wasn't until he was staggering down to the neighborhood convenience store to buy another and stumbled over a patch of root-ruptured sidewalk that he was struck — even before the upturned cement — by the awesome detail of the world he lived in. As he plummeted headfirst toward the walk, witnessing every pockmark and crack, every bit of grit and sand, every twig, even the sharp black and yellow stripes of a dried-up wasp, he saw himself clearly, a sodden drunk.

His injury hadn't required stitches. But his nose gushed blood for 30 minutes. He sat on the grassy strip next to the curb with his red, sopping handkerchief, his nose tipped back like a man listening to the drone of flying locusts, his temples pulsing. And he knew what he was. He knew he had to cure his addiction. As he applied pressure to stop the bleeding, the oak canopy overhead and its silhouetted leaves against a pillowy sky seemed to speak to him, to tell him to get a grip.

In the intervening years he had experienced few cravings. So few that at times he'd even questioned whether he *was* an alcoholic. But now, as he watched Robin walk out the door — a vague, intangible sense in his gut that it was for good, a sense he didn't care to parse and evaluate — he wished for a drink with every ounce of himself.

He wandered outside and stood at the riverbank, gazing at the murky Clark Fork. He rubbed the back of his neck violently. After a time, he commenced to walk the four corners of his ten acres, wondering *what now?* Nothing came but the rationalizations of an alcoholic: *It's been seven years; you're probably fine to have a drink. You need this; you killed a man. If watching your wife walk out on you after that isn't reason enough, what is?*

The old woman whom Edelson continued to call Mrs. Sherwood, despite her insistence on Eleanor, greeted him unsurprised. He could taste the sugar from the porch, and she led him back to the kitchen where hot cinnamon rolls steamed on the counter. She coiled one onto a dessert plate and handed it to him with a fork.

"I saw the news," she ventured after a time.

He nodded. Ate his cinnamon roll without looking up. The sugar he would've found in a glass of whiskey didn't quite leave his thoughts, but the roll did help to satisfy his urge.

8

RANDY MCHUGH INSERTED A NEW BLADE into his Exacto knife and torqued it down tight. He set it on the end table, carefully balanced against the spine of an Ivan Doig novel he'd picked up in Missoula. Then he pulled off his right boot and peeled down his sock, letting it drop to the floor. With his ankle draped across his knee, he picked linty specks from his toes and examined the underside of his foot. A line of hard, white calluses ran perpendicular across the ball. Round and flat, like lozenges. He gripped his stiffly curled toes and pulled them back until the calluses stood in high relief, then took up his knife and began slicing them away, layer after layer, until he'd carved them down to divots.

He started on the other foot. As scraps of compressed flesh glanced off the carpet, he thought of Russell Vining. Such pretty feet. Straight toes, soles as soft as a baby's skin. His sister had hunted down a man with such feet, determined not to pass on the McHugh curse. When finished, McHugh set the knife down and stood to put his handiwork to the test. His toes sat atop his feet like talons, each joint stiff and gnarled, with reddened corns. The balls were large and bulbous. He wandered into the kitchen to get a better feel. The hardwood floor was a painful prospect beneath the pressure points, but a good indicator of his success in easing the chronic pain. He hobbled back to the sofa and pulled his socks and boots back on. The spongy homemade arch supports he'd glued inside the boots gave the most relief.

Randy McHugh was an intensely private man, his timbered acres next to Willishaw Creek and his flat-planed log cabin his sanctuary. He stood now on his veranda looking across the valley, the ribbon of river, the mill steam billowing into the deep purple evening sky, the crescent moon hanging, and shivered at the prospect that people could learn his secrets. That he was glad his elegant-footed brother-in-law was dead. McHugh had suffered agonies since the day Russell Vining had dragged Christen off to Missoula to get married. His sweet sister in that creep's arms made his skin crawl. Christen had warned him about Russell's creditors when McHugh had visited her the afternoon of Russell's death. She swore they wouldn't walk away because her husband was dead. They knew McHugh's involvement, however limited, and would leverage the knowledge. He understood with sickening clarity the absurdity of his long-held belief that the most he had to fear was being attacked by a grizzly while putting his trash out.

Edelson stared at TV, thinking about Christen Vining. He struggled against an urge to go to the Missoula County jail and apologize for shooting her husband, and that bothered him. Russell Vining had brought about his own death — Edelson believed that. But Christen Vining's screeching wail echoed in his head. She woke him in the dead of night with it, the cry of a tormented cat.

He thought also of McHugh, that strange little man with the awkward gait. Christen Vining was his sister. Edelson had pieced together McHugh's comments, his attempts at conversation that suggested bribes, including his offers of free food at the Silver Dog. Edelson had met McHugh's kind before. But the way McHugh constantly solicited him made more sense now. How had Vining distributed his marijuana? How else could a bar owner in a near-ghost town afford a fine little cabin on the Willishaw?

Edelson had only glimpsed Christen Vining as she was being hauled out of the trailer in handcuffs. She might have been a pretty woman once. There was something about her, the way she carried herself, or perhaps the high, pinched cheekbones, that suggested something lovelier than the creature with stringy hair hanging over her red and swollen face and filthy clothes. She had barricaded the door and refused to open it until the FBI arrived and kicked it in. Edelson hadn't been anxious to speak to her anyway, not after putting a bullet in her husband's head. So he waited in his cruiser until help arrived. It had been the longest hour and fifteen minutes of his life.

Gray pressed Mrs. Anton's doorbell, the book he'd read twice under his arm. It took her a long time to open the door.

"Hello, Gray," she said, smiling, her false teeth large and stained.

"I brought your book back. Thanks for letting me read it. I read it twice."

"Did you?" She ruffled his hair. "Well, why don't you keep it then? I can't think of anyone to give it to."

"Really?"

"Sure." She leaned outside and looked up the street. "Is your father working today?"

"Yeah, he always works on the weekend. But Andrea's there." Gray looked up the street too. "She's sleeping. She sleeps a lot."

Mrs. Anton's smile disappeared. "Are you hungry? I have some soup."

Gray nodded eagerly. She stepped aside and he came into her warm house. It was like a pillow factory. Everything padded with ruffles and bright, flowery prints.

Later at Rowena's Secondhand, Gray suffered a twinge of guilt. It was somehow wrong to sell a gift. He hid the book Mrs. Anton had given him in his sweatshirt, along with the book he'd bought the previous week. Snow was falling, the first of the season. Small, heavy pellets dusted the ground, but offered no promise of sticking. Gray pulled his hood up, but the sweatshirt barely fit him any more, and it stretched so tight he could hear the fibers snapping. He shivered.

As he turned onto Main Street he spied Brady and his entourage riding their bikes toward him. He crossed the street and ducked into the narrow alley between the empty Montana Bank building and Rowena's shop. He watched the boys pass, laughing and cussing at each other. He hated everything about those kids, even their hand-me-down Nike shoes.

Inside the store, the old woman appeared not to have moved since Gray was last there. She sat behind the glass counter, smoking a cigarette. A small black and white television lit her prunish face in pea green. "What do you want?"

He swallowed and approached the counter, pulling the books from under his sweatshirt. "I . . . I was wondering if you would trade these books for some others."

Rowena lifted the larger of the two and looked it over, opening the cover and skimming the dust jacket. She set it down with a grunt and picked up the smaller one. Her eyebrows arched in surprise. She opened it and looked at her own penciled price of two dollars, then gave Gray a menacing glare. "Did you steal this from me? This is my book!"

"No. I bought it," he stammered. "Remember? I was here last week. I bought it for two dollars." His limbs stiffened and his skin went clammy beneath his sweatshirt.

"I don't remember you. And someone's been stealing my merchandise."

Gray's mind raced. How could he prove he was telling the

truth? No one would ever believe him. Not against a grown-up even if she was a stupid, old, smelly woman.

"I'm gonna call the police," she hissed.

"I swear I bought it; I didn't steal it." Then he remembered. "I found the skeleton at the river. Remember?"

The woman leaned across the counter and scoured Gray's face with pale, cloudy eyes that gave her a ghoulish appearance — half blind, already decaying. She lingered over his face for an uncomfortably long time, then drew back with a nod. "I remember you." She looked again at the books. "Well, I can give you three dollars credit."

"Three dollars? But you can sell this one alone for three dollars," Gray said, pointing at Mrs. Anton's book. "And that one you charged me two dollars for."

"Hey, kid, I have to make a profit. Take it or leave it."

Gray stared at the books, knowing this was the only place he could trade for new ones. "Okay," he whispered and started down the aisle toward the stinking bathroom, keeping his eyes peeled for the mean cat.

Sitting in his cruiser in front of the Silver Dog, Edelson looked up the street at the falling snow. Robin would be in the mood for Christmas music. She always started playing *Oh, Holy Night* when the first snow came and kept on playing it until New Years Day. He'd complained about that at first, hating to be constantly reminded of the obligatory events and presents the holiday represented. He guessed this year Christmas would be what he preferred. He would drive down to his mother's and eat turkey and potatoes, exchange a small token of affection in the way of leather gloves or woolen socks, talk about Monty, then come home again. Quiet and simple. None of the endless entertaining or the stream of sentimental cards with little square school pictures of big-toothed kids he'd never met. At last he could break away from the shallow ritual of tenuous connections with distant cousins or old college friends. Finally, Christmas could be what *he* wanted.

A group of children raced past on their bikes. By this time Edelson was out of the car and he jumped aside, disturbed that they showed no intent of slowing or giving him right of way. Then the boy, Gray, emerged from the second-hand store next door. The sheriff was immediately reminded of Kristi Blackhorse, her claim that she was an Indian, the arrowhead, and the skeleton. He had heard nothing from Susanville, California.

"Hey, kid," he said. "How ya doin'?"

The boy smiled. "Good."

Edelson pushed the grim images of death from his mind. "How come you're not out riding with your friends?" He gestured up the street at Brady and the boys, now a block away.

Gray glanced at the retreating pack of boys and shrugged. "I don't have a bike."

Edelson wondered a moment what this kid *did* have. Anything? "What's that book in your hand?"

Gray proudly handed it over to him. "*Harry Potter.* She just got it yesterday."

"I've heard of him."

"He's a wizard and he goes to this special school for kids who learn magic. You see, he's got a lightning-bolt scar on his forehead. That's how you know it's him." Gray pointed at the cover to show the sheriff the scar in the picture. "There's an evil wizard that's trying to kill him. He killed Harry's parents."

"Does your dad approve of this stuff?"

Gray gave the sheriff a look of confusion, and Edelson realized his error. A silly question.

"Sounds like a good read, anyway." He handed the book back. "Well, see you around, kid."

"Have you found out anything about the skeleton?"

"No. But I'll let you know if I do, okay?"

Gray smiled. "I tried to find some clues for you. But I didn't see anything."

"Really? You're worried I might've missed something?"

"No." Gray's smile faded. "But I looked just in case. Do you think she was murdered?"

Edelson thought before answering. "I guess I don't know. I hope not. You know maybe she was just taking a walk and had a heart attack or something. It could be that simple."

"Wouldn't someone miss her?"

Edelson smiled. "You're pretty sharp. Maybe I should make you my deputy."

"Really?" Gray jumped up and down as if the sheriff was about to pin a star on his sweatshirt.

Shit. Edelson realized what he'd done and struggled for a way out. "Your dad probably wouldn't like that."

"He doesn't care what I do."

Edelson knew how true that was. "We'll see." He looked up at the white sky, felt the cold pellets against his cheeks. "For now, you better get home, and I better get some lunch."

The sheriff took his now familiar seat at the Silver Dog, near the door, where he had full view of the room through the mirror. An abrupt silence had fallen over the place upon his entrance, and all eyes turned toward him.

McHugh came immediately and placed a napkin on the counter. "The usual?" He lacked his trademark chirp.

"Sure."

"Just be a few minutes."

Edelson felt the cold eyes on his back. The dense air around him.

"You gonna serve this son of a bitch?" A man called to McHugh from a booth along the wall.

McHugh ignored the question.

85

"You got some balls," the man said to Edelson. "Kill a man's family, then expect him to serve you lunch."

Edelson swiveled on his stool and looked at the man. He didn't reply straight away. "A man's got to eat," he finally said.

"Doesn't have to eat here."

Edelson swung halfway back to the bar and spotted McHugh. Looking him straight in the eye, Edelson said, "Kill or be killed is how that was. If he'd waited long enough to find out why I was there, he'd be alive today."

All eyes shifted to McHugh. He held the sheriff in his sights for a long moment, the bar rag suspended between his hands and, for once, he did not teeter on his feet. At last he threw the rag up on the bar and said to no one in particular, "Russell dug his own grave."

A collective breath-letting ran through the room, sending a tingle up the sheriff's spine. By the time McHugh served him, the room prickled with hushed conversation. McHugh set the plate down quietly, as if wishing not to draw further attention to their interaction. He leaned close and locked eyes with the sheriff. "I don't harbor ill will for what you did to Russell. But my sister is a victim. You see your way clear to help her out, it would go a long way with me." He paused. "Not that you owe me anything."

"I don't know what I can do." Edelson said, suddenly re-calling the FBI's overt pleasure in having Christen Vining in custody. Of course, the woman was involved in growing six acres of marijuana, but the quivering, wailing creature he witnessed that morning hardly seemed like a serious criminal.

"If the opportunity arises . . ." McHugh backed away as the man sitting to the right of the sheriff took an interest in the conversation.

Edelson nodded, then peeled the bun back and inspected his burger. He watched McHugh from the corner of his eye as he ate and thought of Vining's vast crop. Vining could not have

86

hid what he was up to from anyone who knew where he lived. Edelson scanned the crowd through the bar mirror. The Silver Dog would make a nice market for that sort of agricultural endeavor.

9

At Chris Samuelson's boat ramp, Edelson took a deep breath and inspected her cottage. Across the flat water, smoke drifted lazily from the chimney. His breath was a wraith in the stillness. Even the highway was deserted, lonely in its remoteness. A handful of red cows nearby inspected pumpkins glazed with frost, puffs of steam rolling across the gourds.

He didn't immediately unload his new and beautiful canoe, but walked down to the water's edge, hoping he might alert the dog, which would in turn alert Chris. He didn't feel right about paddling up on her at seven A.M., unannounced, though she left him few alternatives. No road and no phone. He saw no sign of the dog, so gathered his gear and set off.

As he reached the far shore, it crossed his mind that maybe she had a man with her. And what would he do then? It might be hard to explain his visit on a Sunday morning, in his Levis and fleece. He looked back at the boat launch and decided another man would mean another car. But her lawn looked like the after-scene of a fraternity party. Scraps of cardboard, mangled and punctured. Bottles and cans strewn about, a plastic milk jug crushed flat. Someone had been there or was still. The dog barked inside the cottage. Chris's face appeared at the window, scowling. She opened the door.

"Mornin'," he said sheepishly.

She stared at him in silence.

"Sorry to disturb you." When she still didn't say anything, he asked, "What happened here?"

"Bears. They've gotten into my garbage three times this week."

Edelson began picking up the trash.

"Kept me up half the night with all the noise. One of 'em roamed around for over an hour cracking that milk carton between its teeth. Like it was a damned squeaky toy or something." She stepped outside and helped. She was in her bathrobe, her hair free and fluttering.

When they'd put everything back in the can, he carried it down to the ferry.

"That's more like it. Nice." She kicked his extravagant cedar canoe.

"Nice enough for a cup of coffee?"

She studied him. "I suppose it's worth one cup."

She returned to the cottage and he followed her. The bed was made, though she appeared to have just rolled out of it, her hair fuzzy with sleep. A teapot steamed on the woodstove and a mug on the table gave off the strong aroma of cloves.

"What brings you up to the Flathead this cold morning? Can't be the great canoeing." She handed him a cup of syrupy black coffee. "All I have is goat milk."

"No thanks."

She nodded and sat down next to him at a small table. Her feet brushed his.

"I thought up some reasons to give you."

"I'd love to hear them," she said in a tone that made Edelson wonder if she meant it.

"Naw. None of them are any good. Guess I just wanted to see you." He stared into his cup, embarrassed. "I keep wondering about you. I just had to satisfy my curiosity."

89

"I feel so much better since you put it that way."

He looked at her. She was lovely in a work-worn, supple way. "Why do you live here all alone?"

"Because most men aren't as resourceful as you," she said, failing to hide her amusement.

"Oh, are you . . . you know?"

"A lesbian?"

He felt a rush of blood to his face, imagined himself lit up like a beacon.

"Wouldn't you just love that?" she said, looking at him boldly.

"It could be bad . . . or good . . . depending . . ."

She laughed again, freely and uninhibited, raising in him a sudden tide of sexual excitement. His jeans pulled tight in the crotch.

"No. I'm not a lesbian," she said, smiling as if she knew his state. "I just don't have very good man-picking skills. So I decided to quit trying for a while." She took a long, slow sip of her tea. Her smile slipped away. "Read about your big bust."

He made a prolonged show of examining his fingernails. "Wasn't mine. Feds owned that one. I just got stuck in the middle."

"I dated that man."

Edelson's head popped up.

"No, I'm just kidding. Not that specific man anyway. But lots just like him. Real winners."

"Vining must've been supplying the whole western half of the U.S. with his crop." Edelson leaned back in his chair and pulled his ankle across his knee. "Wasn't doing it alone, that's for sure."

"What do you mean?"

"I doubt the man I shot could distribute quantities like that without an outlet of some sort." Edelson thought again of the popularity of McHugh's tavern, but that alone could not support the quantity Vining had.

Chris stared out her window, as if she could see the drug operation itself churning out carefully measured baggies of marijuana.

"I've got enough to keep me busy without busting up drug rings," he said.

"How many men have you shot?"

Edelson shifted uncomfortably in his chair. "Counting that one?"

"Yeah."

"One."

"Oh. I imagined it was just another day at the office."

"Can we talk about something else?"

She got up and refilled her cup. "Like what? Your marriage?"

His ears followed his face in blushing.

She leaned against the sink, cocking her head. Her hair swept down the length of her, smooth and silky. "Well don't you think I'm entitled to ask? I mean, come on . . . you drop in before I'm dressed simply to satisfy your curiosity. I think it's only fair."

"I don't think she's coming back . . ."

She turned and looked out the wavy-paned window over her sink. "So you're getting divorced?"

The word stung. He wondered how they'd gotten from lesbian sex to his personal problems.

"Look," she said, turning to him. "You seem like a nice enough guy, but . . ."

Edelson stared into his cup.

"You keep coming up here like this and I'm gonna get attached. Especially with that pretty canoe."

Silence filled the cottage.

"You know what's funny," he finally said. "I still don't understand why she left."

Chris sighed and sat down.

"You know?" He looked at her, hoping to see an inkling of understanding. "I thought I was doing okay."

"Well, what did she say?"

He drained the last of his coffee and stood. "She said I broke my promise to let her finish college."

"Where are you going?" Chris poured him another cup. "You finally get down to the real issue, then decide to leave?"

He sat down again, confused but grateful.

"So *did* you break your promise?"

"I don't . . ." He stopped to think about it. "I never promised it in the first place." When he looked up again, Chris was quietly waiting for him to go on. "I don't remember promising that."

"So what's the big deal? She goes back to school. What difference does it make if you promised it or not?"

"We can't really afford it."

"There's always financial aid."

He shook his head.

"What? Are you in debt or something?"

"No!" His response came fast and loud. Too loud to be left hanging there. "I don't carry any debt . . . besides my mortgage. No credit cards, nothing."

She softened. "So what's the problem?"

Edelson looked out the window. How to find a way out of this conversation? It was pointless and, really, none of her damn business.

"You don't *want* her to go back to school."

He looked at Chris again. She had a stubborn, probing way that made him want to shake her. Or throw her on the bed and rape her. "Maybe I don't see why she needs to."

Her mouth twisted in disgust. "So why didn't you just help her go back to school?"

92

"I don't get why she isn't happy being my wife," he said.

"I like to think men and women are two wings of the same bird," she said. She stopped, as if waiting for her words to sink in. She had an urgency about her he hadn't seen before, but not maliciously so. "How can a bird fly with only one wing?"

He scowled.

"You're too damn insecure to let her fly. But it's you who suffers."

"Right." He stood and pulled his jacket on. "That's a load of crap."

"I'm glad we had this little discussion," she said and, with finality, began filling the sink with water.

He yanked the door open. The frigid wind hit him in the face, burning deep into his lungs. "Enjoy your day."

He stomped off, swearing he'd never come back.

At the Missoula County Jail, Randy McHugh sat in the cramped visitor's booth. His hand rested on the intercom telephone, ready. A guard opened a door behind reinforced safety glass and directed his sister toward the chair on the opposite side. The bright orange jumpsuit gave her a jack-o-lantern-like appearance below greasy, uncombed hair and eyes dull and puffy.

"Hey, Wren," he whispered into the phone. It was the name he'd called her since childhood. A name between the two of them, a secret. "You doin' okay?"

Tears welled under her red-rimmed lids. "Get me out of here, Randy."

"I will, hang in there a little longer."

She wiped her eyes and adjusted her chair. "

McHugh frowned. "You need a good lawyer, and I've already gotten a call from someone who claims Russ owes him money."

"Sagen?"

93

McHugh shook his head. "No, who's that?"

She didn't answer, kept her eyes on the table in front of her.

"Sis? Is this someone I need to know about?"

"Yeah," she said, meeting McHugh's gaze. "You should call him, before he calls you."

"First tell me, where did Russ keep the money?"

She shook her head.

"Russ's been growing for years; he had to have made thousands — hundreds of thousands."

"There is no money. Russ —"

"What?" McHugh raised half out of his chair, but dropped back when the guard advanced.

"He lost it."

"He *what*?" McHugh's chest went tight as he thought of how much money he, himself, had given Russell for the pot he sold at the Silver Dog — and that was pittance compared to the quantities he knew Russell was dealing. "How do you *lose* so much money?"

"You know how he was," she said. Her upper lip quivered, despite her attempt to still it.

"That son of a bitch! How could that idiot lose so much?" McHugh thought of Russell's out-of-town trips to Spokane, Seattle, Vegas. He knew the man gambled, and did God-knows what else. Russell bragged about it, even in front of Wren, who'd not been out of Mineral County since the two were married.

She dropped the phone and cupped her face in her hands, sobbing.

"Christen. Christen." He knocked on the glass. "Wren . . . I'll think of something, Wren . . ."

The guard laid a stern hand on her shoulder. "C'mon. Let's go."

"We have fifteen minutes," McHugh shouted through the glass. "We have fifteen minutes!"

94

Gray spent the remainder of Saturday writing out his plans to become a sheriff's deputy. He made long lists in his notebook of things he needed to do to get ready. Lawmen have to be in good shape, so he was up early, palms pressed to the mildewed carpet, back straight, butt in the air, straining through a series of push-ups.

Andrea's muffled giggles came through the door and Gray rolled onto his back, cupping his hands over his ears while he performed his sit-ups.

When he finished with his morning calisthenics, he went to the kitchen. Breakfast was important, he knew, and Andrea had bought corn flakes the day before. He poured himself a bowl and sat at the dinette table. He ate slowly, savoring the sweet yellow flakes, hoping she wouldn't be mad that he ate them.

His father was in a better mood since Andrea moved in. He even smiled sometimes. He seemed less apt to snap at Gray for leaving his things lying around. And he'd never taken a day off on the weekend that Gray could recall — not until today. But for all this, when Gray heard the bedroom door squeak, he froze and waited, his neck hot and his palms aching.

Andrea appeared first, bare-legged, in the same long shirt she always wore in the morning. Then his father, unshaven and smelling of sweat. They walked past him without a word and into the kitchen, where Andrea began making coffee, and Jim Dausman gulped down a glass of water.

Gray watched from the corner of his eye as Andrea ran her bright pink fingernails along his father's ribs, making him spurt water through his teeth. She giggled and tried again, but he gripped her fingers and squeezed until she screeched.

Finally, Jim looked in Gray's direction. "Hey, kid."

"Hi," Gray said without looking directly at him. He summoned his courage and addressed his father. "Do you think I could have a book about the law?" he asked.

"What for?"

"I'm gonna be a policeman."

Jim laughed. "That'll be the day." He looked at Andrea, then back at Gray. "We're goin' to Missoula. We'll be back tomorrow. You be okay?"

Gray wasn't sure if he was being asked or told. He nodded.

"You need anything, Mrs. Anton is just up the street." Jim paused and thought a moment, then looked at Gray with intent. "You don't tell her you're alone, though. Got that?"

"Yeah."

"You do . . . I'll work ya over."

When Edelson had his canoe secured to the top of his truck, he peeled onto the road, spraying gravel down Chris Samuelson's boat launch. He ground his teeth audibly, pulling the short tendons at the base of his neck tight like baling twine. Snow drifted out of the flat sky. Light and peaceful. Pissing him off. As he drove, the snow came with greater force, blanketing the rugged landscape. The intersection of Montana 200 and U.S. 93 was marked by a stunted apple tree, standing alone in the blizzard, catching the icy moisture in its crippled limbs. He turned onto highway 93, figuring to drop down into Missoula. Maybe go surprise Robin.

10

THOUGH MISSOULA IS TOO SMALL to be considered a city, it still reminded Edelson of his disdain for urban life: the traffic, the noise, the barrage of advertisements. But mostly the sprawl. He'd been coming into Missoula for at least ten miles before he reached the city limits. Truck stops and warehouse stores winking neon gave him a headache.

His father had been stationed at Fort Missoula for a year of training when Edelson was eight. The name of the school where he'd struggled through the third grade seemed an accurate summation of the place: Hellgate. He'd been, for that brief time, one of the mighty Hellgate Demons.

Edelson turned onto I-90 eastbound to bypass the airport and, ultimately, his old grade school. He'd drop into downtown at Orange Street, then across the Clark Fork to the university. He had a vague recollection of where Third Street lay.

He parked across from a brick, two-story building. It sat back from the street a little way, flanked by mature maples, now leafless and insulated in white. He understood immediately what Robin liked about the place. Built in the 1930s, it had elaborate Art Deco ironwork over the windows and doors. The building's crisp lines and symmetrical elements gave it perfect proportions. It represented the one thing urbanity could offer the interests of a man such as him — diverse and historical architecture. He found himself wanting to live in this overlooked gem of American design, if only for a moment.

Edelson stood in the street. A pickup sped past, spraying his feet with gravelly slush. He crossed and waited for a group of college students smelling of exotic oils to clear the sidewalk. They were oblivious to his presence, and it occurred to him right then perhaps that was what he disliked about cities — the anonymity. He was the sheriff of Mineral County, a man to be reckoned with. A man with the power to kill someone and yet walk free. That simple truth — ending Russell Vining's life — bothered Edelson. The lines were blurring. Hadn't he acted in the line of duty? That didn't change the fact that a man was dead, and Edelson was responsible. He glanced again at the students, now far down the walk. Of course the students didn't know that about him. He was just one more middle-aged guy, hanging out.

When Robin didn't answer the door, he looked at his watch and wondered where she would be at noon on a Sunday. He tried the knob. Of course it was locked; she was a sheriff's wife. Edelson wandered back to his truck, his anger seeping away in the frigid day, leaving him defeated. Tipping his head back, he closed his eyes.

Gray was on a mission under his father's unmade bed. There was a box he'd seen his father shut and hastily shove under there more than once. Though Gray had wondered about it on many occasions, he'd never found the courage to go snooping. He'd rifled through the closets and cupboards in every part of the house on different occasions, but never his father's bedroom. Jim Dausman had warned Gray of the beating he'd receive for going into his bedroom — a beating he was well familiar with. But now . . . now that his father was away overnight . . .this was his chance. Still, Gray was uneasy about breaching the boundary of his father's private world.

Dirty clothes lay scattered over the floor, some his father's, some Andrea's. Gray dropped to his knees at the edge of the bed and saw that the cavern below was crammed with boxes and papers. He reached and caught the dusty corner of a box, dragging it out into the light. It was filled with his own outgrown clothes. He shoved it aside and reached for a stack of Playboy magazines, lingering over them, amazed. After a half-hour of hot-faced perusing, he held back one. His father wouldn't miss it. He reached for the next box, a green shoebox.

The lid was snug and the contents rattled loosely inside. Gray anxiously pulled the top back and gazed down at his father's treasures. A small, oddly shaped pipe, about three inches long, the blackened bowl sticky with tar. A plastic baggie, mostly empty, small green flakes sticking to the inside. He knew what the bag contained, he'd seen the public service messages on Saturday morning TV, but he'd never known anyone who smoked pot.

Gray sat back on his haunches, disappointed. This was his father's big secret? He knew something about the reality of things; he knew it was a dream that his father was capable of doing anything vaguely fatherly. And now it seemed his father was incapable of having something to hide. It figured.

He scanned the blackness once more and pulled out the last box, dragging with it tattered phone bills and a long bit of cardboard tubing. He opened it, expecting nothing in particular.

Behind his school ran an electric fence that a rancher had put up to keep the kids from tormenting the cows that grazed in the field. A gullible kid, either new or young, quickly learned the magic of electrical conduction the hard way. Gray never forgot the sensation that raced through him one morning in his first-grade year as he laid a damp stick against the wire, the feeling of having all his hair ripped from his body in one swift jolt.

It was the same sort of sensation he experienced that Sunday afternoon, alone in his father's bedroom, when he looked down at the pile of letters he'd so carefully written to his mother still sealed in their envelopes. Unmailed. Unopened. Unread.

Edelson's nose felt like a frozen parsnip when he awoke in the cold cab of his pickup. The windows had fogged with condensation and his arms and legs had rusted in place. He wiped the side window with his sleeve and looked out at the coming twilight. A few cars rolled past with their lights on. Robin's window remained dark.

He started the truck and revved the engine, waiting for the defroster to kick in, and rolled his window down to peer up the street. On the corner a man pulled merchandise into his second-hand store, preparing to close for the evening. Edelson watched passively, thinking it a damn inconvenience to drag that junk outside to sit in the snow all day, then drag it all back in. But as he pondered the man's tolerance for repetition, he spied a bike the merchant was handling. Red, and just small enough to be a kid's. A big kid's bike.

Edelson left the truck running and trotted up the block. "How much is that bike?"

The man paused and looked at it. "Seventy-five."

Edelson stopped short and shook his head. "Never mind."

"It's a nice bike. Practically new."

Edelson turned to go back to his truck.

"How about fifty, then?"

Edelson turned back with new interest and looked at the shiny paint. It was a nice bike. But fifty bucks was still too much to spend on a whim for a kid he didn't even know. "Naw . . . thanks."

"You're kidding me?" the merchant hollered at Edelson as he retreated. "What do you want to pay, then?"

"Thirty."

"Forty-five."

"Forty."

"Take the damn bike, then." The merchant walked the bike toward him.

Edelson fished out two twenties and pressed them into the man's hand.

"And people say *I'm* a crook," the man muttered as he turned back to his store.

Edelson stared down at the bike, immediately mournful for his lost cash. Then he pushed it up the street and put it in the back of his pickup.

Randy McHugh sat alone with a glass of whiskey, looking out on the twinkling valley where a bitter-sharp wind had swept the cobalt sky clean. A neat stack of papers sat on the kitchen table. Tallies of all he owned — one man's net worth. The sultry voice of Billie Holiday, as if she'd been steeped in his drink, filled the darkened room. The pinched wail of muted trumpets carried her forth, even where her frail voice couldn't. He wasn't typically a drinking man, McHugh. He had too often seen thinkers turned to fools. But tonight, with its delicate warmth at the back of his throat like a yellow ember, the whiskey softened the world a little.

His thoughts, which hours ago had raced through different scenarios, now slowed to a gentle, but inconsistent lope. His sister needed money to live on. The Silver Dog he could concede to her. It was never really fair that he alone got it. She was the better at serving clientele, a job she enjoyed. His talent was for numbers. They might've had a fine partnership, but their father hadn't wanted to pass his tavern to a daughter. McHugh laughed aloud. Instead, she married a drug dealer. He was thankful to the sheriff for unburdening his sister of her derelict husband, but it was a fact that Russell protected her while he was alive.

Even still, the sale of his business would cover Christen's defense and leave a nice stake left over for the two of them. The bar was profitable, but it was the extra income from Russell's marijuana crop that made it lucrative. With the loss of his additional income, McHugh would have to find other ways to make the payment on his home. He was hardly in a position now to support his sister too. He leaned back in his chair and thought about his own stupidity for becoming dependent on Russell's illicit activities. He always believed Russell would get himself killed someday, but McHugh had imagined it would be the scum Russell ran with that would kill him over some petty squabble, not the sheriff.

McHugh wished he'd been smarter about planning for this day. He could've saved the money instead of building his cabin, and that would've allowed him to sell the Silver Dog, bail Christen out of jail, and take her away from this place. Start new. Just the two of them. He cursed himself for not preparing.

A clatter came from the back porch, startling McHugh. He set his drink down and listened, the nape of his neck bristling. A noise he would've otherwise dismissed as an animal he now deliberated on. He crept to the hall closet and extracted his rifle. Though he rarely hunted anymore, he'd readied it the morning he heard Russell Vining was dead. McHugh had always held Russell at arm's length, but now he saw the foolishness of that. There was no telling who Vining owed money. Anyone might show up here or at the Silver Dog to collect. McHugh had less than a pound of pot left — he could relinquish it for payment, but how would he make his mortgage?

He made his way to the back of the house, setting his heels lightly on the wood floor. The luminescence of a near-full moon burned through the windows. Hulking pine trees cast their shadows along the wall like gun-toting thugs.

But it was simply the wind. McHugh stood shivering at the back door, looking down at the fallen snow shovel. He pushed the door shut and bolted it. Then he checked each door and window in a circular round through his house, a routine he'd only recently become familiar with.

A storm blew in during the early morning hours, depositing half a foot of pristine snow. The interstate was packed with a bitter ice. And a biting wind raised a fine haze that sifted, apparition-like, over the road. Edelson glided past cautious motorists, the crunching of studded tires beneath him and two hundred pounds of bagged sand in the trunk of his cruiser. As he came into a calm stretch of highway — flat and straight — he found a semi with a jackknifed trailer in the median.

As Edelson approached the cab a young man opened the door and dropped into the snow in front of him. "Son-of-a-bitch SUV was flying down the left lane and started to spin. Just about here," he said, holding his arm out to show the sheriff the prox-imity of the vehicle to his front fender. "I thought he was gonna come right under me. He forced me to hit my brakes." He ges-tured helplessly at his truck. "How the hell am I gonna get it out now?"

"Call for a tow, I guess," Edelson said calmly.

The trucker stared incredulously at the sheriff, puffs of hot steam roiling from his lips.

"Well? What else are you going to do?" Edelson trudged out into the median and inspected the tracks from the other ve-hicle.

"If I'd known the bastard was going to take off, I'd a run him over —" He stopped short and looked away.

Edelson radioed for assistance, then took down the de-scription of the other vehicle. Doubted they'd find it now, but he followed procedure anyway.

When he reached his office, he found a message from the Susanville Police Department and immediately returned the call, but the detective he spoke to had no real information. Kristi Blackhorse's sister had moved out of her apartment back in April, with no forwarding address.

By the time Edelson set the receiver down, his fingers were stiff with cold. He spent so little time at the jailhouse he wasn't in the habit of heating it, and he could see his breath. He pulled out his list, now limp and tattered, to examine the names once more. Lines were drawn through most, a circle around Kristi Blackhorse's, and two stars next to Chris Samuelson's. I can solve this mystery without visiting any more Chrises on the list, he thought. All I have to do is take the boy down to Missoula for a DNA test. Chances are they'd find a match and we'd know who the corpse was. It was a grim prospect. He needed a burger to cheer him up.

Edelson pulled up a stool next to the register at the Silver Dog. He waited for McHugh to finish up with a customer paying his tab.

"The usual?" McHugh said, placing a napkin on the bar.

"I have some questions for you. About your brother-in-law."

McHugh glanced around. "Hang on." He disappeared into the kitchen and returned shortly, followed by his grill-cook. "We'll talk in my office," he said to Edelson.

The sheriff followed him down a narrow corridor to a large room in the back. McHugh nodded at a chair along the wall, and Edelson pulled it up to McHugh's desk. He instinctively ran a palm over the lustrous wood. "Tiger oak. Nice."

"My grandfather's," McHugh said.

"Very nice." Edelson turned his attention to the barman. "How was Russell Vining distributing his marijuana?"

McHugh blinked twice, as if startled, then steadied his gaze on the sheriff. A hard, defiant stare. "How should I know?"

"Be a lucrative side business." He nodded toward the dining room full of patrons.

"What are you suggesting?"

"If you've ever been to your sister's place, I guess you'd know what she was up to."

"*She* wasn't up to anything. She's a victim in all this."

"Not my point." Edelson squinted at McHugh, waiting.

"I got your point. And it's just plain wrong. I'm not involved with what Russell was up to. Not in the remotest possible way."

The two stared at each other a moment longer, then Edelson got to his feet. He nodded. "I'll see myself out."

McHugh watched the sheriff go with a growing sense of hatred for the man. If he was looking for a piece of the action, he was too late. That jackass Vining had seen to it that no one would be profiting now.

He had hoped that Edelson might have a word with the federal investigator on Wren's behalf. Didn't he owe her that at least? After killing her husband. Couldn't the man see she had nothing to do with illegal business? But instead, the sheriff has the balls to come sniffing around the Silver Dog, looking for more victims.

Gray stacked the envelopes neatly and bound them with a rubber band and set them on his bed. Then he rummaged in the hall closet, eventually pulling out his father's prized fire jacket. He was forbidden from wearing it, though he couldn't see why. It never got used. His father only took it out when people came over. Talked about fighting forest fires when he was younger. Dangerous work, he assured the listener. Gray had heard the stories so many times they felt like his own.

He pulled the heavy canvas around his shoulders. Its

smoky scent brought the promise of a sneeze to the tip of his nose and stubbornly perched there. He lumbered down to the bathroom and peered at his reflection, imagined how important he'd be wearing it. But the sight of his scrawny limbs buried under mountains of canvas looked pathetic. He dragged the jacket back to his room, where he wadded it up and shoved it under his bed. Gray threw the letters in after it and rolled onto the floor, pulled his knees against his chest and cried.

His father arrived home late Monday afternoon. He didn't ask about school, but Gray didn't expect him to. He only wished he'd known his father would be gone all day. He would've come home earlier, instead of hiding out in the abandoned Elk Creek schoolhouse a mile or so from town. The ceiling of the hulking building with giant, multi-paned windows, most of which had been shot out, leaked. The gym floor was curling up, one plank at a time. But someone had used it recently; in the basement Gray found the remnants of charred logs. A hobo fire, he imagined. The railroad tracks came right past the place.

He hadn't gone to school that day, but had spent the time in the empty building studying his father's twenty year old road atlas. Planning his trip to California. He'd been as far away from home as Peerless, which he located on the map. Magda and Peerless were practically next to each other in the tiny space along I-90 depicted by a double blue line, but he knew how far apart they really were. His journey would be impossible on foot. California was so far, and so big. He experienced a stinging realization that Andrea was right. How would the mailman know where to deliver his letters without a street address? Dispirited, he dragged himself home. He *had* to find another way to get to California.

"Gray," his father's gruff voice called from the front door about six P.M.

"In here," he said, planning his attack on his lying father.

His father didn't come all the way in, but stood awkwardly in the entryway. "Get your shoes on," his father said. "I thought I'd take you out for a burger. How about it?"

Gray realized he was just staring at his father. "Okay."

"We'll go down to the Silver Dog."

His father was quiet on the drive, but not in his usual neglectful way. He occasionally flashed an out-of-place smile at Gray.

Gray wanted to confront his father about the letters, but he needed to learn more about this outing first. "Where's —"

"She's still in town."

"Oh."

"She . . . she wanted to do some shopping."

Gray chewed at his fingernails.

At the Silver Dog, Jim selected a booth along the wall. A low window provided a view of the snowy alley, illuminated by a bright yellow security light. "Get whatever ya want, Gray," he said.

Gray looked around, watched the barman slip something to a man in a cowboy hat. He turned back and asked quietly, "Can I have a pop, too?"

"Sure. Whatever ya want."

Gray smiled. He had always wanted to have a cheeseburger and a root beer at the Silver Dog. Yet his hatred of his father's deception warned against his hunger and excitement.

When his food arrived, Gray gasped at the size of the burger. "Wow."

"That's a lot of food," his father said.

Gray looked at his father's side of the table. Just a beer. "Aren't you going to eat too?"

"No. I'm not that hungry."

"You can have some of mine." Gray thought maybe his father couldn't afford two hamburgers. It was always the reason he'd given for not taking Gray out to eat, before Gray stopped asking to go.

"No. You eat it," his father said. Then leaned over, pinched a wad of fries between his blackened fingers, and shoved them into his mouth.

Gray's first bite was cheesy, with grease that melted in his mouth and ran down his chin. It was just the way he always dreamed a restaurant-grilled burger would be.

"Listen, there's something I need to tell you, kid."

Gray swallowed and quickly took another bite. He watched his father's face, knowing he was about to tell him something terrible. He chewed fast, swallowed, and took another bite. Maybe his father knew about the missing letters, or his playing hookey, and was just softening him up before giving him a good beating in front of everybody at the Silver Dog.

"Andrea and me . . . well, we've decided to get married."

Gray shrugged. And . . .?

Jim was silent a while, watching Gray with the half-eaten burger suspended in mid-air. Finally, "That's not all. You see, Gray, your mama . . . she was never married to me."

Gray set his burger back on his plate.

"She . . . she was a busy girl. And . . . you're not my kid. Anyway, a boy should respect his mother."

Gray watched his father's lips say the words, but he didn't grasp their meaning.

"You're not my son. I'm not your dad. Your mama was already pregnant. I only agreed to raise you as my kid when I thought we had a future together. But then . . ."

Gray felt the burger in his throat, forcing its way back up.

Jim paused. "Look, this isn't easy for me either. I like you. I mean . . . we've had a lot a years together now." Jim shifted in the booth to face the aisle. He took a slow draft of his beer and spun the cap across the table. "I tried to find your mom. I wanted you to be able to go live with her. I know it's what you want."

"Did you find her?" Gray felt a rise of hope complete his nausea.

"No."

Gray looked down at his unfinished burger, oozing with ketchup and cheese. It was funny almost: the thing he'd always wanted was sitting there in front of him and now the sight of it made barfing a certainty.

"We'll go in to Missoula tomorrow. There's a foster home there."

"What?" The words he heard were strange and stretched. His father's face got blurry.

"Listen," Jim said, holding his hands up as if to calm Gray. "They're nice people. They like kids. You'll be happy there."

"No," Gray said, as tears began to streak his cheeks.

"I'm sorry, kid. I'm sorry." Jim took a swig of his beer and wiped his mouth with a shaky hand.

Gray stood. "I have to go to the bathroom."

"Take your time."

Gray started for the back of the room, then turned suddenly and rushed toward the front door, brushing clumsily past a couple on their way in. He shoved the door open.

"Gray!" his father shouted.

But Gray was sprinting down the icy sidewalk, the wind shoveling his vomit back into his face, his sweatshirt, his jeans. He heard his name two more times, but didn't look back. Then his father stopped calling him.

11

WHEN EDELSON SPOTTED THE BOY he was a half mile west of town, hiking along the frontage road — his gait a belabored trot. The wind peeled white breath past his ears and into the blackness.

The sheriff pulled alongside the boy and rolled his window down. "I've been looking for you."

Gray glanced over his shoulder, giving the sheriff a glimpse of his red-rimmed eyes and cherry nose, then broke into a sprint.

"Why don't you get in the car? It's warm."

"I'm not going to no foster home," Gray shouted. A sour smell like vomit blew into the police cruiser.

Edelson eased off the brake and let his engine pull him along at the same speed as the boy. "Who said anything about a foster home?"

Gray stopped short in the road, forcing the sheriff to brake hard. "Didn't you talk to my dad?"

"Not yet."

"I'm not going to no foster home." He started walking again.

"Stop," the sheriff called. "I don't know what you're talking about. But I didn't come looking for you to take you . . ." He paused, restrained himself from making promises he didn't know if he could keep.

"Just leave me alone!" Gray shouted and started running again.

"Don't make me arrest you."

"Please." Gray turned again, sobbing. "Please leave me alone. I have to find my mom. *I have to find her.*"

"What's this got to do with a foster home?"

Gray's sobs had turned violent, rendering him unable to speak. On his chin was an icing of dirt, tears, and unexplained yellow mess.

"I won't make any decisions until you've had a chance to tell me everything. Why don't you get in the car? We'll go down to my office and talk it out. Okay?"

"I don't want to go to jail," he wailed.

"I'm not taking you to jail. How 'bout if we go to my house, then? I think I have some cocoa."

Gray pulled his shirt up and wiped his nose, then his chin. He crossed to the passenger's side and got in.

Edelson radioed his dispatcher and let her know the boy was safe. One thing the kid needed right off was a bath. Edelson sniffed at the sour smell that hung over Gray like an odorous cloud. Soon the pristine cruiser would be permeated.

Gray blushed with embarrassment. "Yeah," he muttered, "so I barfed."

Peachy waited on the front porch, eternally reminding Edelson that Robin was not there. He hated the cat more every day. But when Gray saw the animal, he cheered up a little.

"This your cat?"

"It's my wife's."

"Can I play with it?"

"Sure." Edelson led the boy up the steps and unlocked the door. When he turned to let the cat in, he found it draped over Gray's arm. The boy's face was buried in its orange fur. And the cat purred as loudly as when Robin held it. "Guess he found a friend."

"What's his name?"

Edelson hesitated, despising the name. "Peachy." He went to the kitchen and filled the teapot, setting it on the stove to heat for cocoa after sending Gray into the bathroom to clean himself. "So . . . wanna tell me what's going on?"

Gray sat on the edge of the sofa, holding the cat tight against his chest. "He told me he isn't my dad," he said.

Edelson pulled his hat off and ran his fingers through his hair. "Tell me everything he said."

The boy started with the letters he'd found under his father's bed and told Edelson everything, also admitting to skipping school to start for California. He explained as if the sheriff might not be aware that it was a long way — too far to walk. When he finished, he looked at the sheriff and said, "I have to find her."

Edelson fought the urge to kick the shit out of Jim Dausman.

The boy sat quietly now, stroking the cat. Edelson wondered if the foster family would take the cat, too. They needed each other — Gray and Peachy. "How would you like to sleep on my sofa tonight?"

Later that night, Edelson, sleepless, wandered out into the living room to look at the boy, curled in a ball on the sofa and wearing a borrowed tee shirt. When Edelson pulled the blanket back, he found Peachy snuggled against Gray's stomach. He retreated to the reclining chair and watched Gray sleep. Edelson had seen his share of kids caught in the foster care system, shuffled from place to place — for years even. Well-meaning folks though foster parents were, still substitutes, temporary guardians. And those were the good homes. He'd seen others that offered no such refuge.

But he had to draw a line somewhere. He was an officer of the law, not a social worker. It was his job to find the boy and bring him to safety. Nothing more. He'd done his part, and now there would be professionals to take the problem from here.

Gray waited in the police cruiser, wearing the sheriff's jacket and a pair of the sheriff's jeans rolled up several times. Edelson had lent him a belt, but had to punch extra holes in it to make it small enough. Gray was curious about the pale yellow house and its wide porch. It looked warm. Not like the houses in his neighborhood. He'd glimpsed the old lady who lived there when she opened the door and greeted the sheriff. He wondered if this was the sheriff's mom. She smiled at Edelson the way mothers do before the two disappeared inside.

Gray wished he had Peachy. Felt bad for it, alone all day outside in the snow. He'd tried to convince the sheriff that it should stay inside where it was warm, but he wouldn't listen. Just said it always went outside during the day. Gray thought the sheriff was a hard case, not mean like his dad, but cold-hearted.

The sheriff finally returned to the car while the old lady stood in the doorway watching. "Gray," the sheriff said as he opened the door, "Mrs. Sherwood is going to look after you today."

"I don't need a babysitter."

"I know," the sheriff said, but waited for Gray to get out, anyway.

"Is she your mom?"

"No, she's a friend of mine."

"How come I don't have to go to school?"

"Tomorrow."

Gray climbed out of the car and followed the sheriff up the steps. Mrs. Sherwood invited him into her house, and he stepped into its warmth, pausing in the entryway. It was filled

113

with beautiful things that scared him. Everything looked breakable.

"Are you hungry?" she said, pulling off the sheriff's jacket.

He shook his head, watching Mrs. Sherwood put away the precious jacket. Hoped she'd give it back. He liked it, felt important when he wore it.

"What do you like to do? I have some puzzles . . ."

Gray shrugged. "Do you have any pets?"

"No."

"Oh." He glanced around again. "Do you have any books?"

"Oh, yes," she said, and led him into a small room off the parlor that was crammed with books. Shelf upon shelf, all four walls, stacked to the ceiling. "Yes, I have lots of books."

Edelson cruised past the Silver Dog, slowly, in his now habitual manner, looking for something to confirm his suspicion that McHugh was involved in Russell Vining's drug trade. He'd taken to patrolling the street regularly, watching for in-and-out activity — people stopping at the tavern, but not staying long enough to eat or drink. Edelson knew he'd need to stake the place out, hide in an adjacent building or something, to see that kind of activity. He drove past anyway, hoping to get lucky. Nothing looked out of the ordinary, so he went to his office to wait for the social worker. He turned up the heat specifically for her, then checked his phone messages, looking out at the llamas that grazed the hillside as he listened. They stood as they often did — stock-still — looking off to the east. Their ears pricked forward, as if listening to something amusing. Edelson couldn't imagine why people in Montana were so fascinated with these animals, but they were as common as magpies. What did people do with llamas? He'd never seen them shorn. He once asked someone if llamas were edible, but was met with a gasp of horror. The woman then informed him that people used llamas to guard their sheep from predators. Edelson looked out at the llama-studded hillside devoid of sheep, and shook his head. Clearly, he was missing something.

The social worker was younger than she sounded on the phone. Or maybe it was just that Edelson always envisioned social workers as matronly older women. She carried herself with such a measure of confidence that it seemed contrived to Edelson. As if she expected a fight.

"Good morning, Sheriff," she said, thrusting her hand at him. Her grip was beyond firm.

"Mornin', Ms. Winborn."

"Where's Gray?" She looked around Edelson's barren office.

"With a nice old lady in Magda. I —"

"Write down the address and I'll go get him."

"Wait, I thought we should talk about the situation first."

"What about it? I have the information I need. I met with Jim Dausman on Monday. I was expecting him to bring the boy today." She snapped her fingers as she spoke.

It annoyed Edelson. "Have a seat, Ms. Winborn."

She huffed impatiently and sat in the plastic chair opposite his desk, pulling her coat tightly around her despite the warmth of the office, her square purse balanced on her knees.

"I . . . have reason to believe a skeleton we found a few weeks back might be the boy's mother."

She turned her eyes on Edelson, at last giving him her full attention.

"We need to run a DNA test to be sure."

"Okay," she said, shifting in her chair. "We can arrange that."

Edelson ran his fingers across his scalp and sat back. "I don't want this kid to end up in the foster care system. Life hasn't exactly been a picnic for him."

She blinked twice, staring. "Where did you think he was going, Sheriff, if not to a foster home?"

115

"Well, I guess I was hoping that if we could identify the body as his mother's, he'd be placed for adoption."

"Yes, if paternity can't be established, he will. But you have to understand something; this kid is ten years old. It's highly unlikely he'll be adopted at his age. Everyone wants babies, not older kids. It's an unfortunate . . . no, tragic, fact."

"Why don't you let him stay with me until we know?"

Sarah Winborn stood abruptly. "I'm sorry, Sheriff, I can't do that. I have a family ready to take him. A family that's been screened and approved, who has been through training."

"Is it a permanent home?"

"No." She pursed her lips. "It's temporary. Until we find a more long-term place for him."

"Leave him with me until you . . ." Edelson paused. "I can be the temporary home."

"But you're not qualified. I don't know your background, I —"

"Qualify me then. I'm the sheriff. Doesn't that count for something? Come look at my house. Qualify me."

"Are you married?"

He sighed. "Yes, but she lives in Missoula."

Sarah Winborn arched her eyebrows.

"It's too far to commute. She's a student at the university," he said quickly.

"Then who's going to take care of him while you're working?"

"I've arranged for that. She's a wonderful woman. Like a grandmother. She'll bake cookies for him and help him with his homework."

"I don't think so, Sheriff," she said, starting for the door. "Let's go pick up his things, then you can take me to him."

"Please," Edelson said with a disturbing hint of desperation. "He was the one who found the body."

She turned back and met his gaze, shuddering.

"He asks me about it every time I see him. If . . . the body is his mother, I want to be the one to tell him. I want to at least see him through that."

Sarah Winborn shook her head. "You could get me fired for this."

"I'm as qualified as anyone. Check me out. But please, give me a chance."

Edelson escorted Sarah Winborn to Jim Dausman's house where she collected three boxes containing Gray's things. Dausman stared at his feet as he answered her questions about allergies, medical conditions, school progress. They came away no better informed than if they'd asked a complete stranger.

"Ten years and only three boxes," Edelson muttered as they loaded them into the trunk of his cruiser.

"I've seen worse," the social worker said.

At Mrs. Sherwood's, the matter was solved between Gray and Ms. Winborn in the kitchen, while Edelson waited silently with Mrs. Sherwood, the sound of her antique clock snapping out each elapsed second.

Finally the social worker emerged and handed Edelson her business card. "I'm going by the school to talk to the counselor." She looked the sheriff dead on. "Don't make me regret this."

Randy McHugh brushed his palm across the giant oak desk; its golden stripes shimmered in the sun. He remembered his grandfather hoisting him up on it when he was a little boy. His first recollections of the bar. The business. Listening to Granddaddy talk about old Montana. The characters coming alive in the sweet haze of his cigar smoke. Always a handful of old timers gathered there, in Granddaddy's back office. Swapping grim predictions of record-breaking cold to come in the winter ahead, or the inevitable collapse of this market or that — leaving people broke. Just like the silver. Nothing lasted forever.

His favorite, Buck Collins, used to tease him. Buck would sit against the wall, too deaf to follow the conversation, shriveled and leathery, like a dried apple. His eyes were ghostly white and penetrating. He'd shove a wrinkled finger at McHugh's nose and accuse him of stealing his good looks. Then he'd clink noisily through his pocket change for a silver dime and hold it out for the boy to take. Just as McHugh would brush the coin with his fingertips, the old man would pull it away and laugh. It was their ritual. If McHugh kept reaching, the old man would relinquish the coin, sometimes six or seven of them in a single afternoon. Then he'd line them along the edge of the desk, glinting silver and rich beyond imagination against the golden grain.

"Something missing?"

McHugh looked up at the realtor, a white-haired man of about sixty. He wore a navy suit with a crisp white shirt, out of place in the Silver Dog. McHugh scribbled his name across the bottom of the contract and set the pen down. He sat back in the heavy chair.

"Remember, no signs on the property. I don't want anyone to know it's for sale unless they're lookin' to buy."

The realtor nodded and gathered the document. "It shouldn't take long to sell. It's a prime piece of property never offered for sale before. A good history. Won't take long at all."

McHugh scowled, then turned his back and looked out at the setting sun.

"I'll just show myself out," the man said.

McHugh watched the realtor appraise the beauty of the Silver Dog on his way out and wondered if his sister would thank him for selling the tavern or admonish him for his risk taking. She'd loved this place too. Perhaps if he'd been wiser — saved the money — he'd have the cash to take care of her now. She constantly nagged him for taking the easy way, his need for instant gratification.

McHugh thought of Edelson, a man with seemingly no end of self-discipline. What would he do? But it wasn't how the sheriff handled his finances that interested McHugh. It was whether Edelson had ever been sexually tormented by a sister. How would Mineral County's hard-ass peace officer handle himself in a situation like that?

12

"THOUGHT I TOLD YOU we don't need a washerwoman here," the sheriff said, eyeing Crystal O'Shea, who was crouched on her front steps chipping ice with a garden spade.

She started, but when she realized it was the sheriff she composed herself. "Last I knew it wasn't against the law to take in laundry. Besides, I could do a little laundry for you, Sheriff."

"I don't think so."

"Oh, you wouldn't have to pay me. I believe in supporting local government."

Edelson stood in her driveway, snow dusting his hat. "I like to know where my laundry has been."

"Suit yourself," she said hotly, a change so sudden Edelson looked more carefully at the woman. "You've done a damn good job of putting me outta business anyway. With all this patrolling up and down my street." She flung an arm out to illustrate his comings and goings. "All I have left is washing. Besides . . . " She turned back to the stubborn layer of ice, whacking it violently with the tip of the spade. Tiny chunks bounced off the side of the trailer, making a faint tinkling sound.

"Besides what?"

She threw the spade down in frustration and got to her feet. Her nose in the cold air was bright red. "You know who that was you found down at the river?"

She had his full attention. "Do *you?*" he asked.

Crystal looked up at the white sky, her lips contorting. Edelson thought she was smiling — a wicked sort of smile. But then he saw the tears. He waited for her to compose herself, but she kept her head tipped skyward, tears streaking down her neck. He finally said, "If you know something, better tell me."

"Or what?" She turned her ruined eyes on him. "You'll arrest me?"

"Yeah," he said.

"Go ahead, then. I'm not the one you should be wasting your time with, but go ahead and arrest me."

Edelson didn't move. He didn't have any hard evidence she was a prostitute — nothing that would hold up in court. Besides, he just wanted her to get out of his county. Save him the trouble of arresting and prosecuting her. She'd be out in a day or two, anyway — further agitated and harder up for whatever drug she'd been recently denied. He squinted at her. "You better tell me what you know. Who should I be after?" His mouth arranged itself into a grim line.

Crystal looked at him, as if she might say something — offer a name maybe. Then she shook her head. "I don't know anything," she muttered and started up the steps. "I was just asking if you did." She slammed the trailer door behind her, leaving the sheriff irked by a Chris for the second time in two days.

Back at his office, Edelson listened harder to Crystal O'Shea's voice in his head. He compared it to the voice of his anonymous caller. Could it be? His recollection of the call seemed so vivid until now. He worked at it a little longer, then picked up the phone and punched in numbers.

"Hello," Robin answered.

"How you doin'?"

"Good. You?"

"Okay." He twirled the phone cord around his index finger, trying to think of what he wanted to say. "You gonna be around for Thanksgiving? Want to get together?"

"Um . . . maybe." Her voice was flat and noncommittal.

She felt a million miles away. Each day he seemed to be losing her a little more. He could hear her disinterest as clearly as if she were speaking the words, telling him what he most dreaded to hear.

"I'll think about it. I've got a lot of work to do. Mid-terms are coming up, you know."

"Please come home." He immediately regretted the words. They sounded so desperate.

"Kip, we've been through this."

"Not really. You said you needed some time. What about counseling? I'm open to it . . . if you are."

She drew a heavy breath, and Edelson felt their marriage slipping away like sand through his fingers.

"I don't know. I . . . I need to talk to —" her words fell away abruptly.

"Who?"

Robin took in a long breath.

"You need to talk to who, Robin?" He pinched the bridge of his nose. She already had someone else? Was that it?

"I have to go, Kip."

He searched for something to say, but she'd already hung up. Edelson set the receiver down and smashed his fist on the desk.

He stood and gathered his hat. It was too early to pick up Gray. *Gray*, he thought. What in God's name was he thinking when he talked that social worker into leaving the boy with him? He didn't know anything about kids.

Gray sat at the table with Mrs. Sherwood, eating a fourth chocolate-chip cookie. It was true that homemade cookies were a million times better than store-bought. Especially Mrs. Sherwood's — the chocolate oozing out, melting on his fingers. The aroma of hot brown sugar had reached him in her library and pulled him out of his wonderland. He was still full from lunch, but it didn't matter. He ate until his belly hurt.

"What are you reading?" the old woman asked, nodding at the book next to him.

Gray looked at it, bound in cloth, soft with age. A paper label was pasted on its cover with curious writing — all its U's looked like V's. Gold lettering up the spine read *Arabian Nights*.

"Oh, that's one of my favorites."

"It's good," he agreed. "Did you see the pictures?" He opened the book and showed her a picture of a bare-chested man with a turban holding a long, curved sword. "That's a skimitar," he said, fingering the sword.

"Spelled s-c-i-m-i-t-a-r." She pointed to the word. "But pronounced 'simitar.'"

"I read four stories already."

"Did you? You must be a very good student."

Gray slumped back in his chair and shrugged.

"You're just being modest," she said and winked at him.

He felt a twinge in his stomach. Like he'd been pinched under his ribs. "I'm not very smart," he said, and worried she wouldn't like him as much now.

She picked up the book and thumbed the pages he'd read. "You must be to have read this much in one day. I wouldn't have been able to read it any faster."

"I'm good at reading," he conceded. "But the rest of school is hard for me. Well, besides computers. We just got new ones at school, and I like them."

"Do you?"

"Yeah, you can play games and write and do a lot of cool stuff."

"Well, then you must be smart," she said, looking thoroughly convinced.

Gray liked Mrs. Sherwood, she was kind of like Mrs. Anton, always telling him he was smart or handsome. "Is the sheriff going to let me stay with him? That's what that lady said."

"Yes, for a while." Mrs. Sherwood's smile faded a little, but didn't disappear. She looked long at him, making him feel funny.

"Do you know about his cat?"

She looked surprised. "He has a cat?"

"Oh, he's so cool." And Gray told her all about Peachy and how he had slept under his blankets all night.

Mrs. Sherwood poured Edelson a cup of coffee and began to clear the supper dishes.

Edelson stared at his reflection in the kitchen window, thinking of Robin, who didn't even want to have Thanksgiving dinner with her own damn husband. Edelson wanted to tell her about Gray. Thought she should know. They *were* still married after all. And taking in a kid, even for a few days, was something they would have talked about. Chris Samuelson popped into his head again. Standing in the sun, her hair blowing in the wind. Garbage all over her lawn.

"That boy is bright," the old woman said of Gray, who'd gone to gather his things. "He read a third of *Arabian Nights*." She pointed a sudsy finger at the book lying on the table. "In one day. That's not an easy book to read."

Edelson picked it up and flipped through the pages. "This is older than the one I read as a kid. Monty and I read it over and over again. It's one of the reasons he ended up in Saudi Arabia. This and Laurence of Arabia." He smiled down at the elaborate pictures. Something about them stood out, caught his eye. He flipped to the title page and gasped. "Do you know what you have here?"

Mrs. Sherwood came to the table and gazed down at the colorful, elongated illustrations. "It was my father's," she said with a fond smile.

"This was illustrated by Maxfield Parrish," Edelson said, running his finger over the byline. "My mother collects old prints of his. They're very expensive."

Mrs. Sherwood twisted her mouth, trying to place the name. "He sounds familiar. Wasn't he famous for his calendars?"

"Wow," Edelson said, turning the book over in his hand, looking again at the title page, noting the copyright date of 1909. "This is a first edition. And it's in great condition. It must be worth a fortune. How many illustrations are in here, anyway?" He flipped through the pages, pausing to study each of the dozen prints.

Gray came in shrouded in his borrowed sheriff's jacket, his shoe laces frayed and trailing behind him.

Mrs. Sherwood laughed. "What do you know, Gray, the book you like is illustrated by a famous artist."

"Put this away," Edelson commanded. "You don't want anything to happen to it."

"Oh, no. I told Gray he could borrow it."

"But this book is worth a lot of money."

Suddenly, Mrs. Sherwood's face had gone stern, cross even. He'd never seen her that way, and she reminded him of his own mother.

"He'll take good care of it. Won't you, Gray?" she said, turning to the boy.

"It's okay." Gray shook his head.

"Don't be silly. Take the book with you." She pulled *Arabian Nights* away from Edelson and handed it to Gray. "I trust you."

Gray looked uncertain, worry jumping from every part of him. "I dunno. My dad said I was a slob."

"Wanna go see that cat now?" Edelson interrupted.

The boy's face brightened and he nodded, gripping the book to his chest.

"Wait for me in the car. I just need to get my things. I'll be right out."

Mrs. Sherwood waited for the door to close then turned to Edelson. "Kip, Gray needs someone to believe in him. It's just a book; it can be replaced. But that child's self-worth is a lot harder to get back."

Edelson nodded humbly and pulled his jacket on. He knew so little about children. What in hell was he thinking — he'd never even liked kids before. He was practically single now, without the first clue about preparing regular meals. The boy would be needing help with his homework, Edelson thought, or perhaps wanting to play a sport. He'd need clean clothes soon. That last idea panicked Edelson. He'd better start a load of laundry straight off when they get home. How could he possibly provide any sort of refuge for Gray, living in this two-bit town on his miniscule salary?

Another glass of bourbon at home this evening, while his cook and waitress ran the bar alone. The nightcap had become routine by now. McHugh went through the numbers again in his head, for the one-hundredth, or one-hundred-thousandth, time. But not more times than he had gone over a conversation with his sister before she married Russell Vining. He believed she might've finally listened if he'd just told her one more time not to marry Vining. *He's a bum, Wren. He'll make you sorry.*

McHugh had pegged Vining for trouble from the start — felt it in his gut. He couldn't stand the way Vining sweet-talked Wren. Lavished her with compliments until she was dripping with love. Made her promises any fool could see he'd never be able to keep. Any fool but Wren. She was too innocent, easily led astray. McHugh knew that for a fact. His face went hot as he remembered her youthful smile, bright and intoxicating. She used to follow him everywhere, like a shadow. And he had lured her into the quiet corners and hidden places of their grandfather's tavern, whispering promises he could never keep.

When he would wrestle with her, not quite sure why, she would work so hard against his grip, but gain no ground. Finally she'd calm and look up at him with her deep brown eyes, smile almost shyly, and say *Please, please Randy*. And he'd let her go.

McHugh threw back the glass of bourbon, but his stomach revolted. He bolted for the deck and vomited over the railing.

"Where is your wife?" Gray asked.

Edelson looked at the boy prone on the sofa with Peachy stretched nearly the length of him, its nose buried in the fold of the boy's neck. "She goes to school in Missoula."

"Doesn't she live with you?"

Edelson scowled. "It's too far to drive back and forth."

"Oh." The boy watched television for a moment, then turned back to him. "Do you have kids that live with her?"

"No."

"How come?"

"Because we just don't."

"Oh." Gray stroked the cat and it kneaded its claws against his shoulder. He watched a few more minutes of television, then asked, "Does your wife come home on the weekends?"

"No," Edelson said, setting his newspaper in his lap and looking at the boy. "Anything else you'd like to know before I read the rest of this article?"

Gray thought a second and shook his head.

Edelson went back to reading about the Democratic primaries. Elections weren't as interesting without his brother around to debate with. Edelson let it go. Had plenty already to worry about. A body to identify. A boy —

"Is this where I'm going to live from now on?"

Edelson didn't set his paper down right away. Why hadn't he thought of this? Of course the boy would have questions. What kind of an idiot had he been to not think of this?

"It's okay, I like it here," Gray assured him.

Edelson peered over the top of his paper. "I don't know. I mean . . . no, not forever."

Gray nodded his understanding. "Until we find my mom, right?"

Tiny volts of electricity coursed up and down Edelson's arms. "I'll do what I can to find her. I mean I *am* trying to find her."

"Did you call California?"

Edelson hesitated, wondered if he should begin laying the foundation for what could eventually end in a painful discussion. "Yeah, I called California. They're looking, too."

"I can't wait to see her," Gray said, turning back to the television.

"We need to go to Missoula tomorrow, Gray."

Gray snapped his face back to the sheriff with an expression Edelson read as panic.

"To see a doctor, that's all."

"How come?"

"Just a checkup," Edelson said, trying to sound unconcerned. "When did you last see a doctor?"

Gray shrugged. "I don't know."

"Well, you'll probably have to get some shots. You know, measles and stuff."

"I hate shots."

"Well, they won't let you go back to school if you don't get them."

Gray grinned. "I could stay here with Peachy."

"I don't think so," the man replied.

13

Before sun-up, McHugh got down to the Silver Dog. He parked in the back alley and came in through the kitchen door, which wasn't his habit. He worked his key in a rarely used door off the back hallway and carted several empty cardboard boxes up the steep, narrow stairway to the second floor. The air smelled of dust and old leather. He dropped the boxes in the hall and looked up and down the corridor at the rows of closed doors. The building had once been the Silver Dog Saloon and Hotel. And while he was aware that the saloon still resembled a scene from the old west, where Clint Eastwood steps from the shadows with a cigarette clenched in his snarl and brandishing a six-shooter, McHugh remembered when they used the upstairs, too. And he remembered when his father closed it up. He'd come up here only once in the intervening years — a memory he pushed away before it prevailed itself on him again.

He sucked in a deep breath, half expecting to see a ghost floating down the corridor, then stepped forward and turned the first knob. The door creaked and McHugh stepped into the room. Dust lay thick as snow. He went to the window and pulled up the sash. A cold breeze burst in, scouring away the stagnant air. He turned a full circle, inventorying the room. And wondered if he should leave the furniture, forget it, give it to the next owner, whoever that would be. Perhaps he would, he told himself. The dresser was empty, as well as the wardrobe.

Antiques, but not of great quality. He'd be lucky to get a hundred dollars for them. He closed the window and pulled the door shut, then stood again in the hallway, gazing down the corridor. He moved to the next room. A pile of books lay in the corner under a heavy blanket of dust. Floral-covered wallpaper, faded to powder blue, curled off the walls. A bare bulb hung suspended in the center of the ceiling. The room was otherwise empty. He heard Wren's childish giggle and relived a memory of the two of them playing on the floor there. He was older than she by a full ten years. She must have been three or four then. Long brown pigtails cascading down her dress. She was a beautiful child. Everyone crooned over her. Made such a fuss about her. And he had eyes to see, even at his young age. He sat on the floor with her, offering up marbles and other delights, just for the pleasure of looking at her.

Gray rode uneasily next to the sheriff — Mr. Edelson. He couldn't get used to calling him that. Sometimes he just called him Mister. He gripped Mrs. Sherwood's book tightly, but couldn't focus on it, or even look at its glossy pictures. He could hardly sit still, shifting and twisting in his seat.

"Don't worry, it won't hurt. It's just a little prick, is all," the sheriff said.

Gray turned to look out the window. Adults all said that, that it wouldn't hurt. But they yelled like hell when they got stuck. The landscape unfolded gradually from forest to farmland. He strained to see the paper mill as they passed. The sheriff did, too, but neither said a word.

After a while, the city came into view, and Gray blurted, "Please don't take me to a foster home."

The sheriff looked over, eyebrows arched. "We're just going for a blood test and a checkup. I already told you."

Gray sat on his hands to keep them still. His stomach was crawling, like it was full to the brim with long-legged beetles.

McHugh cursed the skeleton lock on the third door. It was seized — the metal rotted in the dry air. He thought to move to the next room, but persisted until finally he forced the door with a firm whack of his boot sole. The door flew open, crashing into the wall and bouncing back. McHugh stood in the entry. A chill ripped up his spine, raising the hair up on his neck. He spun around wildly. There was nothing there. He stood stone still then, his eyes darting from corner to corner, inside the room and down the hall. Nothing. His own damn imagination. He let his breath out and moved inside.

The room was nearly empty, except for a few picture frames propped against the far wall and a wicker chair with a caved-in seat. It was his grandmother's chair, the only thing of hers he still owned. He'd been saving it for Wren. Had planned to have it repaired. He ran his fingers through the heavy dust along the back of the chair. Maybe it wasn't too late. He could take it into Missoula next time he went to see Wren. By the time the place sold and he'd bailed Wren out, he could give it to her as a coming-home gift.

His sister was much like this chair, both wasting away, she under the neglectful hand of Russell Vining. She could be beautiful again, too. The refurbished chair could serve to symbolize her new start. *Their* new beginning.

He hauled the chair up and carried it down to his pickup, where he set it in the bed before returning to the saloon.

Edelson tensed with Gray as the needle tucked into the boy's flesh. The nurse yanked the rubber tourniquet from Gray's arm, and the blood squirted into the small vial. The fluorescent lights and stark white linoleum floor glared and Edelson squinted. The scent of iodine burned in his nostrils.

"Almost finished," the nurse said. "You're doing great."

Gray opened his eyes to watch her pull off the full tube

and snap on an empty one, which quickly filled. He grimaced.

"We'll have the results back in about two weeks," she said to Edelson.

"Two weeks? Why so long?"

"It's Thanksgiving next week. We've got a skeleton crew working."

Gray's eyes met Edelson's.

"She means they don't have very many people working," he said to the boy, wishing she hadn't mentioned skeletons. It was only a matter of time before Gray asked again about the one he found. "I think I'll take you to lunch for being such a good sport."

The boy grinned. "Those shots hurt."

"What?" The sheriff feigned alarm. "You're not any tougher than that?"

"I didn't cry," Gray said defensively.

"I know. You did great."

But no sooner had they returned to Edelson's cruiser, than Gray asked, "Did you find out who that skeleton was?"

Edelson was prepared this time. "No, but I have some leads. I expect we'll know who it was before too long."

"Do you have to tell the family?"

"Yes," Edelson said quickly. He stared ahead at the square brick clinic, one hand on the ignition. "Yes, I will have to tell them."

"I bet they're going to be really sad." Gray looked happy himself. The shots were over and he was being taken to lunch.

McHugh returned to the second room to wipe the book covers with an old kitchen rag from downstairs and begin boxing them up, all the while thinking about his crew. They'd come in to prepare for the lunch shift, and his waitress was immediately suspicious.

He'd squeezed past her in the narrow kitchen to gather the newly bleached rags they used for the floor.

"Were you upstairs?" she asked.

"Yeah," he said, not looking up.

"I saw your truck, but I didn't think you were *up there*."

He shrugged and gathered a handful of rags, waiting for the ghost stories to start spilling out of her. McHugh hated that people believed the building was haunted. He hated that people were so morbid and gullible.

"Why were you up there?" she pressed.

"Why not?" He turned to her then, in a challenge intended to make her back off.

She shivered. "Doesn't it creep you out?"

"Does it you? Have you been up there?"

"No." She tossed her head. "But I've heard."

McHugh's jaw worked back and forth as he thought about it now. He had a headache from clenching his teeth — all night and into the day. He hadn't slept, but flipped and flopped and tangled in his covers with a guilt that paled with the morning light, but failed to do him the courtesy of disappearing.

He picked up the last book and blew the dust off. They weren't important books. Some were school books; some were ledgers. There were a few novels with swirly designs on the covers. All were old. McHugh didn't know why he was bothering with them, except that the thought of leaving them behind unsettled him. He heaved the box into the hall and shut the door. He looked down the corridor and decided it was enough for one day. He'd come back before his crew arrived for work tomorrow and finish. He hated the way they eyeballed him every time he walked into the kitchen. As if he had no business exploring the unused rooms of his own tavern. Or worse, that maybe they felt sorry for him.

McHugh stopped at the Y, just outside Missoula — so named

133

for the shape of the I-90/U.S. 93 interchange. He ordered lunch at the truck-stop diner, glancing frequently at his watch to make sure he didn't miss visiting hours at the jail, wondering what the Mineral County sheriff was doing in town. He'd spotted the familiar cruiser headed in the opposite direction a few miles west of the Y. McHugh hoped Edelson would decide to help his sister — how he didn't know. But cops could pull strings. They knew other cops. Had a network — an elite community unto themselves. He didn't trust Edelson, though. McHugh prided himself on his gift for reading people, understanding their motives after a moment's observation. Yet Edelson remained a mystery. But McHugh hoped the vein of decency he thought he'd seen in the man might give way to some sense of obligation to McHugh's family. Being the one who killed his sister's husband and all. Any man could see she was a victim. Any decent man could see.

She looks better today, McHugh thought as his sister was escorted in. *Not so frantic.* Her hair was clean and neatly combed, but there was more silver in it, which startled him. Somehow he'd imagined Wren being young forever. She was once so beautiful — long-legged and willowy, with shiny chestnut hair. Her weight gain he'd attributed to living in Russell's shadow. He never allowed her anything but cheap, fatty food, never a new dress or shoes. Said why the fuck she needs nice things up there in the mountains. McHugh mourned the loss of Wren's figure more than he believed she did. And Russell had never seen her at her most glorious; he never knew what he'd lost. But it pained McHugh over the years to watch his little Wren, once a magnificent specimen of womanhood, inching steadily into middle age and mediocrity.

She smiled at him, lighting his world.

"Hey, sis," he said into the phone.

"I'm so glad to see you. When are you going to get me out of here, Randy?"

"I have a plan, but I'm not telling you yet. Trust me, it'll be all right." He knew she'd be angry if he told her he was selling the Silver Dog. Not because she wanted it, but because she knew he did. He'd tell her when she was out. When the lawyers were paid off and things were okay. When he'd have her all to himself again, with enough cash to move away and start over.

"You're the only one I can count on, Randy. Thanks for not turning your back on me."

In Mrs. Sherwood's small library, pale winter sun reached in through the window, touching Gray's book, open to the same page for nearly an hour. Mrs. Sherwood sat in a chair opposite him, crocheting something frilly and blue. Tiny particles of dust hung weightless between them, sparkling like diamonds in the sun. Gray wanted to visit his father, had wanted to see him for days, even though he knew Jim Dausman wasn't really his father. Gray wondered if he was supposed to feel this way, feel a connection still to a man who had deserted him. Sheriff Edelson acted like he should never want to see his father again. It wasn't nice, what his father did. And if his father didn't want to see him, he shouldn't want to see his father, either. But Gray missed Jim Dausman. He even kind of missed Andrea. Not like he missed his mother; that was different. He missed his mother with a pain that felt like his gut was splitting in two. Seeing Jim was more like a feeling that he wanted to just say, "Hi, how's it going?" Gray missed his bedroom, and his scruffy blankets. He missed being able to watch whatever he wanted on TV. He even missed being alone. He was never alone now.

Arabian Nights slid off his lap and thumped loudly against the wood floor. Gray remembered that it was an important book and scrambled to his feet to get it.

"I'm sorry," he stammered, holding it awkwardly at his waist.

The old lady looked up over the rim of her glasses. "You can lie down if you're sleepy."

"No." His face went hot at the suggestion, like he was a baby or something.

"Are you hungry?"

For once he wasn't. "No." He sat down and thumbed through the book to find his place. She went back to her crocheting. He watched her. At last he said, "Do you think I'll be able to see my dad sometime?"

She bit down on her lower lip, making it disappear, and her forehead creased. "I don't know. I guess that's a question for Mr. Edelson. Or Ms. Winborn."

"Is it bad that I want to see him?"

She looked up. "No. Of course not."

"Do you think he wants to see me?"

"I don't know that I can answer that, Gray, but I have to believe that after all this time together he must miss you, too."

Gray sat back in the chair, confused. Talking about his father made him want to see the man even more. That Mrs. Sherwood thought his father missed him, too, made him feel less guilty. Then Gray remembered again that Jim wasn't his real father. He decided to remind himself about that fact more often.

14

SHERIFF EDELSON DROPPED GRAY OFF at school and watched him disappear inside the hulking building. He pulled onto I-90, headed for Peerless, planning to check messages at his office, but as he came up to the exit he drove on past.

He parked on Third Street in Missoula and looked up at Robin's window. It was just past nine. If he was lucky she'd be up having her morning coffee. She wasn't an early riser.

The rest of the city bustled with activity. Students bundled against the east wind whipping in vicious torrents down the Little Blackfoot River and onto campus had narrow slits in their swaddles for navigation. Edelson crossed the gravel-studded ice, his exposed ears burning with cold.

He knocked politely. Not like a cop, but like a gentleman.

"Who is it?" Robin called.

"Kip," he said.

The door swung open.

"Hello."

"Hope you don't mind, but I needed to see you."

"Is everything okay?" Her eyes roamed his face in a search for clues.

"No," he said, stepping inside, uninvited.

She left the door open a moment. An arctic wind scattered dust bunnies across the pine floor. "What is it?"

"My wife left me."

She slammed the door, dropping her chin with annoyance.

"I need to know if she's coming back. I need to know if there's any chance, or if I should just quit trying." He stared at her with the most earnest gaze he could conjure.

"Do we have to talk about this now?"

"Yes. Yes, we do. This isn't just about you, Robin. You're not the only one who feels."

"Then, no. I'm not coming back."

Edelson staggered a little before catching the doorknob in his fingers. "Okay," he said and stalked out to meet the wind. Its icy sting was no comparison to his wife's rejection.

Winter descended on Mineral County with maniacal vengeance, forcing all but the hardiest school kids to the gym for recess. As his morning break neared, Gray asked if he could go to the library instead. The questions from his classmates were unbearable. Had he really been kicked out of the house? What did he do? Gray tried to shrug it off, pretend his life was the same. But they were quick to point out that they heard the police had picked him up. But he told the truth only to his teachers. They'd begun to treat him like some kind of movie star, giving him tender smiles laced with pity. The nurse pulled him from first period every day to ask how he felt, as if Gray couldn't tell what she was getting at and resented it. *Nasty bitch.* Even the principal greeted him by name. Teachers he'd never met before suddenly knew who he was and suddenly cared about him.

"Of course you can spend recess in the library," Mr. Allen said. "Would you like to take a friend with you?"

Gray shook his head and shoved the pass into his book bag. "I'm not a fucking baby," he said under his breath as the teacher passed.

When the bell rang, Mr. Allen walked with Gray down the

noisy corridor, weaving among the throngs of bored children. Something he had never done before. "Do you want someone to stay with you?"

Gray ducked inside the library without looking back. He missed being invisible.

"Hello, Gray," the librarian said, giving him a long and sad gaze. "How are you doing?"

"Fine," he said, curtly ending any further conversation. "Can you tell me how much an old book is worth?" He pulled Mrs. Sherwood's copy of *Arabian Nights* from his bag and set it carefully on the counter.

The librarian looked it over. "This is an old one."

"The pictures were painted by a famous artist," Gray said.

"It's old, Gray. But I don't think it's valuable."

"Are you sure?" His face must have registered his disappointment, because she quickly responded, "Let me look into it. Can I keep the book overnight?"

"No," he said, pulling it from her hands and tucking it back into his bag.

She gave him a look that was less kind than before. "I'll need to write down the name of the illustrator. Can I at least see it again?"

He produced the book once more and watched as she copied the artist's name onto a piece of pink scrap paper. When she finished, he took the book to a row of chairs along the frost-glazed windows and thumbed through it, scanning the pictures with disappointment. She would know better than Mr. Edelson. She was the librarian, he thought. In a way he was relieved. He didn't really want to steal from someone as nice as Mrs. Sherwood.

On Highway 93 toward Ravalli and the Montana 200 junction, Edelson found himself trapped behind a string of semis moving too slow to satisfy his craving for speed and too fast to get past them without using his lights. His anger burned hot. One moment he wished Robin dead, the next he was happy to be rid of her.

He turned onto 200 and headed westward, winding along the Flathead, thinking it was too soon — not even December — to be this cold. Winter in Montana was a time that most did not appreciate. But Edelson liked Mother Nature's raw, pissed-off mood. He got it, understood it, partook of it. The icy river, steely-blue, biting against its shore, came into sight.

As he neared Chris Samuelson's boat ramp, Edelson understood the pattern of his own behavior. He didn't imagine this other woman could save his marriage, nor replace it. She couldn't change the circumstances of Russell Vining's death. Nor could she change the boy's luck. But there was a gap in his existence that perhaps she might fill. She could flush all the others from his mind. At least for a little while.

He tossed rocks into the water as he surveyed her ferry docked on the opposite shore. Her canoe was where he'd left it, untouched. The wind shriveled his fingers. He admired her independence, her freedom to ignore anyone she chose. He returned to his cruiser and laid a palm against the horn. He imagined the noise wafting upstream on the winter wind to the tiny hamlet of Paradise, the sound never reaching Chris. She didn't appear at the window, or open the door.

In the dim corridor of the Silver Dog's second floor, Randy McHugh listened to his staff below, for nearly an hour prepping for lunch. They knew he was up here, he could tell by the hushed tones of their voices. He kicked the box of items he'd salvaged from the third room. Nothing much, really. Just some old photos of the tavern. One of a wagon and team sitting out front, the driver posed stiffly for the camera. Another of dirt-blackened miners lounging the front steps — one of the earliest photos his father had of the place. And a third hand-colored picture from World War II. A large V for victory hanging over the door. A woman — he guessed his grandmother — bespectacled and wearing a white apron, stood on the upstairs balcony. It was gone now, the balcony. His father ripped it down, he said, before it collapsed and killed someone.

McHugh stepped to the last room, feeling ashamed for letting his imagination run wild the previous day. There were no ghosts in the Silver Dog. He knew it better than anyone. He'd never ceased to marvel over the years that a simple suggestion could produce such staunch believers. Not simply people who thought it was true, but people who swore by their own first-hand accounts. And yesterday, he himself quaked at the memories echoing in his head.

McHugh's father had started the rumor, half-drunk and tired of covering up. What surprised McHugh was that it had worked so well. He dropped the empty box in his hand, producing a mushroom cloud of dust. Most of the second-floor furniture was crammed into this tiny room on the corner. He went to the wavy-paned glass and looked down Main Street. Why had he stayed in this town, anyway? He always swore he'd have the brains to leave it behind. McHugh watched crazy old Rowena unlocking her shop next door.

"There's one person I'll be glad never to see again," he said aloud, tapping the glass, wishing she could hear him. She'd been accusing him of sneaking into her shop and stealing her merchandise since he was a boy. No one was stealing from her. No one was buying, either. What she couldn't find was buried under all that garbage. It was all garbage.

Turning away, McHugh began picking through his stuff, looking for anything worth keeping. His father had not been a meticulous man, and McHugh loathed the condition in which he'd passed things on. This was no exception. Newspapers were stacked three feet high in one corner, brittle and yellow. A fire hazard. He opened several boxes to find Wren's old toys and a few tattered dresses. She and her mother lived in this self-same room until the mother, Dina, passed away. She died on the mattress standing on end against the wall. For years the room had remained as it was on the night Dina died. The haunting moans patrons attributed to her ghost were simply McHugh's father and his inconsolable misery over losing his mistress, Wren's mother.

McHugh opened another box and took out a porcelain doll dressed in a red velvet cape and hood. Her white satin dress now the color of old ivory. He tipped her up and her blue eyes popped open. He caressed the matted curls gently and placed her in the empty box. Wren would want to have her back, he was sure.

"Gray," the librarian called. "You were right. That book was illustrated by a famous artist."

Gray jumped to his feet and ran to the counter. "It was?"

"Yeah," she said peering into her computer monitor. "The price of his work has skyrocketed in the last thirty years. That book you have now sells for three hundred dollars." She turned to Gray, her eyes twinkling.

"Three hundred dollars?" Gray couldn't believe it. He had hoped it was worth twenty.

"Where did you get it?"

"Uh, it was a gift." His words came out rushed, and he looked at his feet.

The librarian kept her eyes on him, waiting for him to continue.

Gray didn't think she believed him. "It was."

"From another student?"

"No, nobody here."

"Well, if it was a kid, the right thing to is give it back you know."

142

"It wasn't a kid," he said.

"Okay. You should probably tell the person who gave it to you, anyway. They may not have known."

The bell rang and Gray dashed out of the library. Halfway down the hall he shoved the book back in his bag. His cheeks burned with excitement. *A $300 book, all his!* He didn't think he could sit through math period.

When Edelson got back to his office he discovered a message from the Susanville police. He immediately called them back.

"This is Edelson. Mineral County. You found something?"

"A lead I thought you'd be interested in." The Susanville detective spoke with a slow drawl that reminded Edelson of the southeastern states. "Nothing much, but you know how it is, any scrap is news. Something little could turn out to be just the thing you're looking for."

"What is it?"

"The sister of that woman you're looking for, Anita Jossey, is in Las Vegas. She was arrested for possession of narcotics a couple of weeks back."

"Who's got her?"

"Oh, she's out now. Been out for a while." The detective breathed heavily into the phone. "You know how it is. With tax cuts and all. Anyone short of a cold-blooded murderer is out the next day. Even a murderer —"

"You get an address on her?"

"No."

Edelson's pencil snapped in his fingers. "Las Vegas, you say?"

"Yup. I've got the officer's name and number here somewhere."

Edelson yanked his desk drawer open and extracted a

newly sharpened pencil and took down the Vegas name and number. "Thanks, I appreciate the call."

"No problem. We all have to work together. It ain't easy."

"Thanks," he said again. "Thanks a lot."

"Okay, then." And Susanville hung up.

Edelson wasted no time dialing the Las Vegas police department. He and an officer exchanged cordialities and Edelson got right to the point. "I'm looking for a woman by the name of Kristi Blackhorse. The sister of Anita Jossey, a woman you recently arrested for possession."

He was put on hold. When the officer picked up again, he was abrupt. "No record of a Kristi Blackhorse."

"Okay, thanks. Can you give me the Jossey woman's address and phone?" Edelson said and took them down.

He sat back in his chair then, thinking about what he'd say to Anita Jossey. He'd need to give her some reason for his call. And he wasn't going to tell her about Gray's situation. Not over the phone, anyway. And not to a woman who'd been arrested for possession of narcotics, who might suddenly get the notion she should care for the boy. He picked up the phone and dialed the number.

"I'm sorry, but the number you have dialed has been disconnected or is no longer in service — "

Edelson slammed the receiver down.

15

GRAY DRIFTED TO SLEEP, Peachy snug against his side. He had asked Mr. Edelson if he was going to always sleep on the couch, but Edelson didn't answer. Gray knew there was an extra bedroom in Mr. Edelson's house, a guest room filled with boxes and other stuff. Gray was liking Mr. Edelson more. He was quiet. Didn't ask him a lot of questions about how he was feeling. Not like the teachers at school, or even Mrs. Sherwood. But in a way that also made Gray feel weird. He wasn't sure if Mr. Edelson really wanted him to be there. He wondered if the lady that came to talk to him at Mrs. Sherwood's house told Mr. Edelson that he *had* to take care of him.

Gray stood at the river, looking over the bank. Sheriff Edelson was sitting on the slope, the sun on his back, reading *Arabian Nights*. Gray called to him, saw the bright colors of the artist's painting on the open page. He took a step closer, and finally the sheriff turned. But it wasn't the sheriff at all. It was the skeleton with those gaping black eyes. Gray turned to run, but his feet were like lead, dragging him backward down the hill. He could smell its rancid odor. He ran harder, trying to go faster, but he wasn't getting anywhere. He looked back to see its horrible teeth, slippery black with mud. Gray screamed as loud as he could. But no one could hear him.

* * *

When Gray came to his senses, he was sitting upright on the sofa, his blanket on the floor. Peachy cowered in the corner near the door, staring up at him with round green eyes.

Mr. Edelson stumbled out of his bedroom half asleep, wearing his undershorts. "What is it?"

Gray gasped for breath, tears now streaking down his face. His heart hammered away in his throat.

Mr. Edelson sat down on the sofa next to him and laid a hand on his shoulder.

Gray tensed. Through sobs he said, "It was coming after me."

"What?"

"The skeleton. It was pulling me into the river."

Mr. Edelson patted him awkwardly on the shoulder. "It was just a dream," he said.

Gray knew it was. But it seemed so real. He was breathless from running.

Mr. Edelson rubbed Gray's sweaty head with a large hand. "Just a dream."

Gray closed his eyes, but the skeleton wouldn't go away.

Edelson awoke before dawn, his foot dead asleep, lying on the floor like another man's limb. The boy was curled against him, snuggled under his arm. He'd only meant to stay with the child until he went back to sleep, pulling the blanket onto his lap and around Gray's shoulders.

"Hey, kiddo," he said softly, trying to extract himself from the tangle. Peachy jumped down and stretched long, kneading the carpet with his claws. Edelson laid the boy down on the pillow, deciding to let him sleep a little longer.

By mid-morning, Edelson found himself at the big warehouse store on the north end of Missoula near the Interstate, and after an exasperating hour of fighting his way through the throngs of people he thought ought to be working, he left with several boxes of food, including an eighteen-pound turkey that he took straight to Mrs. Sherwood's house.

The old woman held the door for him as he made three trips in with the groceries, then followed him to the kitchen and they began to unpack them.

"I didn't ask first, but hoped we might spend Thanksgiving together." He didn't look at her when he said it, but busied himself emptying a bag of oranges into the fruit bowl she kept on her kitchen table.

"As long as you promise to carve the bird," she said.

"You've got a deal."

She paused halfway to the refrigerator with a package of hamburger in her hands. "Will your wife join us?"

Edelson dropped the empty box on the floor at his feet and started to unpack the next. "No."

McHugh looked on as the realtor tried to pound a For Sale sign into the rock-hard ground at the end of his cabin's driveway.

"Ground is frozen," the realtor finally said. "We'll have to nail it to your fence."

McHugh nodded. He could've told him that. But he was curious to see if this man had some secret for setting posts when the temperature had hovered at zero for over a week. His confidence in the realtor's ability to sell his house or his bar sank a little in the face of this display.

"I quit traveling when the chicks hatched," the realtor started again about his chickens.

McHugh had never heard anyone so gaga over their pets in his entire life. And he'd listened to a fair number of pet lovers from behind his bar. Especially not a grown man like this, and chickens for God's sake. "Because of chickens?"

"Oh, you should see them. The wife wanted to find them homes. But they're so cute. She finally admitted she was attached. We named them Oliver, Jasper, Cheetah, Annabel, and Gerald."

McHugh couldn't look the man in the face. He was afraid he'd laugh out loud at him.

"They're smart too." The realtor wiped the sweat from his face with a handkerchief.

"How long have you been in the real estate business?"

"Eighteen years," the man said proudly. "I exceeded six million in sales last year alone."

McHugh was relieved. He was beginning to imagine he'd contracted a nutball to sell his property. "Why Cheetah?"

"She can run really fast." The realtor peered at McHugh as if he were stupid or something. "I'm bringing a client by this afternoon to see the place."

"Already?"

"I've got a guy who's been looking a while. I think this is it. I called him last night and told him about it. He's pretty excited."

McHugh flinched. He turned and looked at his cabin, yellow against the towering pines. Snow-bright under the pale sky. It looked like a photograph. He almost changed his mind on the spot.

"It'll get the price we put on it. Don't worry." The realtor folded his handkerchief neatly and slid it inside his jacket. "What're your plans after it sells?"

McHugh looked at him. Plans? "I don't know. Was thinking to maybe move up to the lake or something."

"Are you interested in some listings up there? I know a couple of very nice places on the eastern shore. Right down in the cherry orchards. Beautiful."

"I don't know. Let's sell this place first."

"That won't be a problem."

*   *   *

In the afternoon Edelson drove up to St. John's to check out an abandoned car someone had called in. He sat along the shoulder behind a dented VW Rabbit, running the plates and identification number. The VW came back clean. Probably just ran out of gas, or broke down. He leaned across the seat and popped the glove box, pulling out a fluorescent green window sticker warning the owner to move it within forty-eight hours or lose it.

As he affixed the sticker to the driver's window, Chris Samuelson's red and white Ford pickup cruised past. He glanced up in time to see her slowing to look at him. She didn't wave. Neither did he, but got back in his cruiser and spun around to follow her.

She stopped at the Gas'n'Go to fill up. Edelson pulled in behind her, tempted to turn his lights on, but reckoned that would really piss her off.

Chris slid out and unscrewed the gas cap. He approached. She watched him through the corner of her eye. "Afternoon, Sheriff," she said curtly when he was a few feet away, but still refused to look directly at him.

"Ms. Samuelson."

She jutted her chin out trying to look mad, but he could tell she wasn't. "How come you were parked at my boat ramp yesterday?"

"So you did see me."

"Yeah, I saw you."

"Why didn't you come out, then?" He leaned against the bed of her truck, trapping her between the gas hose and himself.

"I thought I was rid of you," she said.

"Ouch."

"Well, you're the one who's married, not me."

"Nah." He shook his head and shoved his icy fingers into the pockets of his jacket.

"Nah, what?" She watched the dollars climb steadily on the digital display. Didn't look again at the sheriff until he spoke.

"She's gone for good."

Chris tossed her braid over her shoulder and snapped the stop on the pump.

Edelson looked at the number. Nineteen-ninety-nine. "Bet you overshoot it. Can't get just a penny any more. It's too little gas for one snap on the handle."

She clicked it with her index finger, quick, like a trigger. Twenty even. She tossed him a look of superiority.

"You didn't really mean what you said, did you?"

She replaced the pump handle and began to screw the gas cap back on. "About what?"

"You know what."

"I wouldn't have said it if I didn't mean it."

"Give me another chance."

"You're implying you had a chance in the first place. You're just too stubborn to see that you didn't." She leaned in through the open window and pulled out her wallet. "I have to pay for my gas."

"I'll wait."

She strode inside, sporting an amused smile that Edelson interpreted as a good sign.

She let him buy her lunch at the roadside diner in Magda where Edelson told her about the boy. She didn't interrupt or ask questions, but frowned through the entire story, picking gingerly at her spinach salad. When he finished, she said, "What are you going to say to him when he has to go to a foster home?"

Edelson set his fork down. His pork chops and gravy suddenly seemed less appealing. "I don't know."

"Well you better think of something. That poor kid is going to be devastated."

"More so than he already is?"

"Well, yeah. He thinks you care about him."

"I do," Edelson said quickly. "Why else would I take him in?"

"I mean . . . a lot more than temporarily." She dropped her fork, too.

"I don't just care about him temporarily." But Edelson wondered if she could read his mind. Apparently, she regarded him as shallow and careless about other people's feelings.

"Enough to give him a home — a forever home?"

"I can't do that."

"You should've thought of that before you took him in."

He shoved his half-eaten lunch away and picked up his coffee. "What do I know about kids?"

Her gaze had gone soft. "Obviously enough to know he needs you."

Edelson looked out at the traffic whizzing past on the Interstate. He wished he hadn't made such an impulsive choice in taking the boy in. Kids were only a bother, But there was something about Gray that Edelson found impossible to turn away from. But forever was not in his plan. He'd been rash and now Gray would suffer another rejection because of it.

16

THANKSGIVING, A HOLIDAY EDELSON could take or leave, turned out to be a surprising bright spot. He and Gray arrived early at Mrs. Sherwood's house with a bouquet of orange flowers that she instantly identified as asters. He nodded agreement, as if he'd known that all along. Edelson drank coffee and Gray ate toast and jam while the old woman stuffed the bird. When she gave the word, Edelson lifted it into the oven. A homemade cherry pie sat enticingly on the kitchen table that Gray looked at with pure wonder and excitement.

"I take it you like pie," he said to the boy.

Gray smiled as big as Edelson had ever seen. "Yeah."

"Me, too. Especially cherry."

"Those are Flathead cherries," Mrs. Sherwood said. "From right here in Montana. Have you ever had Flathead cherries, Gray?"

He nodded. "My mom takes me to the lake sometimes to go swimming. She always gets cherries so we can eat them at the beach and spit the pits into the water."

"What can I do to help you?" Edelson asked Mrs. Sherwood, not wanting to hear the boy talk about his mother this way — like she'd just taken him swimming last week, and would again as soon as the weather warmed up.

"You can peel potatoes." She pointed at a pile of wet Russets in the strainer.

It was a job he knew he wouldn't mess up, and he gladly stepped up to the sink and started working on the spuds.

Hours later, when the aroma of roasted turkey had penetrated every nook of the house and Edelson and Gary could scarcely stand another second of waiting, Mrs. Sherwood declared that the meal was ready. Edelson carved the bird as promised and the three convened at the dining room table to look upon their feast: turkey with stuffing, minced cranberries with mandarin oranges and walnuts, cornbread rolls, baked green beans with mushrooms, sugar-glazed carrots, and mashed potatoes and gravy. Edelson watched the boy's excitement with an ungrudging sense of satisfaction.

"I'm thankful for my new friends, Kip and Gray," Mrs. Sherwood said, raising her water goblet.

Edelson didn't know what to say when the old woman looked his way, obviously expecting him to declare *his* thanksgiving. He looked down at the fine bone china, then at the boy, then back to Mrs. Sherwood. "I'm thankful for your terrific cooking," he said and raised his glass.

Gray smiled with embarrassment at his turn. "Pie."

They laughed and ate their fill.

After dinner Edelson and Gray cleared the dishes, but Mrs. Sherwood shooed them out of the kitchen, insisting she could wash up. Edelson suspected it was a strategic decision to protect her good china from two clumsy boys. So they watched football in the living room, sock-footed and stuffed, lying full out on her Chinese carpet. From the glazed look in Gray's eyes, Edelson deducted the boy was not only incapacitated by the enormous feast, but by the annual event most folks took for granted.

McHugh ate a tuna sandwich and read through the offer the realtor had faxed to him that morning. He couldn't believe his house had sold so fast. One prospect, full price. He wondered if he should have priced it higher. It would pay off Russell's debt and give McHugh time to focus on raising the money to prove his sister's innocence in court. The sale of the tavern should take care of that. He was grateful and kept the idea foremost in his mind, refusing with militant fervor to go sentimental. It was worth it. Just a house. People were what mattered, not things. Wren would've done the same for him, he knew it.

He called the realtor. "It looks in order. I'll accept it."

"Wonderful. I'll come by tomorrow to get your signature. The Archers will be thrilled."

"Any chance they can close early?"

"Early?"

"Yeah. I'm ready. Just need a couple of days to move." McHugh gulped down a glass of water between sentences.

"Probably. It's usually the buyer who wants to close early."

McHugh looked out at the dusky purple sky. It was rich. He took it in one last time. "Work out the timing with them."

"Will do."

McHugh hung up and dialed a smudged number from the scrap of envelope he now kept in his wallet. Wren had insisted he contact a man named Sagen and not wait for the man to track him down. She insisted Sagen was the only one McHugh needed to pay off, and that he wasn't anyone to mess around with. McHugh suffered a stabbing fury at his dead brother-in-law for exposing Wren to such scum.

"Sagen," the voice rasped

"I can get your money."

"When?"

"Maybe three weeks. I sold my house, but it takes time to close. I'll have it for you, though."

There was a long silence. Finally, "I'm not accustomed to extending my deadlines."

"You'll get your money." McHugh's voice rattled, betraying his nerves. "But if you don't give me time, then I guess

154

you'll be out of luck," he said to make up for it.

"Don't fuck with me!"

"I'm just trying to be reasonable. I sold my house. The money is coming."

Another long pause. Then, "Vining had title to a couple of places."

"No, he didn't own anything. They rented that place."

"Shut up and listen. They own a trailer down in Peerless and another little place up in St. John's. Get me those titles and I'll consider it interest on the debt."

"I think you're mistaken." McHugh scowled down at his feet. The Vinings never seemed to have any money. He gave Wren cash at Christmas.

"Listen, McHugh, get me the goddamn titles. She'll know what I'm talking about." And Sagen hung up.

McHugh put down the receiver carefully. There were others where Sagen came from and they all needed to be paid. Starting a new life with Wren suddenly seemed less possible.

Friday after Thanksgiving the weather broke. A Chinook blasted up from the south sending the temperatures soaring into the sixties, as if it were May and not November. The snow-packed roads were dry and steaming by noon, sending swift rivulets rushing along the ditches. Edelson spent a good deal of his morning drinking coffee in his Adirondack chair, the wind massaging his face, staring at the lodgepole pines across the river. The trees made him think of a shepherd he'd known. A strange man. Quiet and misunderstood — mistaken for a hard-bitten criminal. The man had been the center of an investigation, and Edelson had started out believing what everyone did, but in the end he found only a generous and fiercely private man. A man who had thought long and hard about the nature of men's lives. Who likened his philosophy of life to the diversity of trees, but was no more capable of committing a calculated felony than Mrs. Sherwood. Edelson had learned some things from this man, not the least among them that what you see isn't always what you get. In fact, it almost never is.

Edelson heard Gray talking behind him and turned to see the boy sitting on the porch step twirling a blade of dried grass. Peachy chased after it, leaping and rolling, then winding up again, his tail swishing back and forth like a lion. And it reminded Edelson that the cat's name wasn't Peachy at all, but Ponce De Leon, because he looked like a lion cub when he and Robin first got him, before the cat grew up and his fur came in long and fluffy. He tried to recall how they'd lost that name to Peachy, but couldn't. Easier to say, he guessed. Gray laughed and urged Peachy again to attack the blade he waved around.

Edelson suddenly remembered the bike. "Hey, I have something for you," he said, getting to his feet. "It's in the garage."

Gray followed him into the cluttered room. Edelson's lathe and table saw sat in the center, the sawdust and wood scraps swept into a neat pile. There was no room for a vehicle. Cans of stain and varnish lined the shelves above his workbench. Piles of cedar were stacked along the far wall, its sweet aroma competing with the sharp odor of mineral spirits.

Edelson flipped the light on and pointed at the shiny red bike. Gray broke into a grin, but it slipped away so quickly Edelson wasn't sure if he hadn't just imagined it. "It's for you," he said.

Gray just looked at the bike, his head tilted a little to the side.

"It's a gift."

"Thanks," the boy said. But his tone lacked the excitement Edelson had expected.

"It's a nice day. Why don't you take it for a ride?" He

stepped over and pressed the garage door opener and sunlight dawned slowly over the bike.

The boy fidgeted, shifting on his feet, avoiding Edelson's eyes.

"I'd go with you, but I don't have one of my own."

"You can ride it," Gray said quickly.

"No, it's for you."

Gray bit his lip.

"What's the matter? Don't you like it?"

Gray nodded. "I like it. But . . . I don't know how to ride a bike," he said in a voice that was so quiet Edelson had to strain to hear it.

Edelson scratched his head and looked at the bike with Gray. It had never occurred to him that the boy wouldn't know how to ride. Of course, he had been neglected, but after all, ten years old and couldn't handle a vehicle this small? He turned and looked out at his long, quiet driveway and the gravel road beyond. "Well . . . I can try to teach you."

He didn't immediately take to the bike, Gray. But Edelson knew he would if he kept at it with him, urging him on, running alongside to steady him. By suppertime Edelson guessed he'd run about sixteen miles. His heart pounded against his ribs and his knees ached. His muscles felt like boiled spaghetti. When had he got so out of shape? When had he grown so old?

The knees of Gray's new jeans were torn, as well as the palms of his hands, bloody and speckled with bits of gravel. Yet, the boy was grinning. A shaky rider at best, but a rider all the same. He didn't cry once. Didn't ask to go in or take a break, just got up and got back on with a determination that made Edelson wonder if he himself had such character, such purpose.

"I can't make supper. I'm dead whipped," Edelson said as

the sun was shrinking behind the ridge. He sucked in a long breath of air unlike that in wintertime up north. Wet and fresh and full of promise. It felt like spring. It made him want to get the yard tools out.

"Let's go to Mrs. Sherwood's house," Gray said, rolling the bike into the garage, and giving it a good rubdown with a rag. The bike, in spite of its hard treatment this afternoon, seemed to have survived with just a few dings.

"Good idea. She can't eat all that leftover turkey by herself."

"Do you think she made another cherry pie?"

Later, as stuffed as he had been on Thanksgiving, Gray drifted to sleep on the sofa as Mr. Edelson watched the late news. Peachy was curled around his head like a muff, purring in his ear. And the boy said a quiet prayer, "Please God, if you're there, don't take this away."

The weekend sailed past, Edelson watching the boy steadily improving his riding skills as he rubbed down his own sore muscles and ate aspirin by the handful. His right knee had always been trouble for him, ever since a high school basketball injury. And it complained about the workout he'd given it.

While Gray finally became so competent even the bike seemed worn out, Edelson puttered in the garage, cleaning up a little and sketching out plans to build a picnic table for Mrs. Sherwood. She had a nice yard with a wide-canopied English walnut, and Edelson thought it would be pleasant to sit outside and have supper when the weather turned warm.

But on Monday morning, Edelson dreaded the week ahead. The results of Gray's DNA test were due back. And the Chinook was gone, taking with it most of the snow, but replaced by a biting arctic cold front, plunging temperatures to sub-zero. It was like a cruel joke — that inspiring bit of spring weather just before a steep descent into the black cave of deep Montana winter. Edelson recalled the ominous predictions told to him by the man who rummaged in his garbage. "It'll be a cold one . . . ah, it will."

The sheriff remembered also his lack of information about the female corpse. Got to get back to work, he reminded himself, can't have the townsfolk gossiping I'm inadequate or worse. His little idyll was over.

17

McHugh spent the long weekend packing his belongings. It was a good time to move; business always slowed during the holidays. He figured on taking up residence in the Silver Dog until it too sold. He'd sooner be camping, but with the bad turn in weather, that was out of the question. And after the sale . . . well, he didn't know. But it was a decision he couldn't bother with just yet. All depended now on Wren and her situation.

He hauled his furniture down to the mini storage in St. John's, a few items at a time in the back of his truck. He knew people he could call upon for help, but he didn't care to explain why he was selling his cabin and moving to the tavern. Once the Silver Dog was sold, he guessed he'd just slip quietly out of town with his sister. Maybe. He thought about Wren often. Wished he'd gone to speak to her on Friday, see how she was doing, ask about the titles to the other properties the man named Sagen had threatened him about. He must have been mistaken; the Vinings had lived so poorly for as long as McHugh could remember. Up there in the rugged nowhere. *His Wren.* Property owners? Never. And it worried McHugh that he was now obliged to convince such a man of his error. For surely others would come calling to collect their debts, and not asking nicely. Wren assured him that only Sagen mattered, but McHugh thought she was naïve to believe that. He told himself he and Wren would get out of this mess somehow. After all, he had sold his house for a tidy sum and the Silver Dog would provide the rest.

By Sunday evening, McHugh's house stood vacant and all that remained in the back of his truck were a bedroll and pack with a few days' clothes, his toothbrush, razor and comb, his Exacto knife, and the box of books he'd salvaged from the Silver Dog — something to keep his mind busy so he wouldn't spend his evenings looking for ghosts or listening for gangster debt-holders.

He slipped up the back steps of the tavern with his bedroll and pack, drawing a curious stare from his cook, Bram, who hovered over the grill in a stained white tee shirt with the sleeves cut off. The man was lavishly tattooed from stem to stern, but McHugh didn't care about that. Bram was a top notch grill-cook, and he also knew how to mind his own business. He'd gone silently back to flipping steaks and frying potatoes.

Tuesday was the slowest evening of the week at the Silver Dog. After the dinner crowd, which was generally comprised of a half-dozen locals tired of their own cooking, the patronage dwindled rapidly. McHugh resumed his post behind the bar, sending the waitress home early. By eleven-thirty only three men remained, one at the bar nursing the same drink he'd bought a couple of hours ago and two playing pool, but not buying.

"Last call," McHugh bellowed, as if they were all deaf. It was his custom — didn't want anyone claiming they hadn't heard him.

By midnight the doors were locked, the kitchen clean, and the night's income stashed in the floor-safe under the worn and rotting Oriental rug in the back office. McHugh loitered a moment in the entrance to the dining room. The streetlamp outside cast a pale glow through the tavern windows and across the glossy bar. The room still smelled of the evening special, chicken fried steak and onion hash browns. McHugh thought briefly of renting a motel room, finally turning and thumping down the hallway toward the back stairs.

He had taken the empty room with the peeling wallpaper for his temporary residence. It harbored his fondest memories of the place — it was the room in which Wren had surrendered to him. She didn't beg him to let her go after their silent wrestling match one night, but watched his face as he slid his hand under her blouse and felt her youthful breast. She took in a long breath as he shoved her clothes aside and tasted the hard nipple.

For all the apprehension his tavern guests carried for the upstairs rooms of the Silver Dog, they held only distant magical moments for McHugh. He wasn't one to waste his time pining for days past. Rather he invested significant energy in diverting his thoughts away from the old days. At least until the recent death of Russell Vining, and the birth of new possibilities.

Harsh white light from the naked bulb stung the room, and McHugh immediately wished he'd brought a lamp with him. He stepped to the window and drew down the shade, silently amused with the knowledge that tomorrow Magda would hum with resurrected ghost stories and it would all begin with one observant citizen's comment that a light burned in the upper rooms of the Silver Dog last night. McHugh found it ironic that his father's devotion to Dina Toomey, his sealing off the upper rooms of the tavern like a shrine where he could be heard wailing for his lost lover, had not protected a blessed memory, but created a sick spectacle. Dina Toomey's ghost, it was widely believed, still walked the upper halls of the Silver Dog, sobbing.

It would boost business anyway. People were morbidly curious creatures.

After rolling out his sleeping bag, McHugh went back downstairs to the supply room and rummaged for candles, re-

162

turning moments later to settle in and review his selection of books. He was beat and didn't imagine he'd read long before sleep overtook him. He pulled out a small leather-bound book that had caught his eye in the stack when he packed them up. He'd thumbed the pages thinking it was a ledger. There were several ledgers in the bunch — hand-written records of business dealings from the nineteenth and early twentieth centuries. McHugh had a collection of them. He enjoyed reading about the Silver Dog when it wasn't just a tavern; it was the general store, the bank, the post office, and anything people needed it to be. His grandfather's business dealings ran the gamut from selling flour and whiskey to property loans and mail order brides. The Silver Dog had been the hub of all things civilized in that part of the territory, a two-day ride by horseback from Fort Missoula and the Hellgate Valley.

He examined the stiffened leather cover of the small book, ran his fingers down the spine, which was imprinted with the date 1960. He turned it over in his hands, surprised that it wasn't that old. Wren had been born in 1960, and she too had begun to show her age. A little harder around the edges. Not as supple. But now his Wren again. He almost tossed the book aside. He'd lived through the sixties once already. But it was a curious little book and he opened it up and read the careful script rendered in someone's best hand. He could barely get the thin pages apart to see its title page. Finally he read the name and laughed. The little book he held was the diary of his father's long-dead mistress, Dina Toomey.

Gray had long finished *Arabian Nights*, but he hadn't given the book back to Mrs. Sherwood yet. Things were good and he'd pretty much changed his mind about selling it and using the money to run away to California, but now he was having second thoughts. Mr. Edelson was looking for his mother and Gray thought that him being the sheriff and all, it would be easy for him. He couldn't wait to see her, to tell her about Peachy and show her his new bike. He was planning to ask for a cat of his own as soon as they were together again. Probably, though, Mr. Edelson would let him keep Peachy, since the sheriff appeared to hate the cat. That was one of the things Gray held against him.

He took the book from his bag and sprawled out on the sofa.

"How far are you?" Mr. Edelson asked from the reclining chair. He was reading the newspaper in his nightly ritual.

"Almost halfway," Gray said.

"Good book, isn't it?"

Gray thumbed through it, pausing at the story of the Fisherman and the Genie. He pondered the picture of the turbaned man, knife in hand, staring in awe at the puff of smoke that would become his heart's desire. Gray knew the first thing he'd wish for if he encountered a genie. He turned to Mr. Edelson. "When do you think you'll find my mom?" Edelson scowled, and Gray understood that he'd made the sheriff angry with the question.

"I'm working on it, kiddo." Edelson set his paper on his lap and looked at Gray. He opened his mouth to say something else, but changed his mind. "I'm still working on it."

Gray hid his disappointment. The sheriff didn't like to say much. He just liked to read his newspaper.

McHugh had never cared for Dina Toomey. Not only had she been his father's mistress and the mother of his out-of-wedlock half-sister, but she had been the ruin of Flora Elliott McHugh, his mother. A woman for whom he'd never given up hope, whose axis made a permanent shift with the arrival of Dina, and whose balance he had longed to see restored. It was the sheer brazenness of his father to move his mistress above the Silver Dog that shook his mother's foundations. It was Randy

McHugh himself who had naively told her that his father had found a new tenant. Just family business, idle chit-chat in the kitchen. The sort of thing they discussed at the supper table in which a boy is eager to participate. Eager to show his maturity.

His mother had been standing at the sink, her fingers slick with chicken fat as she sliced away skin and wrenched out bones. McHugh didn't remember the exact words he'd spoken. Just that a woman named Dina had moved into the corner room of the tavern. But he held a vivid recollection of his mother's head snapping up from her work, her kinky red hair bouncing. The look of maniacal inquisition she gave him. "Who did you say?"

"Dina Toomey," he sputtered, for he knew by his mother's stare that her world had already changed.

Her fingers had gone white where she gripped the boning knife. She was out the door without a word, the thin little blade swinging at her side.

Much later, people at the Silver Dog attributed her as saying, "I'm gonna scalp that bitch like the Injun she is." But those were not his mother's words, just the sensational embroidering of these self-same folk who claimed later to encounter Dina's ghost, as if Flora had actually carried out that threat. His father had intervened — publicly protecting his mistress and humiliating his wife. Dina Toomey remained at the tavern until her death, bearing a daughter whose smile distracted all of the McHugh men.

Flora bittered profoundly after the scene at the Silver Dog. In a headlong gallop toward outright meanness, she turned an acidic tongue on anyone who dared show affection. And when Randy McHugh got the call one day that his mother had passed away at the Clark Fork Retirement Home in Missoula at the age of ninety-three, he guiltily expelled a relieved breath. Dina had become his mother's obsession. Despite the forty-odd years that intervened in their deaths, no one knew Flora without also knowing the wrong done to her by her husband and his mistress. All evil in the world, from an abducted child to a robbery at the local liquor store, could be attributed to the ilk that Dina Toomey represented.

McHugh read Dina's diary now with both curiosity and a welling indignation. She'd written about him. Called him a sulking adolescent with an alarming lack of compassion for others. She worried about keeping the baby away from him. His cheeks flamed as he read, and he cursed her. No one loved Wren more than he, then or now.

His eyes began to burn in the stingy candlelight, forcing him to set the diary down and lay a cool hand over his face. He strained to remember Dina, really remember her. The way she looked — fine-boned and dark. Like Wren. Not like him, stocky and red-haired. He sat up and blew out the candle, then lay back again, remembering.

Edelson nodded to the old man rearranging trash in the bin in front of his jail. Pickings must be slim these days, he thought. The man's long burlap sack, tied with rope and slung over his shoulder, hung deflated. A handful of aluminum cans rattled at the bottom.

The old man paused to watch Edelson unlock the door. He had eyes of such pale blue they looked nearly white. And with the mat of dirty gray hair escaping his knit cap, he bore a striking resemblance to a wolf. "Didn't I tell ya, Sheriff? Eh? Didn't I say it was gonna be a cold one?"

"You were right . . ." Edelson realized he didn't know that man's name.

"Uh-huh." He went back to work sifting through the trash.

"Finding much?"

"No. It's always this way come winter."

Edelson hesitated before going inside. The man looked cold. The tips of his wool gloves were worn away, his blackened

166

fingers emerging, encrusted with revolting yellow nails. "Where do you live?"

The old man stood upright and eyed the sheriff suspiciously. "Ain't no law against collectin' cans. I got a right to do it."

"Yup, you do." Edelson pushed the door open and went inside. The cinderblock building savored the cold deep in its bones, and he felt no perceptible change in temperature from outside to in. He dropped his keys on the metal desk with a clatter and upped the thermostat, knowing he'd be back on the road to somewhere before it made any difference.

He called the federal investigator on the Vining case, but hung up rather than leave a message. The man was clearly not one to share his own information, and Edelson imagined he already knew McHugh had sold his cabin up on Willishaw Creek. Still, he would've liked the satisfaction of telling Morback first. He didn't like finding out what was happening in his own county from the feds after the fact, the way it happened with their drug investigation. Edelson contemplated McHugh again. He had to be involved. Why else would a man so rooted into a community sell a prime parcel of land with a nearly new cabin built by his own hand?

As Edelson listened to ancient Arnella Baker rasp on his answering machine, in her long-time smoker's voice, about an unmarked white van in her neighborhood — three days earlier it'd been a green station wagon — the mail popped through the slot and skated across the cement floor. He stared down at the envelope from the lab. Gray's DNA results.

Ten different explanations to Gray shot through Edelson's brain in the span of a second. All the words he'd mulled and practiced: *The skeleton, she was your mother. Your mother, Gray, has gone on to be with God. I found your mother. You found your mother . . .*

He still didn't know how he would say it. Edelson dropped

the receiver back in its cradle and kicked off from his desk, gliding across the floor to the envelope. He held it in his hand a moment before opening it. He'd have to get the words right. He'd have to figure out how to tell the kid.

He rolled back to his desk and pawed through the pencil drawer for his letter opener. The phone rang. He breathed a sigh of relief and picked it up. "Sheriff's office."

"It *was* Chris," a female voice whispered.

He popped out of his chair, a jolt of hot energy racing through him. "Chris who?"

Silence.

"Please!"

Click.

"Damn it!" He slammed the phone down and stood a time with his hands fixed at his waist, his nostrils flaring, his eyes darting from window to window. He replayed the voice in his head. Tried to place it. But the words had been too fleeting, too unexpected.

Finally he sat again. "I know it was Chris — Kristi Blackhorse," he snarled at the phone. "But who killed her?"

He took up the envelope and sliced it open with a swift flick of his wrist and fumbled to get his fingers on the thin paper inside, unfolding it and pressing it flat against his desk. His skin flushed sweaty. The furnace now hummed behind him, angering him. His heart leapt, then sank, then leapt again as he read the words. *Not a match.*

He sat back stunned. He'd been so certain. Good news for Gray, he thought. Wonderful news for Gray. Edelson wanted to go tell the boy the news. Of course he couldn't. Gray had no idea the sheriff thought all along he'd dug up the boy's own mother. Edelson burned to tell someone. But who, Mrs. Sherwood?

He had a despairing knot in his chest. The only friend he

had in the world right now was a little old lady who reminded him of his mother.

McHugh lounged on his bedroll, bathed in morning light. The clock was advancing into double digits. The floor had become unbearably hard, and he had to piss so bad his teeth hurt. But he didn't get up. The memory had come to him early, with the first golden finger of sunlight on the pine floor. He had been out of sorts, still groggy from sleep. But once the memory tumbled down on him, he relished it.

Wren had been sixteen. She giggled and opened the door of this room a crack, peering out into the hallway, a stripe of light setting her irises ablaze in rich sienna. The two of them, in this very room, despite the threats from their father, who had been guarding the second floor of the tavern like a junkyard dog for over a decade since Dina drew her last asthmatic inhale. Wren had pressed a finger against Randy's chest to hold him still. They held their breath.

He ran his hand down her back and she shushed him, as if he'd spoken aloud the thoughts in his head. She stood poised for agonizing seconds, then said, "He didn't hear us."

He pushed the door shut and she rested her back against it, looking up at him, the moonlight casting her face in marble — like a fine Venetian statue.

"We shouldn't be doing this," she had whispered. But her eyes glistened with excitement.

He put a finger to her lips. Soft as new velvet. He kissed her. She tasted like butter and honey and all things smooth and sweet. It was like drinking from a well of pure delight.

Now, McHugh sat up and ran his fingers through his unruly hair. He put his hands to his temples, pressing inward until he couldn't stand the pain. Then he struggled to his feet, feeling arthritic. "I'll get a motel room tonight," he told himself.

18

THE SHERIFF'S PHONE RANG and he snapped it up, in case it was his anonymous caller again. He prepared to listen harder, try to pinpoint background noises, or anything to identify her. "Sheriff's office," he said.

"Edelson?" A vaguely familiar male voice thundered out at him.

"Yes."

"Detective Darby, Las Vegas Police Department."

Edelson sat down. "What can I do for you?"

"Are you still looking for Kristi Blackhorse?" The detective was all business, which suited Edelson fine. He despised idle chitchat. Especially with people he'd never met.

"Yeah, you find her?"

"She reported her wallet stolen last night. I have her address. Got a pencil?"

Edelson couldn't believe his luck. Just when he thought the trail was cold, that nothing could be added to the mystery of the dead woman, a break. "Yup, go ahead."

McHugh waited in his now familiar visitor's seat at the county jail, watching for his sister. When he caught sight of her through the window his skin sizzled as if he were suddenly hooked up to the Montana power grid.

She sat opposite him and smiled, lifting the intercom telephone to her ear.

"Hey, sis."

"Hi, Ran." Her eyes had lost their spark. "I thought you were getting me out of here."

"Remember the night we went upstairs at the tavern?" He grinned at her. Couldn't help himself. Couldn't contain it.

"Randy!" She tapped the glass as if to hit him and looked away, her face pink.

"I never had so much fun in my life."

She tried not to look at him, but couldn't stop herself from a weak smile of mischief.

"Well it was."

Her smile widened, and McHugh's spirits rose. "You just need to get married, that's all," she said.

"Did that work for you?"

A snort of laughter came through the phone. "No."

"Let's run away."

"You'll have to bail me out first."

He realized the perversity of this discussion. The fact that she was his *sister* flooded back, squelching the afterglow of his unbidden memory of what they had done with each other upstairs at the tavern so many years ago.

Her smile faded to resignation.

"Do you know anything about a couple of titles to some places in Peerless and St. John's?"

The color drained from Wren's face and her eyes went flat.

McHugh paused to evaluate her response, then continued cautiously. "This Sagen guy is asking about them. I told him you didn't have any property."

She sat back in her chair and shook her head. "That double-crossing, son of a bitch," she whispered.

"What did you say?"

She looked at Randy as if suddenly concentrating. She smiled awkwardly. "Nothing."

McHugh studied her. "You know what he's talking about?"

She didn't answer.

"Wren, you have to tell me."

"They're in the safe deposit box. The key is —"

"In the safe at the tavern. I know where it is." He stared through the glass at her, waiting for her to look at him. "You didn't tell me you owned any property."

"They're just a couple of run-down places. Not worth much."

"When did you buy them?" He swallowed back the bitterness of betrayal.

"I didn't. They were in trade for some of this stuff Russell was up to."

"Why didn't you tell me? I could've sold them. That might've helped you out."

"They're . . . they're nothing. Trash. You wouldn't have gotten anything out of them." Wren continued to avoid his gaze.

"Goddamn it."

She looked up at him.

"I sold my house."

"You what?"

"I sold my house," McHugh said.

She opened her mouth to speak, but nothing came out. Finally, "They wouldn't have been enough."

Edelson paid attention as the flight attendant went through the safety procedures before take-off. He flew so rarely he didn't feel he could ignore any announcement. He wished he could have driven down to Las Vegas, but he couldn't afford to take the time — time he needed to think. The commissioner was happy to fill in for him while he was gone. As if he'd long harbored a fantasy about being sheriff, he showed Edelson his Colt .45 with a frightening measure of pride.

"Stop a man dead," the commissioner had boasted.

Edelson had no particular sense of pride in himself, but he knew he could do a better job than the commissioner. The flight attendant was demonstrating the proper way to buckle the seatbelt, which looked like it was the same model as that used in a 1965 Ford Galaxy, and he concentrated on her again.

Later, as the plane roared over the western landscape and Edelson took in the hugeness of it, the endless mountains and valleys of untouched wilderness forests, he found himself itemizing his thoughts. The more rural, more remote the landscape unfolded, the more inspired he felt. The unidentified body, Robin, Chris Samuelson — all seemed such small potatoes compared to the intricate connectedness of nature below him. How the vein of a river becomes indiscernible from the vein in a leaf; or snow sifting across a desert is like the smooth surface of a polished agate. Large and small coming together, becoming one another.

The man next to him crowded over to look out. Edelson pressed back in his seat to escape the man's sharp cologne. The man retreated and smiled at Edelson — a yellow, crooked smile. Edelson nodded and turned his face back to the window.

"Where ya headed?" the man asked, oblivious.

"Vegas," Edelson said, as if it were obvious. He pulled the complimentary airline magazine from the seat back in front of him and thumbed through it.

"I love Vegas."

Edelson didn't respond. Hoped the man would get a hint and leave him be.

"I make it down there at least twice a year. You?"

Edelson put the magazine back and looked him in the eye. "Frankly, I hate the place." He turned back to the window.

His seat-mate laughed. "I like an honest man."

After an hour in the air, Edelson pointed down and said, "Grand Canyon."

His seat-mate practically moved into his seat to press his nose against the window again. "Looks like a big crack in the mud. Like you get at the end of your driveway the day after you wash your car."

Edelson looked down at the canyon with new eyes. Saw the way it jagged off into the distance, and had to admit the man was right.

"I bet there's a colony of ants living at the end of my driveway that march out to the edge of that crack every once in a while and speculate about the time it must have taken for such an enormous crevasse to come into existence. I bet that crack looks just like this one if you had an ant's-eye view."

Edelson chuckled. Maybe he just needed a new perspective on things. His mystery — heck, maybe even his marriage — might look different from Las Vegas.

The peaches slipped over Gray's tongue, mushy and warm with little stings that caught between his teeth. The sharp tang opened the glands below his ears with delicious agony. He nodded across the table at Mrs. Sherwood. He did like cooked peaches after all. At least cooked this way, with cinnamon and crunchy, sugary crust sprinkled over them. Gray felt he was coming to understand something extremely important. There were a whole lot more delightful things in the world than he ever knew or even imagined. He'd always thought of a treat as candy. Something you bought at the grocery store in a plastic wrapper. But the Baby Ruth bar he'd dreamed of when he lived

174

on Big Sky Court seemed like nothing compared to the peach cobbler or chocolate chip cookies Mrs. Sherwood made in her own oven. He would never again drift to sleep wishing for a candy bar. His dreams now were of pies with homemade whipped cream.

"Can't we go get Peachy?" The cobbler reminded him of the cat, which he imagined sitting alone on the porch step, wondering why Gray had abandoned him.

"I'm allergic to cats," Mrs. Sherwood said. "Besides, it's only one night. He'll be perfectly fine."

"But what if he freezes?"

"Mister Edelson told me the cat can get into the garage. He figured you'd be wanting to go see it."

"But he'll think I don't love him. He'll be sad." Gray knew he was putting it all on the cat, when Gray himself wanted to see the cat in the worst way.

Mrs. Sherwood shook her head. "It's just one night."

"Where did Mr. Edelson go, anyway?"

"Just a business trip," she said, getting up and starting to clear the table.

Gray looked out at the flat sky. Wind whipped the branches of a walnut tree so violently it creaked and groaned. "Can't we just go make sure he's okay?"

Mrs. Sherwood untied her apron and hung it on a wall peg near the porch door. She was shaking her head at Gray, but her eyes were telling him something different. "I'm going to regret this. I know I will."

McHugh snapped the radio off with a jab of his finger, but made no motion to pull back onto the highway. After he sat idling for an hour on the shoulder, a semi pulled up behind him. Its heavy diesel engine rattled and hummed, and its emergency lights flashed in his eyes. He tilted his head to get a look at the kid coming up to his side-view mirror. He looked no older than twenty and spit an arc of tobacco onto the asphalt before tapping on McHugh's window.

McHugh put the glass down halfway and looked up at the kid.

"You need some help, mister?"

"No!" The word was sharply punctuated.

"All right, then." The kid turned and started back toward his rig.

McHugh scowled. Found it highly out of the ordinary for a trucker to take the time to check on someone sitting by the road. They had schedules to keep, couldn't stop to check on people who weren't even giving signs of distress. The kid pulled himself up into the cab, reminding McHugh of a chimpanzee swinging up onto a tree.

The lights from the semi burned like the sun in his mirror as it pulled onto the road and crept past, sporting a large, white lion's head on its door and blowing hot diesel fumes over him. The kid was the fourth person to stop since McHugh had pulled over. His faith in mankind might have been restored, if he could cease to be annoyed by the intrusions. He sat in his pickup by the side of the road, six miles east of Magda, because he didn't know where to go. He wanted to be alone, and the Silver Dog was the last place a body went to be alone. He just wanted to think. Think about Wren and Russell. He agonized over the sharp interchange with his sister, wished he could take back the angry outburst. It wasn't her fault. He could see that. He knew she would've told him about the other properties if it might have helped.

Edelson parked his rental car along a residential curb in suburban Las Vegas, pausing to look at the small stucco house, far from the neon and noise of downtown. The yard was neatly kept, decorative cactus bloomed in waxy yellows, surrounded by a bed of white gravel raked smooth. A squat palm tree snuggled up to the front porch, where a woman bent over a pot of geraniums, a watering can at her feet. He squinted at her, wondering if she could possibly be the woman he sought. He'd half expected to find a prostitute or a junkie.

Edelson got out and approached her. "Excuse me, are you Kristi Blackhorse?"

The woman stood and turned, her eyes searching for something familiar about him. "Why do you want to know?"

"My name is Edelson, Sheriff Edelson."

"You don't look like a sheriff to me," she said. Her tone was businesslike, and she neither smiled nor frowned.

He glanced down at his jeans and boots. "Guess not. I'm out of my jurisdiction." He paused to look hard at her, noting Gray in her dark eyes and pinched rosebud lips. "I'm from Mineral County. Montana."

An anguished look crossed her face.

"Came about your son . . . Gray."

"Is he okay?" She spoke now with a maternal urgency that heartened Edelson.

"Yes, he's okay." He looked out at the neighborhood, the rows of white stucco houses all similar in size and shape. The red tile roofs and the cactus-studded yards. It was a nice place, modest, but well cared for. A boy would do well here, he imagined. Could ride his bike along the quiet streets. Edelson turned back to Kristi. "Jim Dausman claims he's not the boy's father."

Her face darkened and her eyes veiled over.

"He's got proof of it."

She glanced over her shoulder at the open front window, then back. She remained quiet and remote.

"He needs a home, your boy," Edelson finally said, perplexed by the woman's silence. "He wants his mother."

She looked again at the window.

"Something in there you need to tend?" Edelson said, craning to see inside.

She shook her head and stood off the porch, walked halfway out into the yard. Edelson followed. She put a hand to her forehead to shield her eyes from the mild winter sun. Her dark hair glistened bronze. She was a beautiful woman, and he could see her reasonable claim to Indian blood.

"I can't really take him . . . not right now," she said at last.

Edelson waited for her to go on, but she didn't. "Why? He's your boy. He wants to be with you." He felt exasperated, even angry at this unexpected stubbornness.

"You don't understand, mister . . ."

"Edelson. And you're damn right I don't understand." He pulled his hat off and ran his fingers over the brim to keep them busy. "He's gonna go to a foster home. He's devastated. Don't you care what happens to the boy?" He looked her straight in the eye as he said it.

"Of course I care," she snapped. "I'm his mother." She looked again at the house, then back.

"What the hell is in there that's more important than what I'm telling you?"

She gave Edelson a rancorous glare. "My husband. He's just back from Wyoming and he's sleeping. He's a long-haul trucker."

Edelson looked up and down the street in a smooth sweep of his head. "Where's his rig?"

"We don't park it here," she said, as if the idea was ludicrous. "This is a residential neighborhood."

He turned back to her. "So what's the problem with taking your boy?"

As he waited for her answer, the door opened and a tall man with pale skin and mussed hair stepped out on the porch. He stood a moment in his bare feet, then ventured out onto the gravel without so much as a grimace. "What's goin' on, Kristi? Who's this?"

"No one," she said quietly.

The man walked up next to her and put his arm around her shoulder, gripping her territorially and pulling her into his side. He cocked his unshaven chin at Edelson. "What do you want with my wife?"

"He was just asking directions," she asserted. She turned to Edelson with meaning, "You think you can find it now?"

Edelson stared at her.

"Get your stuff packed, baby," Kristi's husband said to her, but his eyes remained unmoving on Edelson. "I gotta be on the road in an hour. I think you're comin' with me."

She obeyed, starting for the house, but she didn't go inside. She waited on the porch for the two men to disengage.

The sheriff assessed the trucker a long moment, wondering what Kristi Blackhorse was hiding from the man and why. Edelson had a mind to speak his business outright. See for himself if she had reason to fear. But instinct — intangible and unarticulated — warned him off. He nodded to the trucker and turned toward his car.

19

EDELSON STOOD UNDER A GIANT YUCCA with the tip of his left index finger jammed in one ear, squeezing the phone against his other to hear Mrs. Sherwood over the roar of jets taxiing into the Las Vegas airport.

"Did you find her?" The old woman's voice imparted unmasked hope across the miles.

"No . . . it was somebody else," he said, craning up at the electric blue rent-a-car sign towering over him. "Can you manage without me for another day?"

"Of course. Are you going to keep looking?"

"Yeah." A shuttle turned into the car lot next to him, smoking him in black diesel grit. "How's Gray?"

"He's fine. He and that cat."

"You didn't?"

"I couldn't tell him no," she sighed. "He loves that cat."

"Yes, he does. I think I'll let him keep it." He paused to say something, then let it go. "Expect me tomorrow afternoon." And he hung up, anxious to get on the road.

Guilt over taking the day to drive back to Mineral County didn't weigh on Edelson's mind as it might otherwise have. He'd never been one to take advantage of people's willingness to pitch in. His father had taught him not to wear a welcome thin, let alone out. But something about Mrs. Sherwood left him forever asking favors, or just letting her take up the slack without being asked at all. And the commissioner with his Colt .45 barely crossed Edelson's mind. He needed time now to prepare what he would tell Gray and how he was going to handle the harsh task of relinquishing the boy to a foster home.

Edelson reasoned that he'd followed through on his word to the boy; he had found his mother. And for the first time since the idea took residence in his thoughts, he wished Kristi Blackhorse *was* the dead woman from the river. At least the kid might get a chance at adoption, no matter how slim, if she were. He could cling to the belief his mother had wanted him. But as it stood now, that fantasy could too easily be shattered by truth.

Swinging the car onto Interstate 15, Edelson headed for the U.S. 93 junction, and left the carnival called Las Vegas in his rear-view mirror. He felt his assaulted senses slowly relax and come to life once again. Edelson relished the scenery ahead, especially Idaho. Too far from his own hometown to be familiar in the practical sense, but not failing to offer a comforting kinship by association. He'd see Robin's hometown of Idaho Falls, though.

To get away from thinking about Gray, he thought about Robin and his encounter with Kristi Blackhorse. He wouldn't tell Robin about the bizarre exchange between them, even if she were waiting at home for him. It was not his habit to discuss his work. But she would've asked anyway; she always did. And when he wouldn't satisfy her curiosity she'd accuse him of some shift in mood that only she seemed able to perceive. He'd be pelted with relentless questions about what was bothering him. In the end, she always came to believe his silence was the product of something she'd done, and that he was simply too stubborn or mean or cruel to tell her what it was. Until finally, like the self-fulfilling prophesy it was, he would be angry with her.

It perplexed him still — this synchronic dance they engaged in with predictable regularity. He'd once attributed it to her hormones, but came to regret stating it aloud, although he never let go of the idea. Edelson pondered Chris Samuelson's assertion that men and women were like birds — or one bird, rather. He wondered if he and Robin could ever bring it into unison, to fly together straight and sure.

And Kristi Blackhorse — some goddamned mother. Even Robin wouldn't deny her own blood. Robin would make the best of a bad situation. She wouldn't shrink from her duty. He realized he might not like the institution of marriage, but he missed his wife deeply.

Business at the Silver Dog was surprisingly busy the week after Thanksgiving, and McHugh found a rhythmic therapy in serving drinks and taking orders, skipping down the bar seeing to the needs of his patrons. He'd almost forgotten about Vining's debt holders and the titles, which were laid out carefully in his top desk drawer. He was at first surprised to find them both in Wren's name, not Russell's. Vining was so selfish with what little he got his hands on. But McHugh figured it was Russell's way of ensuring their safety — the dolt. Sagen hadn't called and it was Wednesday already. McHugh had driven down to Peerless and surveyed one property — the trailer — the evening before. It was a modest single-wide. From the 1960s, he guessed. Wren was right; it wasn't worth much. As McHugh sat in the driveway, a woman poked her head out to see what he was doing. She looked vaguely familiar, but he was used to that. He guessed he'd served almost everyone in Mineral County at one time or another, and he could never keep track of the faces. She had smiled sweetly at him, making him wonder if they'd gone to school together, though she looked younger. Maybe the woman was a friend of Wren's. She'd tossed her chin over her shoulder as if to invite him in. He thought she had mistaken him for someone else and pulled onto the street again.

She looked a might disappointed when he waved goodbye.

The other place turned out to be an abandoned cabin that shared a common wall with Shank's tavern in St. John's. Worth less than the trailer, he guessed, due to its abysmal state. McHugh had a nodding acquaintance with Pete, Shank's' proprietor, and stopped to have supper there and glean some information about the property. Pete was a nice guy, but stupid by McHugh's assessment. Couldn't tell him anything about the place, just that his ex-girlfriend had lived there for a while. She must've been a fine one, McHugh thought, because Pete was incapable of conversing on any subject without bringing it round to her in short order.

The phone rang, and McHugh snapped it up. "Silver Dog," he chirped.

"McHugh?"

His good day was reduced to shards with the simple utterance of his name. "Yeah."

"You get those titles?"

"Yeah." McHugh looked out at the lunch crowd, the group of bikers sitting in a line along the bar with braided hair, black leather jackets and chaps, their beefy arms and intense *fuck you* demeanors, and felt no less vulnerable for the company.

"Listen to me carefully —"

"No, you listen to me," McHugh snapped, turning his face into the liquor bottles perched on the back bar and dropping his voice to a whisper. "I'm only making one drop. I've got them, but you'll have to wait until I get the money together."

"You're pretty damn sure of yourself."

McHugh tucked a shaking hand into his pocket. He'd come to believe that these people wouldn't stop with his house, or his bar. They'd take everything he had and would kill him, anyway. A mounting resentment was eclipsing his fear. They had no right to this. "You'll get it, but not until *I* say."

183

"You think we can't touch you?"

Of course they could, and McHugh knew it. "It wouldn't be profitable."

"Maybe I've got enough fucking money to kill you for the pure joy of it," Sagen hissed.

"I guess I'll take that chance."

The line was silent.

"Don't call me here. I'll call you as soon as I have the money."

The line went dead.

McHugh's gut twisted. Had he made a mistake? Had he just pissed off Satan himself? He stumbled back to his office and locked the door.

Southern Idaho presented a windswept desolation as Edelson wound his way back towards Magda. Shallow snowdrifts swirled across frozen ground the color of petrified bark. Despite full awareness of what month it was, Edelson had somehow imagined his drive would wind through rolling summer fields dotted with horses. "Romantic fool," he cursed himself.

He stopped to have supper in Idaho Falls, pulling into Brownie's, an old-fashioned burger joint where carhops still balanced trays of food on car windows. Robin had worked there during high school and anxiously had showed it to him the first time he'd accompanied her home to meet her parents. He scanned the main strip now, much the same as it was fifteen years ago. He'd only been there a few times, for obligatory events — her sister's wedding, or occasional Christmases when sufficient time had passed that he could not decline without seeming cruel. Now that Robin had quit him, he kind of wished for Christmas with Mr. and Mrs. Gallagher — he'd never come to call them Mom and Dad as Robin had with his folks. Now, Edelson thought, he could possibly perch on their scratchy yellow sofa with a cup of weak coffee, his hair askew, and partake of the gift ceremony while their yappy little mutt named Hercules shredded the discarded paper. Maybe he would've given Robin a new set of china this year. She'd been hoping for something formal since the day they married. Or maybe a pearl necklace. Her mother would go on about what a wonderful husband he was, never knowing that, in truth, he was a brilliant failure.

He thought of dropping in on them, but he had no idea if Robin had told them about the separation. Still, after dinner and a short walk to stretch his legs, he thought, what the hell?

The Gallaghers lived on Vine Maple Street in a modest Eisenhower-era house — blocky, with extremely square windows, and devoid of extravagances such as overhanging eaves. Pale blue, not too flashy. An architectural achievement Edelson had only recently learned to appreciate. The house was the same as when they'd bought the place as newlyweds. He tried to fathom living in one house for so long. He could scarcely keep himself in a place for the length of one term as sheriff, his bones rattling with wanderlust long before any community thought to reelect him.

"Kip? Is that you?" Mrs. Gallagher squeaked from behind the screen door. She shoved it open and threw her hands up to embrace him.

He stooped deeply to accommodate her short stature, then stood to meet Mr. Gallagher's stern gaze from the doorway behind her. He held out a hand and the two men shook in their usual businesslike manner.

"Why didn't you call? Are you hungry?" His mother-in-law led him inside. "We have some left-over pork roast."

"What's going on with you and Robbie?" Mr. Gallagher barked at his heels. He was never one to mince words or waste time on niceties. "Can't you talk some sense into her? Get her back home where she belongs?"

Edelson took a seat at the kitchen counter.

Harold pulled out the stool next to Edelson and joined him. "Robbie called and told us she moved out. What a stupid thing to do. She's got everything a woman could want and she goes and moves out." The old man slapped the counter hard, scowling.

Edelson flinched. He'd never seen his father-in-law so incensed over a domestic matter before. The man usually saved his tirades for topics involving conservationists and homosexuals.

Mrs. Gallagher set a plate in front of Edelson, the aroma of broiled fat making his stomach growl. He nodded in solemn agreement.

"Why does she need to go to school? What's she gonna do? And at her age . . ." Harold went on.

"She's thinking about psychology," Edelson said between bites, feeling a sudden urge to defend his wife from her father's harsh judgment. He understood for the first time what she had always said about being forced into an expected role by the people around her. As he listened to her parents now he felt like a jerk for not seeing it — for contributing to it.

"For what?" Harold growled.

Edelson shrugged, not knowing what to say. He'd had the same question.

"She needs to get pregnant," Harold said. "Settle down, give us a grandchild. What're you two waiting for, anyway?" He stared at Edelson.

Edelson paused with his fork halfway to his mouth and looked at each of them. They were remarkably alike — short, stout, and aged, both in faded blue shirts and white canvas sneakers. He guessed it came from decades of living together. "I don't know," he finally said, feeling like a coward for not just saying that he didn't want to have a baby.

Mrs. Gallagher shook her head, disappointed.

"Where's Hercules?" Edelson said, looking around for the annoying little mutt.

"Dog's been dead for six years or more," Harold said, frowning.

Edelson shut up and ate his pork roast, trying to remember how long it'd been since his last visit.

The pages of Dina Toomey's diary proved far more fascinating than any of the Silver Dog ledgers McHugh had read over the years. It surprised him how little he'd known about her — about Wren's heritage. Hadn't known Dina's father was a German immigrant, or that her mother burned to death in a hotel fire in Phillipsburg, a town quite similar to Magda a hundred or so miles to the southeast. It had found a sliver more luck staying alive in the post-silver mining days when the miners struck sapphires.

McHugh read by the pale glow of candlelight, stretched out on his bedroll in Room 2 of the tavern, meaning every night to get a motel room, but letting it slip his mind every morning. In truth, he felt a little safer between the heavy brick walls of the Silver Dog. He knew the place like a lover and could make his way in the pitch black were someone to break in. And he had a loaded pistol under his pillow, another in his office, and yet a third beneath the register in the bar downstairs.

Dina didn't write much about McHugh's father, Archibald, except to say he'd given her a room over the bar. There was a comment about his wife, Flora, wielding a knife at her the night she moved in. A dismissive comment about her being a maniac from the jungles of Texas, who had to be physically restrained by the patrons. McHugh tried to imagine how anyone living in the twentieth century could imagine Texas as a jungle, and the ignorance of it served to vindicate his mother a little. But the lack of jealousy in her words confirmed Dina's status in his father's world.

And yet she wrote so little of the man who had mourned her death with a lifetime's devotion. McHugh began to trace a common thread through her entries that circled back again and again to a man she called Will. McHugh saw that Dina's adoration for Will was uncommonly strong, a bond he likened to his and Wren's. He was contemplating this similarity when he stumbled over a passage that shocked him The words were spare, but they changed everything.

Archie suspects Christen is Will's and I believe he'll throw us both out on the street.

Wren was not his sister. The thought struck him like a sledgehammer. His breathing increased in tempo and he fell back against his bedroll. The years of guilt and torment, agonizing over the depravity of loving his own sister — wasted.

He laid the book down and wiped tears from his eyes. The future took new shape as he imagined a life with Wren — legitimate and devoid of shame.

20

EDELSON BID HIS IN-LAWS GOODBYE as the sun reflected its last pinkish beam in the western sky. He'd only stayed long enough to eat supper and have a cup of coffee, claiming he needed to get back on the road. He might have stayed longer, but neither would drop the subject of Robin's foolishness and the importance of having children to settle a woman down. He'd stared at his father-in-law's lips as he railed on about a woman's duty to her husband with a dawning realization that he himself could have spoken those words. Robin had always joked that she'd married her father, a comment that shamed Edelson now.

He was back on U.S. 93 headed due north, winding through narrow canyons in the black night. It was a dangerous drive in winter, but Edelson's stubbornness often put him in perilous situations. What of Gray? He would have to relinquish the boy to Ms. Winborn and the foster care system tomorrow, an event that would be traumatic for the boy. Kristi Blackhorse he dismissed as one of those women who murder their children for the love of a man — women like Susan Smith, who had sauntered away as her car rolled into a lake, her toddler sons strapped securely in their seats.

Edelson was also disappointed that Kristi Blackhorse wasn't the murdered woman at the river. It was worse, in his mind, that she was alive, but an unfit mother. How could she put her own needs ahead of her son's? The woman's selfishness punctuated the lack of understanding Robin's parents had shown toward their daughter. He felt sure that if he were a parent he wouldn't behave in this self-interested way.

Missoula now sprawled below him, twinkling like morning dew on a black blanket, the eastern sky paling in a chalky exhibition. Edelson fought to stay alert, sucking on a cup of bitter, black, truck-stop coffee. The dregs of the pot. Edelson hadn't felt like waiting for a fresh batch. He'd fall asleep on his feet if he didn't keep moving.

It'd been too dark to see the remote stretch of mountain road he'd traveled that night, and Edelson had endeavored to recreate the scenery from memory — Salmon, Gibbonsville, Darby. He began to regret he hadn't waited until morning. Who knew when he'd get down that way again?

At the Missoula airport, he dropped the keys to the rental car in the night-deposit slot and found his cruiser. He pulled onto Broadway and raced past the first morning commuters into downtown, knowing he was headed the wrong way to Magda. But he also knew why he had left Robin's parents at night. He parked on Third and looked up at Robin's window as light claimed the city. He imagined his wife curled under a mountain of blankets, just her toes sticking out. Her hair tangled around her head, a little snap of spit as she took breath in through her parted lips. Did she sleep so soundly now that she was alone?

He looked at his watch and thought again of Gray. He would let the boy take the bike and the cat to the foster home, but today he'd make the switch early. No point in prolonging it, leaving the boy to worry for days. As Edelson reached for the ignition, a light came on in Robin's apartment. He paused to watch a bare-chested man, rubbing a disheveled head of hair, shuffle into the kitchen. Edelson sat immobile, too tired to experience at first the full effect of what he witnessed. Then he got out and strode across Third Street without looking for traffic. He took the stairs two at a time and pounded on the door with his fist.

The man took his time getting there, but when the knob turned and Edelson shoved his way in and backed him into the kitchen, he awakened and groped for words.

Edelson pulled his gun and shoved the barrel up the man's nose where he stood pinned against the refrigerator, hands splayed out at his shoulders, eyes on Edelson unblinking.

"That's my wife," Edelson breathed.

The man didn't speak.

"Did she tell you she was married?"

He gave a nearly imperceptible nod. "Don't shoot," he wheezed.

"What if I was fucking your wife? What would *you* do?"

"Don't shoot. Please, don't shoot."

Edelson looked down to witness a yellow stream trickling from the man's pant leg and onto the floor in a puddle. He stepped back, pulling his weapon down, but not putting it away.

A breath let out behind him. Edelson turned to find Robin there, her hands clasped over her mouth, tears striping her face in the morning light.

Edelson looked at her, and found himself unexpectedly swimming in sadness. What explanation could she give? He holstered his gun and brushed past her to the door. Turned and looked at her again.

"Was just down to visit your folks." His speech welled with uninvited emotion. "Your dad wants me to talk some sense into you." Edelson paused to collect himself. "It's funny really. I came here to tell you that . . . maybe school was a good idea." He chuckled bitterly. "I guess you neglected to tell me what exactly you were studying."

McHugh waited for the guard to escort Christen Vining to the intercom telephone. He'd been in the waiting room for more than an hour, too early for visiting hours, his empty stomach growling relentlessly, but single-mindedly focused.

Wren seemed surprised to see him. She picked up the phone. "You're here early. Are you here to bail me out?"

He smiled broadly and produced Dina's diary from his coat pocket.

"What's that?" she said, pressing her finger to the glass.

"Your mother's diary."

Her mouth fell open. "Where did you get it?"

"Upstairs at the tavern."

"Did you read it?"

McHugh nodded, aware that he was grinning like a lunatic. He flipped the diary open to the passage and pressed it to the glass. "Look at the third paragraph." It stood alone, the line. He watched Wren squint to make out the words.

Her eyes came abruptly up and met his. She seemed puzzled.

"We don't have the same father," he said, his grin widening.

She seemed not to comprehend.

"We aren't brother and sister, Wren."

She just stared at him.

"Don't you see?"

"See what? That . . . that my father is not my father?" Her dark eyes pierced him, as if to ask how he could be so cruel. So thoughtless.

"Wren, I know this is a shock. But, sweetheart, think of what it means."

She flung a hand over her head and clambered out of the chair. The guard came to meet her. She stumbled backward, toward the door, shaking her head.

"Wren," McHugh stood and shouted through the glass, forgetting the phone. "Wren?"

Gray had left for school by the time Edelson got back to Magda, and the sheriff was glad of it. He collapsed fully dressed on his bed and slept soundly for an hour, then awoke with a start, Robin's lover looming like Satan in his thoughts. But the man had neither horns nor a tail, and his hair, though thick, was quite gray at the temples. Edelson remembered that detail now as he pieced the man's terror-struck face together in his head — the thin lips and sharply pointed nose. Not a devil and, certainly, not Adonis either. Which only served to twist the knife again. Least she could've done was find a better looking man than himself so he could blame the breach on her shallow need for a pretty boy to soothe her wounded pride. That Robin's lover was so ordinary cast a much deeper insult on Edelson's sense of himself.

Someone knocked on the front door and he rolled onto his side. Who could it be at mid-morning on a weekday? Probably a Jehovah's Witness. He waited, but the pounding got louder. Not a Jehovah's Witness, he thought. He got to his feet and went to open the door.

"Sheriff Edelson?" A police officer stood on the step.

"Yeah." He rubbed his eyes and looked at the badge. Missoula. He sighed.

"Sorry, but we've gotta take you in," the officer said. He was insultingly young, the reddened trail of adolescent pimples still visible in his ruddy cheeks.

Edelson looked past him, out to the police cruiser and the officer's partner of about the same age, hunched near the open door, hands out away from his sides, as if ready to grasp an unseen pistol at the first sign of trouble. They both looked terrified. Edelson shook his head. To be sent out to Mineral County to arrest the sheriff, what a mean thing to do to a couple of rookies.

"We don't want any trouble, Sheriff," the officer said in a husky voice that was clearly not his normal range.

"Can I get my boots on?"

The officer nodded and followed him inside. He stood in the living room as Edelson gathered his wallet and keys, then pulled his boots on.

"Any chance you'll let me drive myself in?" Edelson said at the door.

The officer grinned nervously. "Sorry."

"Okay then. Take me in, boys."

The chief of the Missoula Police Department had been waiting for Edelson and ushered him straight into his office, skipping the paperwork. The man sat behind a large metal desk, a relic of the typewriter era, smiling like the two of them shared a dirty secret. He was rotund and white-headed, clearly past his prime and given over completely to the day-to-day management of his staff. He wore thick trifocals with heavy plastic rims.

"So, you found your wife with another man, did ya?" The chief grinned.

Edelson nodded, resigned. "Yeah, but I refrained from killing the bastard like I wanted to."

The chief clucked his tongue. "Good thing. Your wife is a student, isn't that so?"

Edelson confirmed with a snap of his chin.

"Her lover-boy is a professor. Did you know that?" He stared at Edelson intently, as if he took uncommon pleasure in making the unhappy comparison.

"I didn't get to know him."

"He'd like to see you lose your badge." The chief sat back and smiled.

Edelson felt the heat of anger flare in his face.

"But he was remarkably short-sighted about his own ethical dilemma, I'd say."

Edelson squinted at the chief. "Come again?"

"I don't imagine banging his married students would play well with the administration. Do you?" The chief tipped his head to the side as if this were a formal question requiring an answer.

Edelson cringed. "I guess not." He was ready to stand and walk out, let them tackle and cuff him. It couldn't be worse than suffering this humiliation. Banging Robin — the chief is talking about *my wife*. "What's the procedure here?"

"No procedure. I talked him out of filing charges." Gray eyes twinkled at Edelson. "I appealed to his better judgment."

Edelson drew a long breath, relieved, and glad he'd stayed his temper long enough to hear the punch line. But he looked quickly at the chief again. "Why'd you send your boys out to arrest me, then?"

"Oh, don't get me wrong, Edelson. I did you a favor today, but I don't condone your actions. You pull something like that again in my town and I'll nail your ass to the wall." The chief's glib words had been replaced by a stomach-knotting glare.

Edelson nodded, but didn't hold the chief's eye. "You can be assured it won't happen again."

"It better not." The chief shifted in his heavy vinyl chair, a smile dawning over his face again. "You're lucky he saw reason."

Edelson got to his feet. "Well if he has a change of heart remind him that he pissed his pants. He wouldn't want his colleagues to be privy to that." He stopped at the door and turned back. "Think one of your men can give me a lift home?"

McHugh tried to focus his attention on the clerk detailing each document in the transfer of his cabin to the new owners, instructing him where to sign his full name and where to simply initial that he understood it. He didn't understand it, couldn't get his mind off Wren. How stupid, waltzing into the jailhouse and dropping a bomb on her like that. Selfish. He was seized of a sudden with the prospect of losing his identity — what made him who he was, and he understood why she was so devastated. Too late.

"Okay, Mr. McHugh, you're all done." The clerk seemed overly pleased with herself, as if she'd facilitated the signing of a peace treaty. McHugh noticed for the first time her youth — twenty-five maybe.

"I've got a check here for you." She slid a crisp cashier's check printed with First Montana Bank on elegant blue paper across the polished conference table. His eyes followed her slender fingers back to her side, noticing a large diamond ring. He glanced up at her smooth face and wondered what she'd look like after she had a few decades on her. Would she manage to retain her grasp of beauty, unlike Wren? He sighed.

"Is everything in order?" the clerk asked, her eyes on the check.

He rubbed his thumb over it instinctively, to make sure it was real. "Yup. Looks in order."

She stood to escort him out, her heels clicking softly on the tile floor.

"Do you have children?" he asked, peering at her well-formed calves perched over narrow ankles.

"No." She laughed girlishly. "I've only been married since August."

A part of him was glad to know that — that she didn't have kids. A vindictive satisfaction in the idea that after she did, she wouldn't remain beautiful forever.

21

LATER, AFTER HE HAD BEEN DRIVEN HOME by the wet-behind-the-ears Missoula police officer, he drove into Peerless. The winter-bleached sun glanced off Edelson's windshield, stinging his fatigue-dried eyes as he came into Peerless. It was late in the afternoon and his head throbbed. He wished for an end to the day so he could sleep at last. He'd have supper with Mrs. Sherwood when he picked up Gray and the cat, but he would not tell the boy his fate tonight. He couldn't manage it after his long day of torment. He'd call Sarah Winborn and arrange to take Gray to Missoula tomorrow. Then he would take the following morning to talk with Gray and collect the boy's things.

He didn't turn on the heat in the jailhouse, but sat at his desk, his own breath keeping him company like spirits hanging on his lips. He collected messages and confirmed the lack of goings-on in Mineral County while he was away. As if there was no need for a sheriff at all here. And honestly, he thought, they couldn't do much worse than him, anyway.

As he gathered his nerve to call the social worker, the phone rang.

"Sheriff's office," he answered flatly.

"Kip, it's me."

His middle tightened. "God*damn-it* I don't want to talk to you, Robin." His breath boiled out in front of him.

"Please, Kip. I'm sorry, Kip. I made a mistake."

He flared his nostrils in distaste. "A *mistake*? Is that what you call it? A mistake is running a red light when you're not paying attention. That's a mistake! How did you mistake taking your clothes off and sleeping with your professor?"

She sobbed into the phone, and he could tell this wasn't her first bout of tears today. But he wasn't going to let her get him with this tactic.

"A mistake," he said again, more to himself than to her.

"Kip, please listen."

He shook his head. "You have unbelievable nerve to call me. Do you know what that bastard did?"

"I know," she squeaked. "I tried to talk him out of it. I tried to stop him."

"Fifteen years, Robin. Fifteen years we've been together in February. And it doesn't mean jack-shit to you." His anger burned hot and terrible words queued up on his tongue. Every vicious thought he'd ever had but never spoke aloud since the day they met revived.

"Kip, please listen to me. Please."

She was reduced to begging, and he couldn't stomach it. The verbal thrashing he'd intended evaporated in the wake of her unbalanced state. "Give me one reason I shouldn't dump your stuff into the river and wash my hands of you forever."

"Because I love you."

He snorted. "What the hell kind of statement is that?"

"I do, Kip. And I'm sorry. I'm *so sorry*."

A thousand images flitted through his mind, from the first time he laid eyes on Robin as a co-ed in a red miniskirt to this morning, holding her breath and praying silently that he wouldn't blow a man's head off. And it struck him just then, how simple it would've been. He couldn't exactly pin down what had stopped him from making that next move. He thought now of the ease with which he might have pulled the trigger.

"Tell it to your lover," Edelson said and hung up the phone.

No sooner had he paused to look out at the llamas and regain his balance, but the phone rang again.

"Son of a bitch!" he shouted, believing it was Robin calling back. "Sheriff's office," he barked.

"Edelson, this is Ms. Winborn."

He sighed. How did she know he would be calling her?

"Are you there?"

"Yeah," he said. "It wasn't her — the boy's mother."

"I'm sorry to hear that, but that's not why I'm calling."

The sheriff opened his mouth to inquire, but she cut him off. "I picked Gray Dausman up at the school this morning. He's fine. He's getting to know his new foster family right now."

"What? You didn't call me first? You just came and took the boy?"

"Sheriff Edelson, I warned you not to make me regret my decision. I'm sure I don't need to explain that assaulting a man with your service weapon disqualifies you as a suitable guardian."

Edelson dropped into his chair with a clatter and pinched the bridge of his nose between his finger and thumb. "No charges were filed," he said, but it was useless and he knew it.

She remained silent.

"How did you find out about that?"

"How big do you think this town is, Sheriff?"

He took a long breath and tried to think. "I'd like to speak to him. Can I at least come see him for a few minutes?"

"I don't think that's a good idea. I'll send someone out for his things tomorrow."

"Please. Please let me just . . . say goodbye to the kid."

"I'm sorry, Sheriff."

One hundred thousand dollars in one hundred dollar bills. McHugh counted them out for the third time as he stacked them inside an old leather suitcase. He had no intention of handing it over to some thug, but the thug didn't know that. When he finished, McHugh locked the suitcase inside the safe under the floor of his office, wondering all the while about the sheriff and whether he'd found a way to help his sister . . . Wren rather. He smiled at the joy of her not being his sister, and wished it were he who was not their father's child. He could bear that burden for her.

The last half of the neon had burned out, and now the sign over the St. John's liquor store burned *Liq* in a rich red that radiated all the way to the Interstate. Edelson sat in his pickup battling with himself over whether to take the next step in his plan. Mrs. Sherwood had agreed to keep Peachy, though she hesitated a long while before saying yes. He thought they might keep each other company, especially since Gray wouldn't be coming to visit either one of them anymore.

A flash of Russell Vining's dead, staring eyes flitted though Edelson's mind, and Edelson went inside *Liq* and purchased a fifth of gin. He set it on the seat next to him and commenced northward toward the Flathead. Darkness had long claimed the day. Claimed the entire season in truth — sitting as they did on the forty-ninth parallel and careening into the low point of the year. But he saw a light burning in Chris Samuelson's cottage. He gathered his gin and laid on the horn, blaring an obnoxious greeting across the still water. She opened the door and stood silhouetted against the glow of her little house for a moment, then brought the ferry over.

"You've really got to stop dropping in like this," she said, but Edelson could tell she wasn't really angry.

"I called ahead, didn't you get my message?"

She'd launched the ferry with a whoosh and it drifted downstream a bit before the cables took hold and righted its alignment with her shore. "I don't have a phone."

"Oh, yeah." He thumped his forehead with a palm. "Well,

I guess someone out there will be disappointed when I don't show up."

Although she didn't smile or seem to respond to his attempt at humor, as the bottom of the craft scraped along the gravel shore, Edelson jumped down and offered her a hand. She reluctantly took it, and he could read her mind. Of course she didn't need his help, that wasn't the point.

"Are you hungry? I have some stewed lamb."

"Lamb? No one ever makes lamb any more."

She looked up at him wonderingly before opening the door. "You seem . . . I don't know. Out of sorts or something."

"You don't know the half of it." He set the bottle, still wrapped in its paper bag, on her table. "I've had one hour of sleep since yesterday morning."

"What's in the bag?"

"Gin."

She didn't say anything for a moment, but watched Edelson. "You gonna get drunk at my house?"

He frowned at her choice of words. "I thought we could have a drink or two together."

"I don't drink."

He laughed out loud. In fact, found her declaration a fitting end to a perfect string of unbelievably disappointing events.

"Don't let me stop you," she said. "Just make sure you can still drive home."

"No." He pushed it aside. "Would you believe I'm an alcoholic?" He pulled the bag toward him again. Took the bottle out and examined the label. It was cheap gin. He fiddled with the cap, but didn't break the seal, then held it up to his nose as if he could smell the liquid through the cap. "God, but I want some of this."

She watched him.

"I never had a craving for it until my wife left. Now it

seems always to be there. It lurks behind my molars." He pressed his fingertips to his jaw, just below his right ear. "And it slides down onto my tongue when I'm alone." He ran a hand over the label again. Reread it without comprehending it. And as unexpectedly as stepping into a hole, he began to cry.

Chris sat down, but said nothing.

"I'm sorry," he sobbed. "I don't know what's gotten hold of me."

"It's okay," she offered.

"No it isn't." He straightened and took a breath, pulling his face into a hard frown with a mighty effort to compose himself. After a long silence he smiled ironically. "I was thinking on the drive up here that things were as bad as they could get. Then I make a complete fool of myself at your kitchen table. I shoulda quit while I was ahead."

"What happened to you?"

Edelson explained about his trip to Vegas, Gray's unyielding mother. "She was so calm. She just said 'I can't take him.' Like he was a dog or something. She was just so calm about it."

"What are you going to do now?"

"Oh, that's already been decided for me." He went quiet again, battling back a fresh surge of emotion. "I went to Robin's this morning — early. I was just back in town. She had another man with her . . . and I sort of shoved my pistol up his nose and made him wet himself."

"You what?"

"I was tired."

Chris shook her head disbelieving.

"Then I got hauled in by the Missoula police, which really pisses me off because the bastard didn't file any charges. And when I got back to my office, the social worker called to tell me she picked Gray up from school and I didn't even get to see him."

"That stands to reason, I guess."

"Whose side are you on?"

Chris returned to the kitchen and began preparing a plate of lamb.

Edelson thrust his head to the side, cracking his neck. Then repeated the procedure on the other side. He'd told her more than he should have, and he felt humiliated and naked now. "You never said why you live here. How can you stand the loneliness?"

She didn't answer right away, but pondered the question. "There's a difference between lonely and alone, you know."

"Still doesn't explain why you live here."

"What did your wife say when you found her with another man?"

Edelson scowled. Chris was evading his question. "She called to tell me she loved me." He snorted again at the absurdity. "Now answer my question."

Chris brought the plate to the table and set it before him. "I'm not in custody. I don't have to answer your questions."

"You wouldn't have to answer them if you were."

"You're not the first person to try and figure out what's wrong with me." She sat. "Maybe there is something wrong with me, I don't know. But I'm not lonely. In fact I'm a lot less lonely than you are."

He bit into the lamb, bracing himself for a strong gamy flavor. But it was mild and the meat fell apart in soft savory strings. "This is good. I've never had lamb that tasted like this." He took the bone between his fingers and peeled the meat away with his teeth. "What makes you think I'm lonely?" The question seemed ridiculous even to Edelson.

She scoffed. "If your wife still loves you, why don't you take her back?"

"After what she did? Are you out of your mind? That's not love."

"No, that isn't love, but neither is a lot of romance or pas-

203

sion. Maybe she mistook one for the other and now that she's had the chance to satisfy her desire she can see the true nature of it."

Edelson squinted at Chris. "What?"

"I mean the kind of love a man and a woman cultivate through years of companionship is not what you see in the movies. Everyone is out there looking for their soul mate, but it's a myth. It's not real. Familiarity may be boring on the surface, but there's a depth to it, a safety, that can't be found with a new lover."

"Maybe she just realized he had a weak bladder."

"You've got to get over this thing about him peeing his pants. It's not becoming of you." She smiled darkly.

"It's all I've got." He scraped up the last of the lamb and set his fork down.

"No it isn't. But you'll have to set your pride aside to see that."

"Tell me again why you live here all alone."

Chris rolled her eyes. "I'm looking for my soul-mate."

"It's a myth. You could have me instead." He took her hand and ran his fingers up and down her thumb. She tried to pull her hand away, but he stood and brought her to her feet also. Placing his arm around her shoulder, he leaned in to kiss her.

Chris twisted away. "Stop it!"

He let go, feeling once more in one day the sting of rejection.

"You're just getting revenge on your wife."

"No . . . no, it isn't like that." Edelson shook his head and stepped toward her again.

"I'm not interested." She glared at him. "Get out. Please, just . . . leave me alone."

22

GRAY LISTENED TO THE MURMUR OF VOICES, his eyes trained on the shaft of light burning along the base of the door. A restless snore emanated from Cody, his roommate and the son of his new foster parents. They were the same age, but Gray didn't want the best-friend relationship that Cody had suggested. In fact, he despised the instant-brother. Gray felt like the new family pet, a gift for a nerdy son. A boy that Gray imagined spent a lot of time alone on the playground. While he could understand this situation, he didn't warm to Cody even a little bit.

Cody had spent the afternoon showing Gray his toys, the sorts of toys Gray had always wished for back on Big Sky Court. A remote-control jeep that traversed the rocky slope behind the house, rolling full over and righting itself again. Video games, a computer, Legos in quantity to build a life-sized palace. Cody was proud of his things, found great satisfaction in showing them off. But, when Gray started work on a Lego structure of his own, Cody quickly gathered them up and put them away. He didn't want them to get lost. He assured Gray that he would he let him play with them — sometime. After all, they were brothers.

The idea made Gray's stomach ache right in the center. Cody was not only a nerd, but a selfish jerk. He thought longingly of his red bicycle, then crept from his bed and pulled his jeans on over his pajamas. Next, his shirt and socks. He fumbled in the dark for his bag and quietly unzipped it. His fingers roamed the hard square shapes, and he realized with some puzzlement that he still had all his books from school. Why hadn't they asked him to leave them behind? Discerning one from the other was impossible in the dark. Which was Mrs. Sherwood's book? At last he recognized the smooth texture of the worn leather spine, a pair of narrow ribs running horizontally, and dragged *Arabian Nights* out. He shoved the bag under the bed, tucked *Arabian Nights* in his shirt, and crawled under the covers to wait.

He wondered if the sheriff, Mr. Edelson, knew that the social worker took him from school and delivered him to Cody's parents. He wondered if Edelson would still look for his mother now that he was gone. And of course, Gray missed Peachy. The cat must be wondering where he was, Gray thought. He knew how the cat would feel because he sometimes wondered if his mother cared about him any more. He often thought back on his time with her, trying to remember if he'd done something to make her mad. Gray's stomach ached as he imagined Peachy suffereing the familiar pain of loneliness and abandonment.

Gray dozed. When he awoke he came sharply awake, trying to grasp how long he'd slept. There was no clock in the room, and no light came under the door. The house was quiet. He slipped out of bed, the floorboards creaking beneath his feet. Taking his book, he tiptoed to the door and slowly pulled it open. A clock ticked somewhere down the hall. He ventured out, looking for his coat and shoes.

McHugh read the rest of Dina Toomey's diary, the candlelight casting deformed and dancing figures across the bleak walls of his upper room, looking for more evidence that Wren was not his sister. One sentence didn't seem enough now. He struggled to keep his mind focused. Kept slipping back to his prison visit with Wren. He was almost certain he'd heard a man ask to see her as he left the lobby. He had turned to look, wondering if he heard it right. The man was young — mid-twenties maybe. His hair was long and braided down his back. He turned and looked at McHugh with the blackest eyes McHugh had ever seen before — hard and flat, devoid of emotion. Not anyone his sister would befriend, McHugh was sure. But the voice kept coming back to him.

He set the diary down and turned his back to the candle.

Edelson dreamed his phone was ringing incessantly. Then he woke and understood it was not a dream. The clock next to his bed illuminated a bright three-eighteen. "Hello," he slurred.

"Sheriff, you're needed at the Silver Dog," Adeline said in a rush. She sounded breathless with the effort.

"What's the problem?"

"Fire."

"You call the fire crew?"

"Yeah, they're headed there now."

"On my way." He was on his feet and dressed in seconds. He flew down the deserted Interstate and into Magda, lights flashing, engine laboring from its cold start. The eastern sky glowed eerily orange, and Edelson's scalp prickled. He was terrified of fire. As he neared the tavern, tar smoke burned his nostrils. He gulped for breath, knowing the sensation of suffocating was mostly in his head, but unable to still the panic rising in him. The fire engine was only seconds ahead of him, the crew still disemboweling miles of hose onto the street. Edelson could see it was no use. A second floor window exploded, showering the firemen with glass shrapnel. Flames licked the eaves and crawled up the roof. Inside, hellfire — blistering and white. Randy McHugh stood helplessly in the street, his face black, his hair singed, and his hands blistered and bloody.

By morning light, the once-proud Silver Dog stood a smoking

relic, an enormous, and entirely forlorn husk. The fire had con-
sumed the second-hand store on one side and the empty
Montana Bank building on the other. Charred timbers continued to fall, crumbling into the black abyss. What little traffic
Magda enjoyed paused as citizens gathered to gaze up at the ruined landmark in mournful silence. McHugh was not there to
witness the public response. Edelson had ordered the para-
medics to take McHugh to the hospital whether he consented
to go or not. McHugh, for his part, had been unable to utter a
sound as he witnessed the complete destruction of his family
business.

The woman who owned the second-hand store had been
there most of the night as well. She stood alongside McHugh, a
ratty parka buttoned over her housecoat, her feet clad in heavy
woolen socks and slippers, swearing to sue McHugh for the destruction of her property. She swore so many times Edelson had
a mind to arrest her for harassment.

Edelson imagined he'd never prove McHugh's involvement in Vining's doings now — and what did it matter, anyway?

Gray, to his surprise, had found the Interstate only a few blocks
from the foster home, complete with on-ramp and a sign pointing him west. He meant to get to California this time. He'd
dressed warmly, and unbuttoned his coat after only an hour or
so of walking. He kept to the ditch, away from the shoulder
where the occasional car might see him. His icy toes nagged
him until, sometime before dawn, they finally went numb.

He found himself at the Y just after sunrise. He'd been
there before. Once as he waited in the frosty truck while his
father had a few beers at the tavern. And again with the sheriff.
Gray had wandered between the giant rigs that second time,
staring up at them with awe. The sheriff had simply let him.
Didn't rush or nag him to hurry, but pointed out which ones
carried frozen food, and which ones carried milk or chemicals.

208

They'd peered between the slats of one trailer at the manure-caked hooves of what seemed to Gray a thousand cattle. The pungent odor of so many hot, hairy bodies squeezed inside stung his nose. Gray had wondered if that's what it smelled like at the Flying W when the boys went to brand. Maybe he was lucky not to have been invited.

So Gray again slipped among the trucks, their big diesel engines humming in the cold Montana morning. Some were pointed east and some were pointed west. He focused on the westward rigs, figuring they were an indication of destination. He looked for an opportunity to climb in back where, he imagined, their cargo spaces were. But they stood like giant fortresses, closed and locked tight. He couldn't even reach the handles.

He was losing hope of bumming a ride when a sparkling blue rig rolled in and made a wide arcing turn to park at the end. He admired the shiny cab, its white lion's-head design. A wiry man swung down, spit tobacco in the dirty snow, and started for the diner. Gray watched him out of sight then turned back to his truck. It had a sleeper cab, and an idea was born.

Edelson lay on his sofa, his clothes reeking of smoke. He hadn't the energy to undress, let alone shower. Sleep was all he cared about. He drifted in and out a while, unable to let go, let it overtake him. McHugh's stoic silence as he watched his tavern burn gripped Edelson's thoughts often, shaking him awake. Until at last he fell into a dream of cruising through the Montana back country — towering pines and dusty gravel roads striped with sunlight. He came into Vining's place, the battered trailer, the marijuana crop waving gaily in the breeze. Doom sat on Edelson's chest like a sinister spirit. All things moved in an unstoppable sort of slow motion. He watched the chamber snap on his weapon, saw the spray of blood, the man go down. What had happened in truth too quickly to observe came to him now in sickening detail. A dog's barking echoed across his psyche as Russell Vining met his irreversible fate.

Edelson jerked awake and stared up at the light fixture. It wasn't the first time he'd relived the scene in his dreams. How long would the death plague him? Russell Vining was a qualified candidate for a shooting in the line of duty, by all criteria — living on the fringes, paranoid and heavily entrenched in criminal activity. But no one ever told Edelson he'd spend hours lying awake at night reworking the events, searching for the one thing he might have done to prevent it. That he'd mourn the soul of a man such as Vining.

He sat up and rubbed his head. His gun lay on the end table within arms reach. Who would mourn him if he used it on himself? How long would it take for Robin to hear? And wouldn't she want to die too, knowing he killed himself after finding her with another man? He pulled his shirt off, then got up and stepped out of his trousers, leaving them on the floor in front of the sofa. He looked again at his weapon. Loaded and ready. And went to shower.

Edelson found Mrs. Sherwood in her kitchen, which harbored the smoky demise of the Silver Dog laced with the faint smell of cinnamon toast. A pyramid of canned cat food was stacked on the dinette. He took a can in his hand and read the label.

"That cat is getting a lot better treatment at your house."

"I don't think I should keep him," she said. "He's not happy here."

"How can you tell?"

She dragged out a skillet and set it on the stove. "You were up all night with the fire crew?" It wasn't really a question.

"Yeah. Have you been down to see the scene?" He pulled the chair out and plopped down, his balance compromised by his lack of sleep.

"No. It won't be the same now. It was really the only thing historic left of Magda. How did it happen?"

"McHugh claims he fell asleep with a candle burning."

"You don't believe him?"

Edelson hesitated. He didn't trust McHugh. If the man hadn't been so badly burned in the fire, he would have suspected him of burning the building down to collect the insurance — or hide something. "I'm pretty sure he was selling Vining's marijuana. I don't trust him, but I don't have any evidence that he's lying."

"He went to school with my daughter," she said, then smeared butter into the pan and watched it melt. "I'll make you some eggs and bacon."

They retreated to their thoughts as they often did in each other's company, Edelson working through the scene of Russell Vining's death again. And wondering about the remains of the Silver Dog. So much disaster in such a short time. He would've traded places with McHugh, though. He would rather be cleaning up from a fire and dealing with the loss of material possessions than the knowledge that his wife was sleeping with another man.

Finally Mrs. Sherwood said, without turning from the stove, "I miss him. Don't you?"

"You have no idea." Edelson took a sharp breath. Fatigue and raw emotions were a disastrous combination.

"I just want to know if he's okay," she said.

"I can probably find out."

"I don't mean physically."

"I know." He stacked the cat food into three neat towers by flavor: tuna, chicken and liver, and salmon. "You said something that keeps going through my head. You said the boy needs someone to believe in him."

She nodded.

"You know, *I* believe in him. I've never seen a kid — anybody — so determined. From finding his mother to learning how to ride a bike. Gray is not a quitter."

211

"Kip, you should fight this." She turned and looked him straight in the eye. "Get him back."

Edelson held his gaze on the old woman. It was never supposed to be forever with Gray and they both knew it.

"People don't come into your life for no good reason."

"What if I was it for him?" He shook his head. That wasn't what he meant. "What if that kid was the only chance I'll ever get to really make a difference?"

She didn't answer, and Edelson was on his feet and heading for the door. His gut ached, and he wanted to puke. He never wanted kids. This discussion was only confusing things.

"I have to go. I'll call you later."

A thousand hornets couldn't match the sting in McHugh's right hand and forearm. The skin, boiled off the muscle, now oozed hot clear liquid beneath mountains of white gauze. His left hand was singed, but ultimately spared the worst of the damage. Despite the severity of his burns, McHugh ignored the doctor's advice and immediately returned to the ruins of his tavern. The money, he had to get the money. It was all he had left. He hadn't carried insurance on the tavern for years — what he had in his safe was all he and Wren would ever have to start over with now. He stood again in the street as a dirty, red farm tractor dragged his smoking fire-resistant safe from the rubble.

"Where do you want it?" the driver called to him over the clamor of the engine.

McHugh pointed his fluffy white appendage. "My truck."

The operator nodded and deftly scooped the two-foot square safe into his front loader and dropped it into the bed of McHugh's truck with a thud. The back end of the truck sagged six inches.

The driver killed the tractor engine and pivoted in his seat. "Connie and I have a guest room if you need it, Randy."

McHugh's hair stood up in the cold wind; his breath blew down the street in white strings. "Thanks . . . I'll let you know." He looked back at the shell of his tavern. "No reason to stay here now."

The man gazed compassionately at McHugh, making him resentful. He didn't need anyone's pity.

"Better let that safe cool down before you try to open it."

"I appreciate your help," McHugh said, starting for his truck. It had all seemed so unreal, so impossible, to lose the Silver Dog this way. But the reality was dawning, down to the memory of his grandfather's tiger oak desk, the photos and ledgers. Practically the entire history of Magda — forever lost.

McHugh drove into Peerless and pulled up in front of the little turquoise trailer. He wanted answers. He tapped the aluminum door with the toe of his boot and waited for this vaguely familiar face, holding his bandaged arm to his belly like a wounded bird.

Crystal O'Shea opened the door and looked him over.

"Do you know who I am?" McHugh asked.

She pulled the door open all the way in an invitation. "Does it matter?" She was barely dressed — a thin cotton housedress cut low, exhibiting a liberal swell of cleavage. Bare feet and ruffled hair.

He stepped into the cramped single-wide. A built-in couch in a shade of aqua that complimented the chipped countertop angled around the end of the room. The narrow window above it was coated with ice in a swirling paisley pattern.

"Would you like to sit down first?"

First? He turned to her, then it came instantly clear. He'd seen her before, at the Silver Dog.

She sat down and tilted her head up at him. "You're Randy McHugh, aren't you?"

"I am." He took a seat next to her on the sofa.

She gestured toward his bandaged hand. "I heard about the Silver Dog. How bad are your burns?"

"Bad enough they wanted to take me to Missoula and stick me in the hospital."

"Why didn't you go?"

"I have business to take care of." He studied her face. "Crystal, isn't it?"

"Yes. What business do you have here? People usually see me for pleasure." She slid her hand over his thigh and brought it to rest on his penis.

He opened his mouth to speak, but didn't. Felt himself harden and lengthen beneath her fingers. So she was a whore. He wondered how he'd never gotten the nerve to visit a woman such as this in all the years he'd been alone, unable to let go of Wren and look for a life-mate. Why hadn't he come here? There was nothing — no one — to stop him.

She moved in on him, until their thighs pressed together from hip to knee, and worked her fingers against his crotch. "Your pleasure can be my business," she said.

"I think you might know my sister."

She laughed, and he thought it sounded a little bitter.

"I guess you don't remember me," she said.

"I've seen you at the tavern."

Crystal frowned. "I know your sister. We were friends in school." She pulled her hand back and let it rest on his leg.

He looked at it, immediately mournful about the lost sensation. There was something in the touch of another human being at this moment in his life that was both unexpected and intensely necessary. "Why did you stop?"

"Why are you here?"

"You think I won't pay?"

She slid her hand back in place, but the simple acknowledgement of the business transaction ruined it for him and the pain in his hand drew his attention away.

"Never mind," he said, getting to his feet. He'd only come there to find out how his sister came into possession of this trailer, but Wren wouldn't have anything to do with a prostitute. If Wren had known this was what her tenant was doing, she would've kicked her out, he thought. But why hadn't she told him about the property?

Crystal looked at him confused. "I don't get it."

"My sister . . ." He looked at the door, thinking he should go. He didn't know how much to say to this woman. Was she just a renter, or did she know the Vinings and their business?

She patted the sofa. "Sit down. Please."

McHugh hesitated, then obeyed.

She started again with her soft caress on his inner thigh. "Does it hurt a lot? Your hand?"

He moved his mouth to say yes, but no sound came. Crystal pressed closer and brushed her lips across his skin just below his ear. He breathed deep and closed his eyes. She kissed his earlobe so slightly it felt like he'd been brushed by the wings of a dragonfly. For a prostitute, she was remarkably tender. The way she touched him, delicately, opening his shirt, leading him down the hallway to her nest of tangled sheets and flannel blankets. He stood to be undressed, then lay back on the bed to watch her unveiling. A little stretched in places. Worn, but still shapely.

She kissed his mouth with full lips, letting her hair dangle down, the ragged ends tickling his face. She set about rubbing her hands over the length of his body, not rushing, but bringing up in him a yearning that had been with him forever. Until he nearly pled aloud for her — for Wren. He imagined his penis purple-blue in its irrevocable need for satisfaction. Finally she slid onto him and brought forth a volcanic response.

23

McHUGH LAY NAKED IN CRYSTAL O'SHEA'S BED, the sheets gritty and smelling of untold sex acts. Exhaustion had swooped down and gripped him like an owl out of the night, and he longed for sleep, but knew he had to get up. Crystal sat beside him in her cotton housedress, smoking a Camel Light and examining the chipped red paint on her toenails.

"I always wanted to make it with you," she said.

McHugh looked up at her surprised. He couldn't recall having ever spoken to her before this morning.

"Christen always talked about you like you were a god or something."

He smiled to himself.

"I asked her to introduce us, back when we were in school. But she wouldn't. She said you were hers. I always thought that was weird. No one talks that way about their brother, you know?" She pulled the blanket up around her waist. "I wish she could see us now."

McHugh frowned, aware of the betrayal Wren would feel. "Why?"

The prostitute crushed out her cigarette and slid down next to him. Ran her fingers through his hair. "When I first saw you, that night you came and sat in my driveway, I didn't realize who you were. Not until you were gone. Then I knew Christen sent you to check on me."

"Why would she do that?"

Crystal rolled the point of her tongue smoothly over her upper lip, thinking. Her eyes were cast downward, shielded by her lashes. Finally they came up to meet his. Deep blue with large pupils, startling McHugh with their intensity. "You don't have to play dumb with me."

"What d'you mean?"

"I don't believe for a minute you don't know the deal here."

McHugh pushed himself into a sitting position with his left hand and laid his burned limb across his stomach. He was beginning to wish he'd filled the prescription for painkillers the doctor had written for him. The pain itself was not beyond his tolerance, but the relentlessness was grinding him down. Spreading to the back of his neck and the space between his temples like hot grease. "Well, believe it." He wasn't in the mood to play guessing games.

She laughed sarcastically.

"Look, I only came here to find out if you knew how my sister ended up owning this place. Since you rent from her —"

"*Rent?*" Crystal snorted.

McHugh paused and looked at Crystal more carefully.

After a moment locked in each other's gaze, Crystal's eyebrows went up as if she'd experienced some sort of revelation. "Maybe you *don't* know."

"Know what?"

"Shit." Crystal rolled over and got out of bed. She picked through a mountain of dirty clothes in the corner, at last extracting a flannel robe that she draped around her shoulders. "You think I'm stupid? I'm not gonna end up like the one they dug out of the riverbank." She tossed McHugh's jeans onto the bed and stood expectantly in the doorway. "Do you need some help getting dressed?"

McHugh's pride suffered a deflating prick, but he had no

time to rebuff the woman. Someone had come in, unannounced and brutally, from the sound of the slamming door. A tremor ran the length of the trailer.

Crystal whirled around to look down the hallway. "Sagen!"

McHugh flew to his feet. He whisked his jeans up and was holding them to his front when the voice so familiar to him from the telephone shouted down the hallway, "McHugh? Is that you?"

A long-faced man appeared in the doorway, black eyes twinkling with malice. His hair pulled back in a braid. A hooked nose, like a hawk. Couldn't be, McHugh thought, recognizing the man from the courthouse — the man who'd asked to see Wren. Couldn't be.

"Well, well, well. Look what we have here," Sagen smiled. "Crystal, you've been holding out on me."

"No," she stammered. "I never saw him before. Not until this morning." She'd shrunk beneath the man's shadow, small and vulnerable against the wall.

"Well isn't this just my lucky day, McHugh *and* his safe," the man called Sagen glanced briefly at the prostitute, then back to McHugh with a widening grin. "And I thought you burned your bar down and then skipped town." His face went immediately dark and he produced a small pistol from his coat pocket. "Get dressed. We're going for a drive." He turned to Crystal. "You, too."

Gray was roused from a shallow slumber as the diesel engine roared to life. In the moment he had an urgent, panicky sensation, trying to recall where he was. As his senses sharpened, he remembered climbing into the truck and pressing himself against the cold outer corner of the sleeper cab. A blanket heavily laden with the odor of an unwashed body pulled over the length of him. He peeked out to see the man — not really a

218

man, but a grown boy — perched in the driver's seat, fiddling with the radio buttons, trying to find anything but static. The man finally clicked it off with a dirty comment that reminded Gray of Brady. Then the driver proceeded to dig into a can of chew for a thick black plug, which he tucked into his cheek, giving him the appearance of a greedy hamster. The driver sat back and waited while the engine rattled. After a few minutes, his cell phone rang and he pulled it from his pocket.

"Hanchet," the man said and paused to listen. "Your lucky day, I'm at the Y right now. Another hour and I'd be tipping into Idaho." He paused again. "Yeah, I can crack a safe."

Gray shifted under the blankets, a hard metal object digging into his back. The man turned in his direction and scanned the space Gray occupied. Gray froze, and after a moment, the driver turned away and stared out the bug-smeared windshield. Gray let his breath out quietly, a revelation coming to him like a bright sunrise: this idea might not have been so brilliant after all. Tears pricked the backs of his eyes, and he wished he'd kept walking. What if this man was a kidnapper? Or a murderer? His father had once told him about a boy who was taken right off the street in front of his house and cut to pieces with a hacksaw, then left in the woods for the wolves to eat.

"Where?" the man barked into his phone, pulling Gray's attention back. "Yeah, I know the place. Hard to get a rig in there." He went quiet a moment, then, "It better. The last thing I need is to get tangled up with some legal shit."

Gray understood immediately that he'd picked the wrong truck.

"I'll be there in an hour. You better have cash." He pocketed the phone, revved the engine, crept forward through the maze of slumbering semis.

Minutes seemed like hours as Gray inched into a new position, slowly and silently so as not to attract the driver's attention, the sharp object still poking deep into his spine. The rocking of the truck brought to mind Jonah in the belly of the whale — darkness, odor, confinement. Not understanding where the beast roamed. Simply bouncing, rumbling, and lurching. Gray could scarcely believe his error: climbing into a stranger's truck. A stranger and more likely a murderer. The truck erupted with a guttural roar that struck terror deep in Gray's heart. Why hadn't he just called the sheriff? He would have helped, Gray was certain of it. Tears rolled into his ear. His heart rapped maniacally against his ribs, just the way it had on that unforgettable afternoon at the river when the skeleton snapped into sight. He wrapped his arms around his head and cried. Mourned the moment he did this damned dumb thing.

McHugh sat squished between Crystal O'Shea and Sagen in the front seat of his own pickup, the barrel of Sagen's pistol pressing deep into his ribs. Crystal scraped and hammered the gears of his old four-by-four truck. She didn't know to start in second, and when McHugh took the gear shift in hand and yanked it down hard to save his transmission, Sagen wrenched the gun painfully against his kidney.

"Let her drive," he barked.

Crystal drove cautiously through town. He'd threatened to paint her window with McHugh's brains if she caught the sheriff's attention.

McHugh wondered how she could believe that threat. Like Sagen would actually kill him right in the middle of town. But fear has no logic, and he could see that Sagen reigned like a king over the prostitute.

"Take the westbound," Sagen said as they neared the Interstate. "Let's hope you're better at driving than you are at keeping the sheriff busy, or I may not have reason to keep you around."

Crystal concentrated on her task, grinding the truck into third, then fourth. McHugh suffered a fleeting thought that it didn't matter anyway. But pulled himself sharply back to his entanglement; it wouldn't do to give up. His opportunity would come, and he had to be ready for it.

Cars sped past them in the left lane, but Crystal kept the speedometer to a crisp 55 until Sagen finally yelled, "C'mon, pick it up. We don't have all day." He turned then to McHugh. "What's the combination to that safe?" Sagen's sour breath hit McHugh full in the face.

"I tell you that and what's gonna stop you from killing me?"

Sagen smiled calmly. It was the sort of crazy smile people don when they conclude that everyone around them is stupid and only they can see the truth. "Ain't no reason to keep you alive anyway." He shook his head, looked out the window, then looked back. "I'd given up on you. Christen told me you were stupid, but Christ. You fucked the whole thing up. You were supposed to mortgage your bar and spring your sister, *then* sell your house and give the money to me." He went quiet, as if thinking. Then, "I'm gonna get a great deal of pleasure out of killing you, you perverted son-of-a-bitch. She told me how you raped her when she was sixteen."

The back of McHugh's throat went dry.

Crystal gave McHugh a sidelong glance that reacquainted him with the shame that lay just below the surface of his life, and he suddenly felt as though he was the whore.

"She's not really my sister," he said.

Sagen shook his head. "Sure, you dirty fucker."

Crystal had accelerated to 70 and was now keeping pace with traffic. She moved into the left lane to get around a semi and as they came nose to nose with the rig, Sagen waved his gun pleasantly up at the driver.

"There's my boy now," he said.

McHugh tilted toward the passenger window to get a look, but was met with the cold gun barrel in his eye socket. He sat back with both eyes closed, waiting for Sagen to remove it, a flash of brilliant blue at the forefront of his brain. He'd seen that truck before. It was the man who'd stopped to help him on the road.

24

THE SEMI SLOWED, TURNED, sped up, slowed, turned, sped up, for what seemed like forever to Gray, until at last he felt a change in the roadway. It was softer, crunchier. He pledged that if the driver stopped again, he'd slip out the passenger door and run for his life. And just as Gray's plan was laid, the rig lurched to a halt, blowing air from its brakes like a steam train. This time the driver killed the engine. He sat a moment, staring at his side mirror, then got out, leaving Gray in the sudden quiet.

Gray didn't move, fearful that Hanchet would return without warning, but as the minutes passed, he conjured up his nerve and took a look outside. Through the grimy windshield, he watched the trucker climb the rusty fire exit on the backside of the ruined and familiar Elk Creek schoolhouse.

Relieved by the familiarity of this landmark, Gray gathered up *Arabian Nights* and turned to move the object that had bruised him so painfully on the ride. He gaped at the long-barreled revolver that jutted up from the heap of dirty clothes he'd been lying on. He pondered a moment and then tucked the gun into his pocket, barrel first, the large, blunt handle sticking out like a cowboy's six-shooter, and scrambled down the passenger side of the truck. He paused in the frozen morning, his breath lingering with him, wondering which way to go. The school sat parallel to the Interstate, the railroad tracks and a wide field with overgrown trees. Gray started toward the road, but heard voices and halted. Footsteps came near, crunching in the frozen gravel. Gray ducked beneath the trailer where he watched in amazement as a man with a gun ordered another man — the man who had brought him his ill-fated burger at the Silver Dog — into the school. A woman followed behind, picking her way cautiously across the icy ground.

As they vanished into the building, Gray turned and sprinted towards the Interstate. He knew what he had to do — find Sheriff Edelson.

"Hanchet, this here is Randy McHugh," Sagen said to the truck driver, pointing at McHugh's temple with his pistol. "The perv I was telling you about. He's been kind enough to bring us his safe. I'm confident we'll find cash in it."

The trucker sneered at McHugh. "Ain't you the guy that was parked on the side of the road a week back?"

Sagen motioned McHugh down to the basement and into a cavernous classroom with a cement floor coated in an inch of ice. The blackboard was scratched with directives for visitors to fuck themselves and to wage peace.

Crystal slipped on the ice and landed hard on her knees. McHugh reached a hand to help her, but Sagen reeled him back by his jacket collar, and placed the gun cold against his ear once more.

She whimpered and got to her feet, then inched along the wall.

"Hey, Sugar," Hanchet said, taking notice of Crystal. He looked her over ravenously, then spit tobacco onto the ice where they all watched it freeze into a hard ball. McHugh felt a little sick that both he and Hancet shared an intimate knowledge of Crystal.

"Think you can take care of a body?" Sagen said, eyeing McHugh.

Crystal turned to look at McHugh, pure agony on her face.

"Shit. You didn't tell me you was gonna waste someone," Hanchet said.

"Just get him tied up for now." Sagen tossed a rope he'd carried in with him to the trucker. He looked again at Crystal. "Tie her up, too. I don't trust her."

"She can't do nothin'." Hanchet took the rope, but before he could tie McHugh's hands behind his back, Sagen stopped him.

"Wait." He gestured at McHugh. "Take off your shoes and socks."

"What?" McHugh stared at the man.

"Just do it, asshole." Sagen thrust his gun in McHugh's face.

After struggling to get his boots and socks off with one hand, McHugh sat on the ice, his pale skin burning with cold.

"See that!" Sagen pointed the gun at McHugh's disfigured toes.

"Shit," Hanchet whistled with amazement at the talon-like appendages.

Sagen turned on McHugh with authority. "What are the odds, you s'pose, that you and Christen would both have feet like that if you weren't related."

McHugh's stomach dropped. How had he overlooked that certainty? The chances were almost nil. He'd read up on the condition years back. It afflicted fewer than a quarter of a percent of the population — and it was hereditary. Wren had made Russell show her his feet on their first date. She had hunted down a man with beautiful feet, determined not to pass on the McHugh curse.

"You're so fuckin' stupid, you perv. Waltzing in to the jail and telling her she wasn't your sister." He turned to Hanchet with a mild smile on his face. "Tie him up."

McHugh's breath seemed to fly away from him in the wake of this revelation. She'd told Sagen about his visit. What else had she shared? What other secrets had she betrayed? Hanchet tightened the rope around his wrists until McHugh cried out. His burned wrist pained him badly. The trucker shoved him down on his side and tied his ankles, too.

"Why not just kill him now? Why bother tying him up first?"

Sagen stood watching, his gun still pointed at McHugh. "No, we'll do that last."

Edelson entered the Interstate at Nine Mile Creek, determined to find some official task to keep him from losing his mind. Nine Mile Creek sat at the base of the pass, just where the steep grade flattened into sweeping curves. He loved those switch-backs, and always took them faster than was prudent, but today he paid no attention. As he emptied into the straight-away out-side Magda it was his habit to slow and peak through the dense trees at the derelict Elk Creek School — a beautiful relic of Georgian design, slowly being beaten back to dust and clay by the jealous side of Mother Nature.

But today he didn't notice the building. Instead, he caught sight of McHugh's pickup parked next to what looked like the back end of an eighteen-wheeler. Finally, Edelson thought, I've caught McHugh carrying out whatever part he played in Vining's drug business. Edelson picked up his radio and called Adeline, but she didn't answer. Disgusted with the county's lack of resources and sole reliance on two people 24 hours a day, he accelerated towards the next exit.

Gray's legs burned with cold, the snow so high it reached his bare skin, finding its way into his pant legs, down his socks and settling into his shoes. He lifted his knees to clear the weeds in the field, and skated cautiously across the frozen ditch. When he reached the embankment below the Interstate he pulled himself up, gripping dead weeds in his numb fingers. At the shoulder of the road he paused to get his breath. He turned to look back at the building, now a quarter mile behind him, to check that a murderer, or a man with a gun, wasn't hot on his tracks. And was astonished to see the sheriff's cruiser bouncing down the road toward the school, like the cavalry riding in to save the day. In his joy he forgot his tiredness, his freezing toes, and his nagging stomach. He trudged back down the bank toward the ditch, anxious to tell Mr. Edelson what he'd seen.

Crystal sat down next to McHugh and pulled her jacket tight around her. She stared at the open doorway where Sagen and Hanchet had gone.

McHugh waited until their voices were a distant muffle as they climbed the stairs, then turned to her and said, "Untie me."

She stared incredulously, as if he'd asked her to sing a hymn.

"Untie me."

"Are you out of your mind?"

"You really wanna watch them blow my head off?"

She turned away and didn't answer.

"Look, you untie me and we both might have a chance of getting out of here."

"He'll kill *me*." Her voice had dropped to an angry whisper.

They sat quiet a moment, McHugh running through scenarios in his mind. His eyes scanned the empty room for any object he might use to cut through the rope.

"Tell me the combination to your safe," she said without looking at him.

He shook his head, not so surprised that the money was all she cared about. "Untie me first."

"No."

"Do it for my sister — your friend."

227

She turned an intense eye on him. "Your sister is the reason we're both here."

McHugh bit his lip, unable to fully accept that statement. How could he believe the word of a thug or a prostitute? He shook his head. "I don't believe it."

"Fine. Die believing what you want." Crystal bit off a fingernail and rolled the sliver around on her tongue.

Hanchet appeared in the doorway, a curious grin on his face. "You wanna wait for me in the truck, sugarbaby?" he said to Crystal. "Maybe I can talk Sagen into sparing you the show." He put his finger to his temple like it was a gun and pretended to pull the trigger. His head snapped back and he wilted onto the floor, then came up grinning.

McHugh erupted, struggling against the ropes, his bare feet slipping on the ice.

"Down, boy," Hanchet sneered. "Maybe we'll let you go if you tell us the combination to the safe."

McHugh shook his head.

"We'll get it open one way or another," Hanchet said and left them alone again.

McHugh's chest heaved, and he sat back in a hot fury. "They'll never get that safe open. It's over a hundred years old. No one's broken into it yet."

Crystal put her hand on his shoulder. "Listen, we do need to work together."

McHugh noticed her sudden change of heart, but said nothing.

"But I don't trust you any more than you trust me. If I untie you, you'll ditch me. I'll be washing up on the riverbank like Chris."

McHugh scowled at her. "You know who that woman was?"

"Just tell me the combination to your safe . . . and then I'll untie you. But you have to go first."

"How do I know I can trust *you?*"

"You have any other choice?"

He waited for her to look him in the eye and then said, "If you double-cross me and I get out of here alive, I'll hunt you down and kill you myself."

She blinked in rapid succession, but said nothing, waiting . . .

"Right 22, left 83, right 19."

She repeated the combination, twice.

McHugh turned his back to her so she could work the knots.

She leaned close, as if to begin, then whispered in his ear, "Christen and Sagen were planning to take off together. You screwed it up for me, too, by not bailing her out like she was expecting. I thought I was finally going to be free of them. I've been a slave for them, doing their shit-work for two years. Remember the old sheriff? How'd you like to screw *him* — and for free? Now Sagen's gonna take the money and run, but your sister will still be here. She'll find a new pimp to manage her business — if she hasn't already."

"You bitch!" McHugh shouted, struggling to face his tormenter.

She pulled away as Sagen thundered down the stairs and into the room. He stood, nostrils flaring, eyes bouncing suspiciously between the two of them. "What the hell is going on?"

Crystal shrugged meekly. "I just told him the truth — about his sister."

Sagen glared at her.

"About how we all work for her."

He looked again at McHugh. Contemplated him a moment, then turned back to Crystal. "Quit screwing around and get the combination to his safe. Hanchet needs to be on the road and I don't have time to fuck around anymore." Sagen handed her a crowbar. "Knock him around a little."

229

She took the weapon, gripping it so tightly her knuckles turned white.

Sheriff Edelson coasted into the gravel lot behind the familiar pickup sitting next to a dense clump of Douglas firs. He walked a circle around the vehicle, confirming it was McHugh's by the black and peeling safe in the bed. The semi he'd glimpsed from the Interstate was squeezed tightly between the school and the steep embankment behind it in a utilitarian space not intended for a truck of that size. From where he stood, Edelson could see it was a deliberate attempt to conceal the vehicle. The rear doors were open, a toolbox sat open in the back, but there was no one in sight. He recognized the unusual lion's head emblem. It was the same truck he'd found jackknifed outside Peerless a few weeks back. He remembered the kid, his frustration with the driver of the SUV.

The place was quiet with a surreal quality, like a bad dream in which crows circle the sky, but make no sound. And an icy wind tears your skin raw and putrid.

With his hand gently touching his weapon, Edelson stepped up to the rig and peered inside at the assortment of tiny tools. A stethoscope was laid out next to the box. He nodded, wondering why McHugh would need help opening his own safe.

His senses were heightened, the crisp air tight in his lungs, a keen awareness of danger coursing through him, reaching every part of him, as if delivered through his blood. His eyes moved quickly, scanning his surroundings. His ears were tuned to a frequency he only got when he came face to face with an enemy.

He sensed movement out of the corner of his eye . . . at the tracks. He turned, his gun drawn now. He looked again. It was a boy. It was Gray. How did he get here? Edelson stepped forward, shaking his head. Go back, he thought. *Go back, Gray.*

Don't come down here. He opened his mouth to speak, and felt cold steel at his neck, just below his right ear.

"Good morning, Sheriff." The voice rippled across his eardrum, pulling him back, dividing his attention. "I'll take that." And Edelson's gun fell away from his fingers.

Gray had stopped short in the weeds, still tiny in the distance. Edelson could see his mouth gaping, his chest heaving.

Edelson pulled his left hand up slowly from the wrist, and held it stiffly at his waist, palm facing the boy. He tapped the air once in a halting motion. Don't do it, he warned silently. Don't yell, boy.

Gray dropped suddenly to his belly, as if he'd heard the sheriff's thoughts.

25

THE IMAGE OF MR. EDELSON led away by that man with the gun left Gray stunned, his ribs aching. He lay in the cold, hands red, cheeks stinging, and asked himself, what would the sheriff do now?

Not a single damn idea came to him.

Edelson moved stiffly at the command of his unseen captor. He sensed the man was much smaller than he by the proximity of his voice and the placement of the gun barrel, which had slipped from his neck to his ribs, just below his right shoulder blade. The two of them stood looking down the basement stairs.

"I can't tell you how disappointed I am to see you here," the gunman said.

Edelson remained silent, knowing his best hope was getting the man to talk. Talk led to information, and information led to options.

"Downstairs," the gunman ordered, giving Edelson a shove that caused him to stumble before getting his feet under him. "Hanchet," the man hollered. "Hanchet, get up here. I need your help."

The young truck driver appeared at the bottom of the stairs, shaking his head uneasily. He looked up at the sheriff and uttered, "Jesus Christ!"

"Get some rope for our friend here."

"What're you gonna do with *him?*" the trucker said, not moving.

"What d'you think?"

"Oh, no. I ain't gonna help you waste the sheriff. Forget it, Sagen."

The gunman stopped short on the steps, yanking Edelson back by his collar. He stood taller than the sheriff now, and the gun barrel pressed against the base of Edelson's skull, at the hollow between his tense and ropey muscles.

Edelson caught the trucker's eye and nodded. Not so much an agreement, but a confirmation that it would be a very unwise choice.

The trucker looked away, and Edelson knew he had a fighting chance.

Hanchet disappeared and Sagen gave Edelson a hard shove to get him moving again, pushing him down the stairs into the basement, directing him to the classroom on the south side of the building. A row of high windows, long smashed out, brought the cold December into the room. Edelson tried to glimpse the boy out along the tracks. Hoped he'd run for help, but knew there was little chance he'd reach it in time. And he prayed that Gray would be okay. Above all other things, he ached for the boy to make it to safety.

McHugh was bound hand and foot and sitting against the wall. Edelson stared at his bare, deformed feet, bluish with cold, and understood the man's see-saw gait. Their eyes met in a silent exchange — an assessment of the situation. The prostitute gasped when she saw the sheriff.

"I don't know about this," Hanchet said, returning with a rope.

"Shut up!" Sagen shouted, his agitation on a rise.

Edelson noted the panic in the man's voice, the pitch a little higher than it had been when it first penetrated his ears.

The man who had spoken that chilly greeting was now hurriedly ordering the trucker to tie him up.

Tightly bound, Edelson got his first glimpse of the gunman. Then he was shoved to the floor. He landed on his side and tried to get to his knees, get his weight under him, when he was kicked squarely in the ribs with the steel tip of Sagen's boot. He lurched, a brilliant pain spreading through him, and coughed. The man kicked him again, and Edelson heard a cracking, then screaming. He thought it was his own voice for a moment, which scared him, for the pain was unlike anything he'd known, but then realized it was the prostitute, shrieking at Sagen to stop.

To Edelson's surprise, he did stop. And stood watching as Edelson retched and collapsed in a heap of nauseating pain.

"What'd you do that for?" Hanchet said, staring down at the sheriff.

"Just get that damn safe open." Sagen towered over the sheriff, seeming not to know what to do next. "Why'd y-you have to s-show up here?" he stammered. "Now I have to k-kill you. And they'll be all over this place." He pulled back and gave Edelson another blast in the kidney, then followed Hanchet out of the room.

Edelson worked at his breathing. Shallow. Hard. He rolled up painfully to a sitting position and braced himself against the wall with his chin tipped toward the ceiling. He counted out 20, 30, 40 seconds in his head, waiting for the pain to lessen. He spit red, then inched himself upright.

Crystal O'Shea was at his side, peering curiously at him. Not in a friendly manner that would denote concern. Simply a morbid curiosity.

"He did that to me once," she said. "I know how it feels. It feels like you're going to puke your liver up."

Edelson rolled his eyes toward her. Pondered the truth of her statement.

"If you'd have just let me do a little washing for you, sheriff, this wouldn't have happened," Crystal said.

Edelson looked over at McHugh. "What are you doing here?" he wheezed.

McHugh didn't answer immediately.

"He's here because his sister sent him to his doom," Crystal volunteered, and not without a hint of joy.

McHugh looked away.

She stood and shuffled carefully across the icy floor near the doorway. She still clutched the crowbar in her hand.

"Russell Vining owed this guy, Sagen," McHugh said, pointing toward the door with his chin. "When you shot him and Christen went to jail, he . . . he called me to collect Vining's debt. I told him I didn't have anything to do with Russell's shit, but he wouldn't let the matter go."

Edelson squinted at McHugh. "Guess he'd have to have something on you, otherwise why pay?"

"Look, I was just trying to clear things up for my sister. So she wouldn't have these thugs after her. He didn't have anything on me." McHugh glanced at Crystal, who was listening intently to his explanation. "I sold my house and . . . I was selling my bar to pay him off. So he'd leave Christen alone."

"Yeah, well, your sister is headed for prison." Expanding pain had diminished Edelson's already shallow capacity for diplomacy.

"What do you mean?"

"The feds believe she was an equal partner."

"Exactly!" Crystal interrupted. "That's what I've been trying to tell him." She had made her way back across the room and sat down with her face next to McHugh's. "She knew you'd sell everything to bail her out, but she was planning to leave with Sagen."

"Fuck you," McHugh growled.

"Look, I know how she is; we were best friends. There

235

were three of us. Don't you remember?" She paused for McHugh's reaction.

McHugh leaned against the wall and closed his eyes.

Edelson watched through the open door as the two men came down the stairs and rummaged in a closet in the adjacent classroom, talking about a small tool one of them held in his hand. He imagined Gray was long gone by now.

"Face it," Crystal continued. "if she can force her best friend to become a prostitute and have her lover murder Chris, what's to stop her from screwing you over too?"

Edelson turned to Crystal. The way she said that name. She was the one; suddenly he was sure she was his anonymous caller. "Who is she? Who's the woman from the river?"

Crystal looked over at Edelson and held him in her gaze. "You still haven't figured that out? You're not a very good sheriff, are you?"

"Who is she?"

"Maybe you should ask Sagen. He killed her."

"How'd my sister force you to be a whore?" McHugh asked, as if her words had just taken root in his brain.

Crystal brought her attention back to McHugh. "She always had what we needed, not just pot." She glanced at the sheriff, as if contemplating her admission, then back to McHugh. "Heroin, coke — the good stuff. Me and . . ." she looked pointedly at Edelson again, "Chris. Christen knew what she was doing. She covered us when we didn't have the money — until we owed so much we could never pay her back, and we couldn't stop, either. So she put us to work. Sagen stuck me in that trailer down in Peerless to keep the sheriff distracted."

"Chris who?" Edelson repeated.

Crystal ignored him. Spoke directly to McHugh. "She doesn't care about you." She looked toward the door. "She doesn't even care about Sagen. But he's too stupid to figure that out. He believes she's in love with him."

"Chris who?" Edelson shouted.

Sagen thumped back down the stairs and into the classroom. His black eyes moved from Crystal to McHugh to Edelson and back to her. "What the fuck is the matter with you? I told you to knock him around until you get that combination." Sagen yanked the crowbar from Crystal's hand and swung it down hard on McHugh's shoulder.

McHugh gasped, his eyes bugging. He drew a ragged breath.

Crystal shrank against the wall, small, even next to McHugh.

"Go wait outside," Sagen said to Crystal. She got meekly to her feet, shoulders hunched, and went up the stairs. He turned back to McHugh. "Wanna tell me the combination?"

McHugh didn't respond. He told himself to hang on, not pass out, until he had the chance to murder Sagen and the whore with his bare hands, just as soon as he got them around their ugly necks. Through blurred vision, he watched the thug leave the icy room. Then a shadow moved across his face and he looked up at an unexpected sight. A boy, poking his face through the broken window and looking at them. "Hey, boy," he called softly.

The sheriff turned to look, and in a harsh voice said, "Gray, get out of here! Run for help."

The boy paused, then held out a gun, teetered it over the sheriff as he adjusted his aim, and dropped it onto the man's shoulder. It bounced and skated on the icy floor, coming to rest several yards away from Edelson.

The sheriff looked up at the boy again. "You're the best friend a guy could have. Now go, and make sure no one sees you."

And Gray vanished.

The sheriff scooted in anguish toward the gun. "God, I hope this thing is loaded," he panted.

Gray crept along the lip of the ragged schoolyard, urgency and euphoria fighting for prominence in his head. *The best friend a guy can have.* The sound of those words filled him with glee, with a warmth in his belly like after one of Mrs. Sherwood's huge cookies. But he couldn't spend time thinking about the sheriff's praises. Couldn't forget the sheriff needed him. He galloped back through the high weeds, toward the tracks, heading back to the Interstate where he might flag down a passing car. But then he remembered the sheriff's cruiser. The radio. He'd seen Mr. Edelson use it. He changed course and headed for the Douglas firs and the cruiser beyond.

Gray could hear Hanchet talking to the other man near the semi, so he was careful to keep out of sight. The patrol car sat at the entrance to the parking lot, behind the pickup. He reached it easily and slipped inside, pulling the door shut quietly. He slid under the steering wheel and lifted the police radio out of its cradle. He pressed the button, just like Mr. Edelson did, and said, "Hello?"

He waited. Nothing. He pressed the button again. "Hello? The sheriff is in trouble. He needs help." He let the button go and listened. Still nothing. He craned around to see the front of the radio. Twisted a knob, accidentally turning it off, then quickly twisted it the other way. "Hello?" he said again.

"Who is this?" a static-riddled voice blasted out at him.

Terror shot through him like an electric shock. He reached up and turned the volume down, his fingers shaking wildly. He pressed the radio to his lips and said, "This is Gray. The sheriff is in trouble. He's at the old school and —"

A figure was suddenly standing over him, rapping on the window. The radio flew from Gray's hands. He shrank back. It

238

was the woman from the cellar. She had her face and hands pressed to the window, staring down at him.

"What are you doing?" she called through the window.

"Where are you?" the radio spat.

Gray flipped the radio dial off. He pulled himself up on the seat and opened the door. His rubbery fingers barely able to pull the latch.

"I asked you what you're doing," she repeated.

Gray swallowed. "I — I was just playing." His voice was small. He could barely hear himself.

"That radio is not a toy. You'll get arrested for using it."

Gray looked only at his hands. He knew the woman was with Hanchet and the other man. He'd seen her go into the building with them. Was she going to take him back to the schoolhouse? Hold a gun to *his* head? Like the man from the Silver Dog? And the sheriff?

"Get out of here. Go home!" she said as if she were addressing a bad dog. "You don't need to be messing around with this stuff. The sheriff will throw you in jail."

Gray scrambled out of the car and made a beeline for the frontage road.

"Go on," she sniped after him.

Edelson worked at the rope, sawing a taut cord against the dull edge of the gun barrel; it was all he had. He thought of Robin briefly, and conceded that he had been a terrible husband. He was a 1950s sort of man living in the 21st century. He had been selfish in his marriage, and now that it was too late, he wished he could do things over. He sawed furiously against the ropes. He and Robin were never a team, never equals. But Gray, now, Gray was his kind, and struggling with the cord helped him push down worry about the boy. He remembered the army knife in his pocket, which may as well have been in another state for his ability to reach it with bound hands. He turned to

McHugh. The man seemed to have given up completely, hunched over, his head between his knees. Edelson remembered him in the early hours of the day, standing stoically in the street watching the fire finish up his saloon, his arm burned, the skin peeling away. McHugh had lost his formidable will.

The young truck driver appeared in the doorway. "Where's the whore?"

"Sagen told her to go outside," Edelson said, then wondered what compelled him to answer the question. An instinctive nature to serve, he guessed.

Hanchet looked distrustfully at the sheriff, and Edelson seized his moment.

"You don't want to be involved with the murder of a law man. They won't stop looking; the case will never go cold. And when they find you, you'll get the death sentence. This is Montana."

Hanchet turned toward the door, but he didn't leave.

"If the wrong man finds you, you'll never even *see* the justice system."

"Shut up," Hanchet said.

"It's not too late. You can —"

"Shut the fuck up, I said!"

Gray wasn't far down the frontage road when he knew he couldn't leave Mr. Edelson behind. He looked back to see the woman on the bed of the truck kneeling in front of a safe. She seemed so weird there, as if she was a safe cracker. He veered off into the ditch and ran through a narrow field, panting over high weeds, to the railroad tracks. Then he circled back to the schoolhouse, buffered by the fir trees, and crept to the window where he'd earlier found the sheriff. He leaned against the cement footing and peeked in.

"How are you going to dispose of my car?" the sheriff was asking the truck driver. "A dozen people have probably already seen it from the Interstate. Maybe more. Let us go and we'll testify that you couldn't go through with it — that you did the right thing in the end."

Hanchet paced in front of the door. He turned in Gray's direction, and the boy ducked below the window.

"Look, it's the difference between a plea bargain and the death penalty," Edelson said. "It's as black and white as that. You'll never get away with killing me. You have to know that."

The truck driver didn't answer, and Gray strained to hear Edelson. Death penalty, he thought. That should convince him. Way to go, Sheriff.

"That whore is gonna talk," McHugh said.

"Shut up!" Hanchet barked again.

Gray waited until the voices went quiet, and peeked in to see that Hanchet had disappeared; this was his chance. Where the sheriff sat was a long drop and he was scared he'd fall and break a leg. He leaned through the window, whispering.

Edelson craned up. His eyes went wide, angry even. "*Get out of here!*"

Gray hesitated, then turned on his belly and put his feet through the window.

"*No!*" the sheriff said, but Gray knew he had to do it.

He dangled a moment, suspended above the icy floor from his fingers. They might have hurt from the steel window frame, but they were so cold he couldn't feel anything. He closed his eyes and dropped. Hit flat on the soles of his feet, bruising his knees against the wall, then slipped back and landed sharply on his tailbone. He suppressed a yelp, tears stinging his eyes, and scrambled quickly to his feet.

Edelson shook his head, protesting or disbelieving.

"Untie us," McHugh said.

Gray went straight to the sheriff and pulled at the knots. They were tight. They looked like they'd been tied by an Eagle Scout. He yanked and pulled, but he couldn't budge them.

Hanchet's voice riffled down the stairs. It was high and whiny. Something about the patrol car.

Gray panicked. They were coming. He worked at the knot. It wouldn't come.

"Get the knife in my pocket," Edelson said, straightening his leg to give him access. "Saw it."

Gray fumbled to get his hand inside the sheriff's pocket and dragged out the entire contents, spilling loose change onto the icy floor. He scooped up the pocketknife and pulled at the blade. It was stiff, the kind he hated. Made to protect children. He dug his fingernail into the groove and forced it, ripping his nail bloody. Red pooled at the tip, but Gray moved quickly to saw at the cord.

"Hurry," the sheriff insisted, watching the doorway.

"Let's just get on with it," Hanchet said as the two men spilled out of the stairs and stood arguing in the narrow hallway outside the classroom.

"He saw that goddamn sparkly truck of yours," Sagen spat.

Gray gave the rope a last hard cut with the blade as the sheriff pushed him away. But there was no place to hide in the vast, empty, ice-covered room. He looked up at the window; no way. He turned and caught the mournful gaze of McHugh as the two men advanced into the room.

"This is where they shoot us," McHugh said.

The shorter of the two men halted. His black eyes peeled Gray to the bone. Time ceased, and Gray stood suspended in mid-move. No crazy mistake he'd ever made in his life could measure up against this one.

Edelson watched helplessly as Sagen advanced on the boy. He searched behind him for the knife, spinning it with his fingers before catching the blade.

"*Who* are *you?*" Sagen shouted. The question seemed to remain frozen in the thick air.

Gray, paralyzed with fear, his mouth open and his arms and legs bent as if for action, riveted his eyes on Sagen.

"This has turned into a fucking carnival," Sagen harped. "Let's invite the whole goddamn county." He bore down on the boy, nose to nose. "Why don't you speak?" And he swung his fist, hitting Gray across the temple, lifting him off his feet and sending him skidding into the wall, where he came to rest beneath the blackboard. Like a dead cat, limp and quiet.

Hanchet and McHugh were clamoring, but Edelson could not distinguish one from the other. His blood had come up like lava, hot and unstoppable. He forced the knife blade down on the rope, cutting deep into his own flesh as it finally snapped. Supported by the rage of vengeance, he came to his feet. He gripped the gun, as comfortable in his hand as his own service weapon. Once more, percussion deafened him. And Sagen stepped backward. Looked first at the sheriff, then down at his own belly. He fell against the door jamb, a statement perched on his lips, and slid onto the basement ice. His feet jerked, his body twitched. But he found no words.

In the seconds that followed, Hanchet was gone. Edelson struggled out of the knots and collected Gray. He sat on the ice with him, rocking him a little, murmuring to him through his own pain. He almost didn't hear the shouting from McHugh.

"Untie me," McHugh's voice finally broke into the sheriff's consciousness. "They're getting away with my money."

26

EDELSON RECALLED THE FAINT SOUND of McHugh's truck peeling out of the gravel lot — a disjointed memory — a detail in the frenzy that had followed his shooting Sagen. What he remembered were those moments he cradled Gray, afraid for the boy's life. Only now, days later, were the pieces coming together in his mind. Adeline had taken Gray's call for a prank, but she was a cautious woman, and Hanchet had made it only a quarter mile down the frontage road before the Missoula County Sheriff met him. The safe was empty.

Edelson searched Crystal O'Shea's trailer for clues to where she might have fled. The only trail the prostitute left were the footprints in the snowy field between the Elk Creek Schoolhouse and the Interstate. Apparently, carrying a wad of cash in the pockets of her thin jacket, she'd made it to the Interstate and hitched a ride. A driver going west left her off in Pasco, Washington, where she seemed to disappear.

In Crystal's bedroom Edelson found several photographs taped to the inside of her closet door. One stood out, made his stomach knot. He pulled the picture down and carefully folded the tape over the corners. He ran his thumb back and forth across the glossy surface, as if to erase the image, but the girl only smiled back at him. He turned it over and read the scribbled name: Chris.

* * *

McHugh sat across from Wren in the too-familiar visitor booth, the phone pressed to his ear, looking for some glimmer of the woman he'd secretly and shamefully loved.

"They lied," she said of what Sagen and Crystal had said about her. "Why wouldn't they?"

But McHugh saw only her hypocrisy, her cowardly turning against the one man who loved her and wanted only to keep her safe.

"Randy — baby — just get me out of here and we'll start over somewhere else. You said yourself that we're not brother and sister."

He believed not a word of her sudden sincerity. He wanted to ask if her memory of their lovemaking so many years ago was as ugly as Sagen had recounted, but could not bring himself to final ruin.

"They ran your story in the paper this morning," he said. "The Vinings and their prostitutes. One dead, one missing — with all of my money. With everything I had left in the world." He paused, the bile rising in his gullet as he thought of that whore escaping with his cash. "You'll be convicted, you know. The prosecutor is sure of it."

Wren's face crumpled. He'd never spoken to her that way. "It wasn't me, Randy."

"You never loved me, Wren," he said, hanging up the intercom phone and getting to his feet. He would move away without her . . . to Colorado. Wyoming maybe. Somewhere. The place didn't really matter. He would try to forget his saloon, his misspent, comfortable life. All he loved in Magda was destroyed.

Still, he kept a tight grip on his promise to the prostitute. One day he would find Crystal O'Shea, and on that day, her life would end.

Mrs. Sherwood opened the door before Edelson knocked. She

didn't appear surprised by his unannounced visit, but then she never did. She smiled, and he followed her inside. She led him back to the kitchen and poured him a cup of coffee. Strong, with a generous helping of real cream, the way he liked it.

"How long has it been since you last heard from your daughter?" He shifted uncomfortably in his chair.

She stood at the cupboard, her back turned to him, and she didn't answer for a long time.

Edelson pulled out the photo he'd found in Crystal O'Shea's trailer. He fished in his shirt pocket for the arrowhead he'd found near the dead woman and matched it again to the one around the neck of the girl in the photo. But he didn't need the arrowhead to know who this girl was. He'd seen her before in a hundred photos. He'd heard about her childhood, her talents and her dreams. Told to him on many evenings by her proud and lonely mother. Only Mrs. Sherwood had never mentioned that her Chris and Crystal O'Shea had been buddies. He slipped the picture into his breast pocket and laid the arrowhead gently on the table.

Mrs. Sherwood stared down at it, then picked it up and held it to her chest. "Her father gave it to her when she was just a little girl. Eight or nine," she said, her eyes shut tight, her voice barely a breath.

Finally, the woman composed herself, took a sugar cookie and bit into it, looking out the window at the Christmas lights her neighbor had strung along the eaves of his house. As Edelson started to speak, she interrupted. "I thought I'd lost it. I don't know how it got in here. Isn't it funny how things seem to move on their own?" She looked at Edelson, her eyes pleading.

He sat back. "It happens to me all the time." Unhappy as his next words might be, he could not let her go on believing her daughter might come home, even though he suspected that Mrs. Sherwood already knew she'd never see her Chris again.

"I can take you to Missoula to make arrangements for her burial," he said.

Her hand trembled. "Are you sure . . . I mean . . . couldn't it be someone else?" But she didn't seem to want him to answer her questions. Instead, she studied the arrowhead. "I feared it was her the moment I heard about the body at the river. She wasn't the same when she came back from Portland — she spent time with people that . . . she wasn't that *kind* of girl." Mrs. Sherwood brushed tears away.

"People make mistakes," he said, reaching across the table and putting his hand over hers.

After a long moment, she pressed the arrowhead into his hand.

"I can't take it," he said.

"No, give it to Gray. For luck. Ask him to take care of it for me."

Edelson stood in Sarah Winborn's office, which was practically across the hall from the Missoula chief of police, constantly glancing into the waiting room to make sure Gray was still there. "The boy belongs with me, and I'm not going to be a *foster* parent. I'm going to be his *dad*," he said for the 100th time. Since the incident, five days earlier, Edelson had kept the boy with him, scarcely letting Gray out of his sight.

Ms. Winborn stood next to her desk holding a handwritten list of violations to prove the sheriff's unworthiness — his failing marriage, his assault on a college professor. She started to interrupt him, but paused and cocked her chin up at Edelson with a faint smile. Not a sly *you'll never win* smile, like he was expecting, but an admiring sort of smile. "Just because you've been decorated for your bravery doesn't mean you'll make a suitable parent, Sheriff."

He shook his head, dismissing the reference to his recent commendation. "I mean it. I'm gonna raise that kid."

Her silent stare unnerved him.

"I spoke to your wife," she finally said.

He closed his eyes and took in a breath. Here it comes, he thought.

"She was surprisingly amiable about you in spite of everything." The social worker sat down and pulled her chair forward in a businesslike manner. "She thinks you'll make a terrific father. I wouldn't have guessed I'd get such a hearty endorsement from her, and frankly, her opinion of you is worth a lot to me. But not hers alone. Mrs. Sherwood seems to share your wife's confidence."

Edelson smiled, he could imagine exactly what the old woman had said. "Kip needs that kid, and that kid needs Kip."

"If it weren't for the prominent role I expect Mrs. Sherwood to play in the boy's upbringing, I wouldn't be so quick to agree to this." Ms. Winborn raised an eyebrow at Edelson.

Edelson nodded, bowed his head in respect and, for once, didn't jeopardize his good fortune by opening his mouth.

Gray followed Sheriff Edelson through the snow and weeds between the Elk Creek schoolhouse and the railroad tracks. He stepped high, but it wasn't necessary in his new cowboy boots. They matched the sheriff's. Gray needed to tell him that Lanny McDeer had invited him to branding at the Flying W next fall. Lanny's grandpa owned the ranch, so it was a real invitation. But this wasn't the time for such news. Gray couldn't remember losing *Arabian Nights*. It had been with him when he got to the Interstate, but he guessed he lost it on the way to finding Mr. Edelson in the basement. He only remembered it the next day, when Mrs. Sherwood took him up in her soft arms and told him he was a hero, just like the sheriff. He wanted to squirm away — 10-year-old boys with some experience loathe cuddling — but he decided not to worry about whether he was too big to be treated that way because he liked her.

They searched and hunted, but Gray didn't give up. Edelson didn't, either. Finally, the boy saw the book, face down on the ice in the ditch he had hid in. He picked it up, but its pages came apart in his fingers. The beautiful pictures were warped. The cover wet and blackened.

He drew a deep breath, tears messing up his vision. "It's ruined."

The sheriff took *Arabian Nights* and turned it over in his hands. He nodded. "We'll buy another one."

Gray didn't even stop to think. "But it's special, remember. And I stole it from Mrs. Sherwood. I was going to sell it and go find my mom. The school librarian said it was worth three-hundred dollars." He no longer felt like the celebrity he'd become, but the same worthless boy he'd always been.

The sheriff put his arm around Gray's shoulder. "You know, Gray," he paused to look down the Interstate a moment. "I've been thinking about your mom. I don't know why she left. But if you go off trying to find her, you might miss her if she comes back. I think the best thing to do is stay right here. Right where she can find you when she's ready."

Gray thought about it; the idea made sense.

"I've been thinking maybe I should stick around here, too. Stay in one place for a while and get to know the community better. Maybe the two of us could do that together. What do you think?"

Gray looked up at the sheriff. "You mean stay with you until my mom comes?"

"Yeah. I'd like that. And you can call me Kip. You wanna do that?"

Gray thought about it, thought about his old dad, who seemed almost a memory after all that had happened, and nodded.

Edelson hoped he could provide the stability that Gray needed.

And here in Magda, too. Still, as he scanned the Elk Creek School, he knew that while it had once been a small pleasure to look at, it would now remind him only of pain and death. He'd killed two men since arriving in Mineral County a few months earlier. Neither man was worth his concern, but their deaths would continue to haunt him, and he knew that. He'd have some rough times ahead.

It was the boy who gave him hope, a sense of purpose — a new beginning. And Chris Samuelson — perhaps she could somehow figure into this new life he would build with Gray. Chris had showed him where he'd stumbled in his marriage, where he'd let Robin down. But he could learn. He could rise to Chris's expectations. He could be her kind of man, he knew it.